shall be executed entirely in conjunction with Party B, but Party A shall ultimately control the Slave's training, excepting that training shall be conducted on the grounds of the mansion owned by Party B, unless permission is given by Party B otherwise. During this period, Party A may utilize any facilities or other slaves of Party B to assist in training the slave or for Party A's own carnal pleasure.

At dawn on the Solstice, if the servitude of the Slave to Party B is extended indefinitely, Party A shall be declared the winner. If servitude is not extended indefinitely, Party B shall be declared the winner. In the former case, Party B agrees to submit to Party A in classic fashion for the period from dawn till dusk on the first day of the year 19—. In the latter case, Party A will serve Party B under terms identical to those agreed upon by the slave, excepting that servitude shall last from dusk on the night of the Solstice to midnight on the ninetieth day following.

Also by N. T. MORLEY:

The Limousine
The Castle
The Parlor

THE CONTRACT

N. T. MORLEY

The Contract
Copyright © 1998 by N. T. Morley
All Rights Reserved

No part of this book may be reproduced, stored in a retrieval system, or transmitted in any form, by any means, including mechanical, electronic, photocopying, recording or otherwise, without prior written permission of the publishers.

First Masquerade Edition 1998

First Printing February 1998

ISBN 1-56333-575-1

Manufactured in the United States of America
Published by Masquerade Books, Inc.
801 Second Avenue
New York, N.Y. 10017

CHAPTER 1

Sarah's house always had the best coffee I had ever tasted—I didn't doubt that it was something very expensive from a faraway country, which she had imported. Rank hath its privileges.

There, beside Sarah's chair, knelt a naked and hooded Tina. She was an astonishing piece of work—not quite nineteen years old, blonde and delectable. Her body was simply magnificent, and the posture in which she now knelt accentuated every enticing attribute she possessed. Tina was a fairly small young woman, not over five feet tall and perhaps a little over a hundred pounds, but she was gifted by the Goddess with extremely large breasts, firm and ripe, and capped with firm dark nipples—unpierced. Those nipples were fully erect, showing her arousal. I wondered what filthy thoughts were going through that girl's head. Tina's belly was flat and smooth; her navel also sported a piercing, this one a bright jeweled ring. Her legs were shapely and delicate, and incredibly inviting, especially given the way they were spread wide in her position of extreme submission. Tina was on her knees, her thighs far apart. And her pubic area was smooth, without a hint of hair anywhere—Tina's crotch was freshly shaved. This gave me a perfect view of her pretty pussy, the most beautiful thing about Tina. It was well pierced—three times through each lip. Tina's large, erect clitoris crowned the beauty of her pussy—with its thick, shining ring pierced vertically through the hood.

She was beautiful. At that moment, in fact, she seemed to me the most beautiful creature I had ever seen. Perhaps it was my randy urgency talking, though. I wanted to spread that slave out and plumb her depths, to feel the silk of her pussy wrapped around my rod. To sense the droplets of her juice dribbling down my shaft and soaking my sheets as I penetrated the girl again and again. Oh, what a delight it is to have access to a beautiful, pierced and collared slave.

Did I forget to mention Tina's throat? How could I? It was slender, delicate, fragile. And across it was padlocked a thick leather collar, displaying her status to all.

Of course, I had yet to see Tina's face.

The Contract

Tina wore a black leather mask that left her mouth exposed, but covered the rest of her face. There were no holes for her eyes, so Tina was as blind as a slave can be. The hood also covered her ears, and I knew from experience that it was fitted with earplugs. No matter what we said, Tina could not hear us.

These slave-hoods were custom made for Sarah by the finest crafters, and over the years I had known Sarah, I'd had the pleasure of possessing many a hooded slave on loan from the great Mistress.

Once again my gaze lingered over the beautiful sight of Tina's cunt, pierced lips parted and exposed between her wide-opened thighs, showing me the firm bud of her entrance. I longed to linger at that entrance and then slowly push in, feeling the pierced lips part to make way for my shaft....

I didn't doubt that the ritual of Tina's piercing had been a wonderful sight. For a moment, I thought about Tina bound naked to a table, thrashing and moaning while Sarah's workers clamped and then pierced each of her cuntlips three times...each time drawing a scream and a shudder from the naked slave as she submitted further further...deeper into submission to her Mistress....

But apparently not deep enough.

I took another sip of coffee, letting my eyes remain on Tina's naked form, considering what Sarah had just told me.

"So you think Tina is willing, even hungry, to submit

—but held back by some psychological block to being completely and wholly owned by another woman?"

"In a nutshell, that's more or less it. I'm afraid so," the Mistress sighed. "But deep inside, I sense her love for me, her desire to give herself totally to my service. When it comes down to this sort of resistance, I can usually break the slave's will with a few weeks of... *creative* work. But I've tried everything. She is submissive, as you can see, but some part of her rebels. She rebels much too often. Sometimes when she is servicing me orally, she seems to drift off, her concentration wanders. This is a good excuse to punish her, of course ...but it grows tiresome. Other times, she is more explicitly rebellious. She actually tried to strike me once."

"Strike you! What did you do, Mistress?" I let an amused look cross my face. "Did you strike her back?"

Sarah looked perturbed, otherwise ignoring my joke. "Of course I had already struck her many times. That's hardly the point, Carlton. I was forced to isolate her until she had cooled down. Later, she was obedient again, and she apologized. And she did indeed achieve her penance in a most extreme fashion. But, as before, that's hardly the point. I think that act of rebellion was only a symptom of a larger, more insidious syndrome of resistance in the girl's spirit. I know she hasn't submitted totally. And I can't seem to break her will."

"Has she been offered her freedom? To be released from the Contract?"

Sarah reddened slightly. Her legendary control had been shaken by this slave. "I'm afraid…well…I have become very attached to this slave. I adore disciplining her so, and I would hate to lose her."

"You've fallen in love with her," I said. "Therefore, the thing to do is to offer her freedom."

Sarah looked irritatedly at me. I smiled genially and laughed.

"I offered her freedom from the Contract. She refused, telling me she wanted to stay. But that was months ago, before I realized how rebellious she really was. If I offered it to her now…"

I looked directly at Sarah. I considered her ageless beauty, her captivating but severe face framed by golden blonde hair, pulled up into a rather severe bun. She looked as magnificent as ever. She wore a black business suit, but one that was cut a little tighter and shorter than would have been appropriate in an office. The black skirt came a little higher than mid-thigh, showing me Sarah's beautiful strong legs with their black-seamed stockings. Her shiny black shoes, also less conservative than one would see in an office, sported four-inch heels. I didn't doubt that Tina's luscious tongue had lazed around every inch of those shoes and many other pairs that Sarah wore, as well as Sarah's bare feet. And since Sarah was close to six feet tall—in her bare feet almost as tall as I—those four-inch heels would put her well over the height of the slave. Sarah's jacket was tight across her large breasts, and underneath it she wore a low-cut peach silk camisole, the lace plunging low between her breasts to show her ample and inviting cleavage. As the jacket fell open slightly I saw that Sarah's nipples were quite visibly erect through the delicate camisole. And several times, when she shifted in her seat, I could see the lace tops of her black-seamed stockings becoming visible just under the hem of the skirt. I had some trouble keeping my eyes off Sarah's inviting thighs.

I wanted Sarah almost as much as I wanted Tina. She and I had been lovers many times, sharing passionate and violent lovemaking through many days and nights. Sarah knew the tricks necessary to make love to a man without ever giving up her dominant position. She never failed to please me immensely. But still, after each extended session of lovemaking, I felt acutely aware that Sarah was absolutely in control, even when kneeling and using her mouth to bring me off. Don't mistake my meaning—Sarah was an exquisite lover, satisfying me many times before bringing our passion to an end. Often I came four or five times during a night with Sarah. But somehow she gave herself to me as a lover, never giving me a hint of submission even when she did the same things to me that a slave might. That made my trysts with Sarah a thousand times more satisfying than a similar session with a slave, for I knew that every movement, every action, everything done to me was done for Sarah's own pleasure. She sucked my cock and swallowed my come because she wished to do so. She took my cock inside her because she wanted it. But even so, I longed to see her given a taste of her own delectable medicine. I wanted to have Sarah submit to me. I wanted to place her in chains and make her my slave for all eternity. What a delight it would be to see Sarah, the dominant Mistress—pierced, shaved, and collared, on her knees before me, servicing my prick with her eager mouth....

"My dear," I said, interrupting my own fantasy, "Now is precisely the time you must offer her freedom. If she takes it, what have you lost?"

Sarah looked at me hard, dangerously stern. "She will not be offered her freedom unless I am sure she will not accept! She has been here for nine months."

"Ah! Then you have only ninety days left. By the end of the one-year Contract period, she must be yours completely, to commit to you for eternity. Or she will go free, never again to service you eagerly with her tongue." I let my eyes laze over Sarah's thighs. The place where the hem of her skirt rode up slightly showed me the lace that framed her delectable thighs. She looked uncomfortable, and so I went on tormenting her. "You have only ninety short, precious days in which to seduce her—to break her will—or she will fly away like a bird..."

"That's enough, Carlton!" Sarah brushed away a tear.

"Please, don't talk about that. I don't wish to lose her. I have grown so very fond of her."

"So what do you need me for?" I asked her. "Unless it's simply to savage your willing body with my manhood…"

Sarah gave me a devilish smile, shifting her body invitingly and letting her knees fall open slightly, showing me a few more tempting inches of her thighs. "That part goes without saying, Carlton, though it sounds like you've been reading too many Victorian porno novels if you put it that way."

"Of course," I growled, licking my lips as I looked over Sarah and Tina—both soon to be my conquests.

"I sense that her resistance might be breached if she had a change of erotic energies. I think some part of her wishes to submit to a man, to have the stern hand of a man on her body before she gives herself over to me. She doesn't even realize it yet, but I believe that's what she needs. She came here as a virgin, you see."

I listened carefully, surprised.

"I have not let her be taken yet."

My eyes widened.

"You mean…you have brought me a virgin, dear Sarah? You are asking me to deflower this young woman?"

"Hear me out, Carlton. Tina has not yet been taken, and I sense that she wants it. I can certainly sympathize—I can testify to the pleasures of a good stiff prick inside my cunt."

I chuckled. "More on that later."

"But you must know that her virginity was one of the most alluring things about her. Perhaps this was part of why I've fallen for her. I know her submission will not be complete unless she gives up her maidenhead. Something in the girl yearns for thrust of flesh—and the act will seem more complete to me as well as Tina if she gives up her virginity to a man. I could easily enough strap on my very own peter...."

"Oh, yes!" I raised my eyebrows. "Please do."

Sarah arched her back slightly, letting me see more of her cleavage. "Soon, dear. Very soon. But for Tina's deflowering to be accomplished to my taste and hers... we need a man to wholly dominate her while taking her maidenhood from her. In cooperation with me, and with my full participation. I firmly believe that only then will Tina give herself up to my domination." Sarah reached out and cupped Tina's delicate leather-clad chin in her hand, touching the girl's lips with her thumb. Obediently, Tina began to lick and nibble at Sarah's thumb.

"You see how good she is? But wait until you see her on a bad day. She's a monster!"

Sarah turned more fully toward me, the expression on her face telling me that she was quickly growing tired of talk.

She sighed wearily and stretched back in her chair, making her jacket fall open. Now I could see much more of Sarah's incredible breasts, for the camisole she wore was quite sheer. Her eyes burned into mine. "Carlton, of course there are other men I could call on to initiate Tina...but I want *you* to do it. *She* wants you. I know her tastes, her desires, her needs. You are the perfect man to be her first. Rough, arrogant, brutish, and domineering. Without a hint of subtlety about you. But, even so, you have an appreciation for the finer elements of a girl's submission."

Sarah looked away, and I saw the grin on her face. She knew that I had taken the bait—and now that I was hooked, I would not get free until I had possessed this delicious creature.

Sarah's face took on a sour look. "I suppose I have preserved her virginity as a trophy, a prize. Some part of me is aroused by the thought of you being her first. And she is quite ready for the pleasure. Tina is almost nineteen, and it is time for her to give up her virginity. And so I offer it to you."

I finished the coffee, my face expressionless. With Sarah, there was always some bargain to be had. So I played the game with my poker face, even though Sarah had already seen my expression of excitement when I contemplated Tina's virginity, so ripe within her succulent body.

"And why should I be inclined to exert myself on your behalf? After all, it's a great deal of effort to deflower a young girl properly, especially one as oversexed as you describe."

Sarah laughed. "Carlton, she's a virgin. You see her."

"I certainly do. But for this service…I would demand a tribute."

Sarah sighed. "That you be permitted to use my slaves should be reward enough, you arrogant, brutish bastard."

"Thank you," I said. "But I still demand some form of payment. Call it ego."

Sarah was silent for a while. Then she said, without emotion, "What would you like?"

I made a show of considering my options. Then I looked into Sarah's beautiful eyes and held her gaze unflinchingly.

"I would like you, Mistress. You will serve me for one night, midnight till noon. Your body and mind will belong to me, totally. You will submit to me—naked, collared, shaved, and chained. On your knees. And your slave will watch."

Sarah's gaze did not flicker. A smile crept across her face. She seemed to be considering it, considering the possibility of being a shaved submissive on her knees, worshiping me.

Then she laughed.

"Carlton. You and I have made love a hundred times. You know how I am. I go to bed with men out of my own insatiable desires. I let you fuck me like the whore you are, in any position you or I choose. I've even knelt many times before you and sucked your cock until I brought you off in my mouth or across my breasts. I've even kissed your ass, in the most literal sense of the word. And the figurative one as well." Here, Sarah licked her lips, and I remembered that time in Venice. "I don't insist on being dominant in the bedroom with my lovers," she said. "But I have never been your slave—and I won't be. Not even for a night."

I noted that she had said she would not be *my* slave. Did that meant that she had submitted to other men? The thought excited me.

I laughed. "You're being awfully coy, Mistress. This agreement would assume, of course, that the slave is yours—that she extends the Contract indefinitely at the end of the year."

"That makes no difference. You still shan't have me collared or in chains."

"And if I did not require that your slave watch you submit?"

"Still impossible as payment. But perhaps I could offer alternative terms? You can take one slave from my stable for a year. Any slave except Tina."

I snorted in disgust. "That's hardly payment!"

"All right. Forever. You can take one of my slaves into permanent servitude. Except Tina."

I pretended to consider it. "Still not good enough. I'm asking only for one night, Mistress. A night, with you on your knees in proper submission to me…it seems perfectly reasonable."

"That form of payment is unacceptable."

"It has been a pleasure doing business with you, Mistress. Kindly send your servant for my coat."

Sarah's face brightened. "But perhaps we could turn this into an interesting wager."

I paused, listening.

"My final offer." Sarah smiled evilly. "I see no reason not to give you what you want. I would let you have my body from dusk till dawn. I would be shaved, collared, and chained. As you require. I would give you my servitude for a night. But in that case, our co-domination of Tina becomes a wager."

"A wager!" She had hit the right spot.

"Yes. If we are unsuccessful in turning Tina, if she does not continue her servitude to me indefinitely, then *you* will be the one to serve. If the slave's Contract is not extended indefinitely, as is the custom, I must be repaid for her servitude during those ninety days. You will find yourself on your knees, with all proper marks of submission. After all, if she does not stay in the Contract, then I have given you the last three months of a slave I truly adore. Therefore, I will be repaid in full: you will submit to me for three months. As a slave. To be trained as I see fit and released at the end of the period."

"Those are hardly fair terms, my dear. Unless you are willing to respond in kind." Ninety days of Sarah's servitude would be a greater prize than I could even imagine. I could feel my cock bulging hard in my pants as I contemplated it—a full ninety days to use Sarah mercilessly, however I wanted…. It was intoxicating.

Sarah's expression told me that this was her final offer. "One night of my servitude against full repayment of the use of my slave for ninety days." Sarah relaxed into her chair and let her knees drift apart. She gave me her most receptive gaze, seductive and hungry, though she still spoke of power and control.

I considered for a long time.

"You would be collared for me?"

"In proper submissive form," she said in a sultry voice. I could tell from the way she said it that the possibility was more than a little exciting to her. Had I found a hidden submissive streak in the Mistress? Perhaps it was just the excitement of the wager.

But I knew I would win. I could tell from everything about Tina that she would submit to me completely and would renew her Contract at the end of the period. By the time I was done with her, she would give herself over to eternal servitude.

I smiled, envisioning Sarah's delicious body open to me, freely given, freely taken.

I thought of her slave, receiving my punishment and returning sexual servitude. Submitting to me as she had never submitted to her Mistress.

I thought of the prestige I would receive when it became known that Sarah had knelt before me wearing the collar of a slave. That she had willingly lowered herself to her knees before me.

I smiled, having no doubt in my mind that Tina would become Sarah's completely, and then Sarah would become mine for that heavenly night.

"You drive a hard bargain," I said to Sarah. "But I agree to your terms."

Sarah's body relaxed. Her face and breasts grew flushed as she ran her hand slowly down her body. It came to rest at the hem of her skirt, tugging it up slightly to show me that she was not wearing panties underneath.

"Finally, we've reached agreement on a Contract," she sighed, reaching out to stroke Tina's face. "You're so difficult to argue with, Carlton. But it's exciting to fence with you." Sarah's hand crept up, lifting her skirt a bit farther. She spread her legs, showing me the lace tops of her stockings, the straps of her garters…and the pink slit of her cunt, dusted with wisps of blonde hair. She slid her hand up to her slick pussy, stroking it.

"Now perhaps you'll be so kind as to fuck me before I go completely mad with lust. All this wagering has made me incredibly wet." Her eyes fixed on the bulge in my pants. My cock was hard at the sight of Sarah, offering herself to me. And at the thought of her submission to come. By the time I was through with Sarah, she would learn to love life on her knees before me—as would Tina. "I see you're also in need of some relief."

"Would it be proper to let the slave watch?"

Sarah smiled and stood up slowly, hiking her skirt up higher as she walked slowly toward me. "I wouldn't have it any other way."

THE CONTRACT

Partial text of the Contract
entered into by Party A and Party B:

Party A agrees to train the slave for the period of ninety days, ending at dawn on the Winter Solstice, 19—, within the boundaries of the Contract of servitude already signed by the slave and Party B. Said training shall be executed entirely in conjunction with Party B, but Party A shall ultimately control the Slave's training, excepting that training shall be conducted on the grounds of the mansion owned by Party B, unless permission is given by Party B otherwise. During this period, Party A may utilize any facilities or other slaves of Party B to assist in training the slave or for Party A's own carnal pleasure.

At dawn on the Solstice, if the servitude of the Slave to Party B is extended indefinitely, Party A shall be declared the winner. If servitude is not extended indefinitely, Party B shall be declared the winner. In the former case, Party B agrees to submit to Party A in classic fashion for the period from dawn till dusk on the first day of the year 19—. In the latter case, Party A will serve Party B under terms identical to those agreed upon by the slave, excepting that servitude shall last from dusk on the night of the Solstice to midnight on the ninetieth day following.

Signed in blood.

CHAPTER 2

Sarah summoned her attending slaves with a ring of the bell on the end table. Then she leaned over me, pulling her skirt up all the way, slipping her jacket off so that all that covered her breasts was the peach silk camisole. Now I could see her inviting pussy, framed by its blonde hair, and the twin globes of her large breasts, the nipples fully erect and visible through the camisole. Two slaves, naked except for their black leather collars, appeared behind Sarah. These slaves had been introduced to me as Shade and Whisper, and they appeared to be Sarah's personal servants, for the time being.

They were very similar in appearance—each a little

taller than Tina, perhaps five foot three, with pale skin and bright blue eyes. Their hair was cut in almost identical fashion, hanging straight in a bob around their pretty faces. But Shade's hair was jet black, while Whisper's was pale blonde. The two slaves had a similar build—with slender waists, slim hips, and pert, firm derrieres. Both women were very pretty in an aristocratic sort of way, with full lips—Whisper's perhaps a bit more full and inviting than Shade's, but Shade's were exquisite nonetheless—and small, upturned noses that were now pierced through the center. Both women had smooth-shaved pubic regions. They differed, however, in one of the attributes which Sarah most valued in her slaves. Whisper's breasts were of fair size for a woman of her build—and crowned with unusually large and dark nipples that looked quite good with those large rings through them. But despite those wonderful nipples, Whisper's breasts were smaller than Sarah or I usually liked. If she had not carried herself with such an exquisite sensuality and had such delightfully kissable lips, I doubt that she would have caught Sarah's eye. Shade, on the other hand, had breasts that were strikingly large for a woman her size—so large that if they had been even slightly larger, they would have been less than aesthetically pleasing. As they were, though, Shade's breasts were perfect on her—much larger than Sarah's or Tina's, yet enticingly firm. They were capped with nipples that were almost as big as

Whisper's, and already quite erect. Her large breasts made her cleavage excitingly deep, and I wondered what it would be like to slide my hard cock between her enormous breasts.

The two women also differed in their piercings. While each bore a silver ring through her septum and a stud through her lower lip, Shade's nipples were not pierced. However, her cunt made up for this, with what looked like four—perhaps five—rings through each lip and one through her clitoris. Whisper, on the other hand, had thick silver rings through her large nipples, but no visible piercings in her genitals. Together, the two slaves were a pleasing combination, and I planned to explore their bodies extensively at my leisure while I dallied in Sarah's house.

"Yes Mistress?" the slaves said in unison. "How may we serve you?"

"Unhood Tina," she ordered them. "I want her to see what's going to be done to her before long. And let her hair down once the hood's off."

As the slaves removed Tina's hood quickly and unfastened the pins that held her hair, Sarah stood before me and let her hand slip down to her pussy, her legs parting slightly. I watched, enraptured, as she rubbed her fingers through the silk of her blonde pubic hair, then began to touch her cunt. She eased one finger between her lips and brought it out glistening wet.

"She is ready, Mistress."

"Thank you. You two may watch, as well—you might learn something."

"Thank you, Mistress." Both of the slaves spoke, as if two speakers in a stereo sound system. They lowered themselves to their knees alongside Tina. I glanced away from Sarah, with some difficulty, to see the wide-eyed Tina, her hair mussed from its imprisonment in the leather hood. She watched with astonishment and fascination.

As they did, Sarah took the hairpins out of her chignon and teased her golden mane, letting it fall across her shoulders. She looked even more beautiful with her hair down.

Sarah crawled on top of me, her knees alongside my thighs as I sank into the easy chair. She reached down and took hold of the bulge in my pants.

"That's one thing I like about you, Carlton," she said. "You're so fucking well-hung." Sarah began to stroke my hard cock, and I let out a little groan of pleasure. Tina watched in obvious fascination.

"Has she ever seen you fuck a man before?" I asked Sarah.

"Of course not," she said. "*You've* never been over before."

I chuckled at Sarah's sarcasm. Suddenly my back arched as Sarah gripped my cock through the strained fabric of my pants, rubbing up and down eagerly. A dark spot was beginning to form at the head of my penis where my precome was leaking through. Sarah suddenly dropped to her knees alongside the chair and got my belt and pants undone in a matter of seconds.

"You bastard! For some reason whenever I get around you, I'm seized by the desire to give head."

Then Sarah pulled my cock out of my undershorts, a look of pure, unmatched hunger on her face. She grinned as she stroked my naked cock with her hand and prepared to swallow it. But Sarah liked torturing me, making me wait for her to pleasure my cock with her mouth. In fact, the way Sarah gave head, it was more like *she* was the one taking her pleasure. My delight at feeling her sucking my cock was merely an unfortunate side effect.

The head of my cock glistened with precome as Sarah eased her lips around the thick shaft, breathing warmly over it without actually touching my cock with her mouth. She guided it slowly up and down with her hand, bringing it close to her mouth, letting it hover between her lips, even drooling on it slightly at one point. I could feel her breath ruffling my pubic hair and sending shivers through my body. Then she let her tongue snake out. I groaned as I felt the first tentative contact of her mouth with my cock—just a faint shimmer across the underside where the head met the shaft, near the glans. I shuddered with anticipation—but I knew Sarah would do this in her own sweet time.

"You're as cruel as ever, Mistress," I breathed, hardly able to control myself.

She laughed lightly and began to rub my cockhead over her face without ever letting it slide between her lips. She stroked the shaft up and down against her cheeks, then down her throat, stroking my shaft with her silken skin. She let her warm breath caress me. Then she slipped the strap of the camisole over one shoulder and shrugged it down, easing one divine breast out of the thin lacy garment.

My moaning became uncontrollable as she pressed the head of my cock to her erect nipple. She teased the head with her firm bud, playing with it and smearing precome over her nipple. I knew well how sensitive Sarah's nipples were—and how much she was enjoying this. She slipped off the other strap of her camisole deftly, exposing both her breasts. Then, while I moaned, she slid my cock between her tits. Sarah pressed her large breasts together and stroked my shaft in and out between them, holding my cock in a firm silken embrace. I ran my fingers through her hair as she squirmed on top of me, sliding my cock in and out. Then she pushed her breasts down, letting my cock jut out from between them. My cock was long enough to allow her mouth access to the head. I felt the flicker of her lips against it, and I moaned louder.

Then, Sarah began pushing her body up and down again, thrusting my cock against the entrance to her glorious mouth. She was driving me mad with her teasing. When she finally took the head of my cock between her lips and sucked it inside her mouth, I was wholly and totally her prisoner.

Then Sarah's hunger for cocksucking took over. She drew my shaft quickly into her mouth until the head pressed against the entrance to her throat—and, without hesitating, she swallowed it down, deep-throating it expertly. I groaned softly as I felt my cockhead imprisoned in the tight, wet grasp of Sarah's throat. She took me down until her lips pressed around the base of my shaft, my pubic hair doubtless tickling her nose. Then she just held it there, without a hint of struggling, plainly loving the feel of holding my cock prisoner in her warm embrace. I was already very close to coming, and I knew I couldn't take much more of this before I shot my load into Sarah's waiting mouth. But the Mistress was much too devious for that.

Instead, she just held my cock as long as her breath lasted, which was much longer than I would have thought possible. The pressure all around my cock was enough to drive me mad—but not enough to bring me off. My impending orgasm drifted away. Only when she sensed the tension in my body lessening did Sarah ease herself back up to take a breath, letting my cock slip halfway out of her mouth. It glistened with Sarah's spittle and the red streaks of her lipstick. She let me suffer there for a moment, tormented by the exquisite pleasure she was causing. She swallowed my cock again in an instant, taking it all the way down her throat and pumping it rapidly. Then the cocksucking began in earnest.

Sarah thrust my cock rhythmically down into her throat, swallowing without effort, eagerly gulping at my hard flesh. I squirmed in the big chair, clawing at the velvet arms, until I heard the material ripping. The chair probably cost five thousand dollars, but Sarah didn't seem to care—she didn't pause for an instant. She stroked my cock into her mouth, and when she sensed me getting close to my orgasm again, she held it, deep inside her throat, letting me feel my manhood embedded within her, imprisoned by her clever mouth. My orgasm vanished once again. Sarah slipped my cock out of her mouth and held it with her hand, rubbing it over her face, smearing lipstick and spittle over her cheeks, panting hungrily as she lapped at the shaft and rubbed the head with her thumb.

I opened my eyes long enough to see all three slaves watching in awe and admiration—particularly Tina, who appeared to be in some great difficulty, her face and breasts flushed and her pussy glistening.

Quickly, Sarah pressed my cock between her breasts again and began to slide it in and out. That was almost enough to bring me off—but not quite. Little spasms went through my cock, and droplets of come shot out across Sarah's breasts—but she paused long enough for me to catch my breath without coming. Then she smiled up at me cruelly.

The Contract

In an instant, Sarah was on top of me, hiking her skirt up all the way. She spread her thighs around mine and guided my cock to her entrance with her hand. She rubbed my cockhead against the entrance to her pussy, which was slick and wet with desire. Slowly, she nuzzled the head in and began to lower herself on her shaft.

I looked up at her, captivated by this vision of beauty. Then she pushed her body down, moaning in pleasure as she took all of my shaft into her pussy. Being tall, Sarah had a very long if snug pussy, and she could accommodate all of my shaft with a minimum of effort. She took my head in her hands and guided my mouth to her nipple, feeding me her breast. I began to lick and suckle, nibbling lightly, as she moved her hips back and forth, working my cock like a lever without thrusting. I knew well what Sarah was up to—I knew from experience that in this position, my cock curved just right to stimulate the spot inside her pussy which caused her immense pleasure—one of the many reasons she was so interested in fucking—perhaps the dominant reason, if you'll excuse the pun. I could tell from the look on her face and the flush of her breasts that she was hitting that spot now, pressing my cock against it, bringing herself closer without the rapid thrusts that would surely bring me off. Even so, my cock was enveloped in pleasure, the hot sleeve of her cunt holding me firmly and administering intense sensations with every movement of Sarah's body. I suckled on one breast, teasing the nipple of the other with my hand, feeling the small movements of her taut body against mine as she approached her crest.

Suddenly Sarah began to pound rapidly, thrusting my cock into her pussy. I knew she had reached the point of no return, that she would come at any second. Her breasts bounced hopelessly; I abandoned my suckling and took her tits in my hands, squeezing and kneading them, pinching the nipples as she rose and fell on top of me. Then I heard her moaning uncontrollably and felt the spasms of her cunt around my cock. She was coming, and I felt the warm spurt of her juice that sometimes came when she fucked me in this position, soaking my pubic hair, coating my cock in slick fluid. I was very close, and Sarah knew it. The second she was finished coming, she came to rest on top of me, pressing her lips against mine. Her tongue slipped into my mouth, teasing my own tongue out so she could suck it hungrily. She thrust her body back and forth just enough to keep me on the very edge.

"Not yet," she told me. "I want to see Tina's face while she watches you do it."

Sarah pulled herself off me slowly, then reversed the position quickly, snuggling her bare ass back against me. She leaned forward and reached down with her hand to guide my slick cock back inside her. As she did, I watched her sumptuous cheeks part and reveal the tight pink bud of her asshole, and I thought how delectable it would be to penetrate that as well. I had certainly done that to Sarah—but it wouldn't do to suggest it right now, not while I was so completely in her thrall. Instead I relaxed and let Sarah take first my cockhead, then all of my shaft into her pussy as she sat down on top of me. She leaned back and turned her head to kiss me, stroking her tongue in and out of my mouth. Then she turned her attention back to Tina, as did I.

Tina's discomfort was evident. She still knelt in the submissive position, with her legs spread. No doubt the hours she had spent in that position had caused her muscles to cramp by now. But that wasn't the real source of her discomfort. By the bright red color of her face and breasts, it was clear that Tina was extremely aroused. If that hadn't given her away, then the faint slick stain on the carpet under her spread legs would have done it.

I held Sarah close, my hands resting on her breasts and toying with her nipples as she squirmed in my lap.

"Masturbate her, Shade!" she ordered, looking at the slave on the left. "While you kiss her and touch her breasts, Whisper. But don't block her view of us."

The two slaves moved quickly to obey. I knew that Sarah was enjoying the torture of making me wait for my orgasm at least as much as she was enjoying Tina's visible distress. But the sight of the two naked slaves going to work on Tina's bound vulnerable body was enough to keep me more than satisfied with the current state of affairs.

Whisper moved and began kissing Tina, her head turned at just the right angle to allow her an unobstructed view of us as we fucked, while she pinched and stroked her nipples. Shade's hand came up between Tina's thighs and began rubbing her clit. Tina was obviously very close; she immediately began moaning and it was evident that she was about to come. Sarah began to thrust her body against me, pushing my cock rhythmically into her as she turned her head to kiss me hungrily again. Then she turned back to watch Tina moaning and thrashing in climax on Shade's stroking hand. Sarah leaned forward so her feet touched the floor, crouching over my cock so she could thrust it into her quickly. My back arched and I squirmed in the chair, my hands gripping Sarah's waist as she fucked me. Then I was coming, as I heard Tina's groans reach a crescendo of orgasm. I could feel my cock pumping in to Sarah's tightly gripping cunt, as she watched Shade and Whisper bringing Tina off.

Exhausted, Sarah leaned back against me, turning to kiss me one last time as Tina fell back, crumpling to the ground, spent.

My eyes fluttered closed, my own exhaustion taking me over as my cock surged its last seed inside Sarah. Sarah whispered to me, "Don't fall asleep yet. There's still a show to be had." Then she sat up again and pulled my cock out of her slowly, putting her hand between her legs to stanch the flow of semen dribbling from her pussy.

With the authority of full ownership, she walked over to Tina, who lay on the ground with her face up. Sarah crouched over her facing me, so that I could see everything. Sarah took her hand away from her pussy, spreading her legs and lowering her cunt onto Tina's face.

Tina moaned softly as Sarah pressed her cunt up to her lips.

"That's right, you little slut. You want this, don't you? You wish it was you he was fucking. You wish it was you taking his come in your tight little pussy. Don't you?"

Tina's only response was her squirm of her pleasure as Sarah rubbed her cunt over her face. Sarah reached down and ran her hand, slick with come, through Tina's lovely blonde hair. I couldn't see everything, but I knew that after my prolonged torture, I had filled Sarah's cunt with great volumes of come. I watched as she rubbed her pussy over Tina's face, obviously savoring the feel of her cunt dripping my come onto Tina. Tina lapped obediently at her Mistress's pussy, but Sarah's hips moved just enough to keep her from getting a hold, so that her cunt oozed all over Tina's face and into her hair. Sarah stroked Tina's hair softly, and I knew it must be growing slick with sweat and come.

"Yes, you little minx," Sarah cooed. "You like that. Taste it. Feel it all over your face." Finally she settled down on Tina's mouth, and I watched her body relax as she eased herself into the pleasures Tina could bring her. Tina lay on the ground and began worshiping her Mistress eagerly, her mouth no doubt filling with my come. I could see the flush of her thighs and the squirming of her body that told me she was becoming aroused all over again as she serviced Sarah.

"You know how to do it. Come on, make me come again. Come on, you little bitch...."

Sarah's hips rocked back and forth as Tina served her with her mouth and tongue. "Clean him off," said Sarah dismissively to Whisper, who crawled toward me quickly and knelt beside the chair. She took my soft cock in her hand and guided it between her lips, then began licking and sucking it all over. It was covered with the slickness of Sarah's juices as well as my own, but Whisper did not hesitate to do as she was told. Soon, as her warm mouth enveloped my prick, I felt myself getting hard again.

"Go ahead," Sarah said breathlessly as she rocked back and forth on Tina's face. "Bring him off again, if you can. Just make sure you clean up every drop."

With that, Whisper began sucking me in earnest, and my cock surged to its full potency once again. Whisper had some difficulty swallowing my entire length, but she managed to take it into her throat until her lips curved around the base. Then she began pumping my cock into her suckling mouth, working the base of the shaft with her fist as she did. She took the time

THE CONTRACT

to lick around the head, teasing me closer to orgasm, then she swallowed it again and began pumping in earnest, determined to make me come.

"Oh, yes!" Sarah sighed, watching as Whisper gave me head. Sarah was plainly very close to her second orgasm, and Tina was obviously working her tongue enthusiastically.

I knew that Sarah had entertained the occasional male visitor—myself among them—but I couldn't imagine how Whisper had become such an accomplished cocksucker without hundreds, perhaps thousands, of hours of practice. I wondered whose cocks she had serviced before—or was it the Mistress's strap-on that Whisper had eagerly swallowed again and again and again?

Sarah's hips began rocking more quickly as Whisper pumped my cock. Sarah's face went bright red, and she took hold of her breasts, pinching the nipples. Shade was still kneeling, awaiting further orders. Sarah reached out to grasp Shade's hair and pull her close. Sarah began kissing Shade eagerly as she gasped and moaned in orgasm. Then I felt myself nearing. Whisper seemed to sense it, too. She obediently kept the same rhythm, thrusting her mouth down over my cock, and as I moaned my orgasm Sarah laughed in glee. I felt my cock spasming, shooting into Whisper's eagerly waiting mouth, as Sarah pushed Shade's face down to her breasts. Shade obediently began suckling her Mistress's nipples, moving quickly back and forth between them and squeezing Sarah's breasts with her hands. Sarah watched me coming, watched me writhing in ecstasy as Whisper obediently swallowed every drop of my come.

Then Sarah moaned her pleasure, and came long and loud on Tina's eagerly working mouth. She began to caress Shade's face and hair as she whimpered in the final throes of her orgasm. Whisper had finished me and was reverently kissing my softening cock, rubbing it over her face, licking it clean and drying it with her hair.

Sarah settled down onto Tina's face for one last pleasurable minute as she finished her orgasm. Then she lifted herself off the panting slave. Tina's face was slick with come and juices, her beautiful blonde hair matted with them. Shade helped Sarah into the easy chair opposite me, and Sarah lay there, her legs spread and her pussy glistening visibly, glistening with Tina's spittle and the other juices that filled it. Sarah snapped her fingers and Shade quickly produced a Gauloise from a silver case on the coffee table. Sarah let Shade put the cigarette between her lips, which were messy with spittle and the pink of her smeared lipstick.

Whisper finished with me and went back to kneel reverently with her fellow slave at the side of their Mistress.

Tina remained on the floor, her body clearly in a very uncomfortable position. Her eyes flickered over me, but as I met them she turned away, blushing.

THE CONTRACT

Sarah and I looked at each other for long minutes as she enjoyed her cigarette.

Then: "Show Carlton to his quarters, Shade. Get him some clean clothes and towels. And if he should require anything more…please don't hesitate to see to it with the utmost enthusiasm. He is your Master now. And Carlton—"

"Yes, Mistress?" I said with a faint tone of sarcasm.

"Pay particular attention to those breasts," she told me. "They're quite a handful."

I saw Shade blushing slightly as she rose to do as she was told, her gorgeous breasts swaying before me.

CHAPTER 3

Watching that pretty slave's bottom wiggle going up the stairs put more dirty thoughts in my mind than I would have had otherwise. Certainly I was all but spent from Sarah's and Whisper's ministrations, but I had yet to sample the sweetness of Shade, one of Sarah's few dark-haired slaves. And I felt sure I could summon enough strength to use her properly, though it might be a bit of an effort. So as the naked girl led me up the spiral staircase, I took great pleasure in following just far enough behind her so that I could see the inviting lips of her cunt between her legs as she walked. Like the others, she was clean shaven. It would be delightful to pass the remainder of the afternoon with my cock sliding slowly into Shade's pussy.

Despite the fact that my cock had been well attended to by Sarah and Whisper, I felt it stirring as I contemplated the long hours before dinner, long hours I could while away with Shade squirming delightfully underneath me.

Shade showed me to a room on the top floor which was as luxurious as any I had ever stayed in. As luxurious as I would expect in Sarah's house. And the room seemed to be designed with one basic purpose. The four-poster bed, for instance, was large enough for three or four slaves to entertain their Master or Mistress without too much crowding, and there was a sunken tub with gold fixtures big enough for that same number of slaves to accompany their Lord or Lady at bath. My needs at the moment were much simpler, though, and I didn't require many preliminaries.

Once Shade was inside the room, I didn't give her the opportunity to close the door behind us, but slipped up behind her immediately and pushed her onto the bed so that she was bent over its side. My arms circled around her as I put my lips to her ear.

"You were the only one who missed out down there," I said. "You must feel...neglected?"

"No, my Liege," sighed Shade, her waist bent over the edge of the high bed so that her pretty bottom wriggled invitingly against the hardness of my cock through my pants.

The Contract

"Then you wouldn't welcome the chance to follow your Mistress's orders and service this need of mine that's sprung up?"

I could feel Shade's cheeks growing hot against my lips. She pressed her buttocks back against my hard shaft. "No, my Liege…I mean, yes, my Liege…. I would gladly service your needs. If you were to desire it."

"Well I desire it." I lifted myself off her. "As satisfied as I was by your Mistress's sweet pussy, I'm still quite curious about yours. Stay right there in that position." I began to take off my clothes.

"My Liege," said Shade breathlessly. "Shouldn't we… Shouldn't we at least close the door?"

"I don't think so," I said as I disrobed. "Let everyone in the house know what a hungry little slut you are …and how well you service your Mistress's guests. Make sure you make a lot of noise while I fuck you. You can make noise, can't you?"

"Y-Yes, my Liege."

Now naked, I returned to Shade and lay against her, the long shaft of my cock pressed between her delicious cheeks. She gasped as I began to kiss and gnaw at the back of her neck. As I moved against her, my hard cock slid in and out of the crevice between her firm cheeks. I wondered if I should take her there, should explore her enticing bottom rather than thrusting my cock into her pussy. Perhaps, I decided, but that would come later. For now I wanted to feel the warmth of her mouth and her breasts and her cunt—I could deal with her pert little derriere later—perhaps much later if she proved herself as eager a slave as I thought she might.

I let my arms circle around Shade's body again and placed my hands on her exquisite breasts. They were indeed wonderfully firm to the touch, despite their great size. And from the mewling whimper that Shade gave as I began to caress them roughly, they were quite sensitive.

"You must be quite proud of these."

"Yes, my Liege," Shade breathed, squirming against me as I played with her large nipples. "Very much so."

"I wonder why your Mistress hasn't pierced them," I mused. "Has she told you?"

"Yes, my Liege," Shade gasped as I pinched her nipples. "She says she likes them sensitive like this. But if she pierced them, I would come every time a man looked at them."

"Really! And men look at them all the time, don't they?"

"Yes, my Liege. And…women."

I spread my hands out over Shade's breasts, exploring every inch of their smoothness. "The other slaves? Your Mistress?"

"Yes, my Liege."

"Ah!" I got her meaning. "But you enjoy having men look at them even more?"

Shade was blushing, obviously embarrassed, but she managed to sigh, "Yes, my Liege."

The Contract

I began to stroke Shade's breasts rhythmically, paying particular attention to the way she moved when I worked her nipples. To think of it! I had been lucky enough to jump the one slave in Sarah's stable who truly preferred men. If I knew Sarah, Shade might get the occasional dose of male flesh, but the little vixen probably didn't get enough cock to satisfy her. Well, I could cure that for a short while, at least. "You say she thought you'd come so easily if she pierced your nipples. Do you climax from having your nipples played with?"

"Ohhhhhh...ohhhhhhh!..." Shade was lost in a haze of ecstasy as I stimulated her nipples. That was my answer. But still, after a while, she murmured, "Yes...oh, yes, my Liege."

"What a rare gift!" I tweaked her nipples harder. I jiggled against Shade and felt the pleasure of her parted cheeks around my shaft. "Can you play with them yourself and make yourself come? Without touching your clit?"

"Yes, my Liege," she whimpered. "If I'm being fucked."

"Ah! A sensitive cunt as well! But if you're not being fucked—if your legs are spread, you're not rubbing them together, and nothing is against your pussy or your clit, nothing in your cunt at all...can you make yourself come then?"

Shade was wriggling against me, overwhelmed with the sensations I was causing in her nipples. "S-Sometimes, my Liege. If I am very aroused. The Mistress is training me to do it on command. Without touching my clitoris."

How wonderful! I had happened not only upon one of Sarah's slaves who was desperate for cock, but one who could do exciting parlor tricks as well.

Her firm ass rubbed against my cock as she squirmed in pleasure underneath me. I desperately wanted to part those cheeks and enter her back door, to fuck her in the ass while I made her come with my hands. Or perhaps to roll her over and enter her pussy with my face buried between those glorious mounds. Or possibly to guide Shade to her knees before me and see if that pretty pierced mouth of hers could work the same magic that Whisper's had so recently worked—if she could use those lips and that tongue and the throat that lay beyond to pleasure my cock until I came in her mouth. But I had other, slightly more exotic things in mind, and I would have plenty of time to explore all the delights of Shade's body. I moved back, taking my hands off her breasts; she gave a little sigh of regret as I released my hold on her tits. Shade looked back over her shoulder at me, and I considered her lush body, bent over with both her smooth-shaved slit and the puckered pink ring of her asshole open to my explorations. But instead of doing the obvious, and pushing my cock into one of those willing openings to take my pleasure from Shade's body, I told her to turn around.

"And get down on your knees," I continued. "Legs spread very wide, as wide as you can make them. Lean back against the bed. Put your hands on your breasts."

My cock throbbed erect and eager, ready for whatever deviance I could come up with. Shade obeyed, kneeling before me and leaning back against the bed, her hands on her breasts.

"Play with your nipples. The way you like to do when you're by yourself."

Shade obeyed, pinching them very hard and rubbing each nipple back and forth between thumb and forefinger. As she did, a look of ecstasy crossed her face, and she moaned faintly.

"How often does the Mistress make you try to come with just your nipples stimulated?"

"Every night," said Shade. "Most nights I do it in front of her, for her enjoyment."

"And how long does it take you?"

"Sometimes only a few minutes. Sometimes as long as an hour. Other nights I can't do it at all, and she makes me practice for at least a couple of hours before administering my punishment. When she's watching, sometimes she has the other slaves service her. Oh!..."

"And does it feel good right now?"

"Very good, my Liege.... Oh!..."

"Perfect," I said. "I'm going to put those big tits to their proper use. Well...*one* of their proper uses." I bent over, pursed my lips, and let a thick drop of spittle fall from my lips onto Shade's breasts; she gasped and started a bit, but accepted this slight degradation as a symbol of her place as a slave. She looked up at me, eyes wide, lips slightly parted, breathing heavily as she played with her breasts. I let several more drops of spit fall into the deep valley of her cleavage.

"Rub it in," I ordered her. "Smear it all over."

Obediently, Shade rubbed my spittle over the center of her breasts with her fingers, until her milk white flesh glistened. Then she returned to stimulating her own nipples, groaning as she pinched them. My little display seemed to have aroused her. Crouching over Shade, I moved forward and slid my cock between her gorgeous breasts, into her deep cleft. I knew that within minutes her sweat would provide the proper lubrication, but the spittle was needed to get it started—and besides, it was such a delight to spit on the breasts of a willing slave. From Shade's response, the novelty of this sensation had aroused her at least a little. But as I laid my long, hard cock between her tits, Shade gave a hungry wail of excitement and began to squeeze her nipples more eagerly.

"Have you ever had this done to you before?" I asked her as I stroked my cock against the swells of her breasts. They were such delightful breasts that I couldn't believe no man had wanted to fuck her there before.

"No, my Liege," she said breathlessly, seeming painfully aroused by the prospect. "Never."

"Big beautiful tits like this," I grunted, "and no man's ever fucked them? I can hardly believe that! Push them together around my cock."

Shade obeyed, moaning as she imprisoned my manhood between her breasts, pushing them together eagerly as she continued to play with her nipples. Her face and cleavage were bright red, and I didn't doubt that they were flushing as she neared orgasm. Such an eager little vixen. I began to slide my cock in and out into her caressing breasts, panting as my pleasure mounted.

"It's true, my Liege," she gasped. "No man has ever done this to me...oh...oh...you're my first...."

There seemed to be a lot of this going around. But I forgot all that as I looked down at Shade with her glorious breasts in her hands, stimulating her nipples hungrily as she received my cock eagerly between them. Shade was moaning rhythmically now, the stimulation of her nipples bringing her closer to her climax.

"You're going to come now, aren't you?"

"Soon, Master...very soon...."

My hips pistoned rapidly, sliding my cock into the embrace of Shade's breasts. I fucked her faster, getting very close myself. Her sweat dribbled down her neck and slicked up my cock, making the passage between her breasts easier. Shade's fingers worked their magic on her own nipples, and as she readied herself for my load, her moans grew louder and louder. Finally, she threw back her head and cried out, and I could see from the spasms of her lower body that she was climaxing. Even so, she did not lose the rhythm of our bodies pumping together—if anything, her ministrations became more perfect, urging me on to orgasm.

"Yes...yes...here I come!... Oh!" I gasped as I felt my cock spasming. I thrust between her breasts, keeping perfect time as the first stream of my semen shot out onto her throat. Shade shuddered and moaned as I came on her. The next stream spurted over her breasts, covering her cleavage. Shade looked down to watch me come, her lips parted; and the next stream of my come splashed across her face, slicking her lips. Then another stream, this time splattering into her hair and across her cheeks. More streams soaked Shade's dark hair, and a shudder of final orgasm went through me. As I finished, a few more spasms sent my semen gushing into her cleavage again, and my last thrusts spread it over her breasts. She leaned back more heavily on the bed, utterly spent, as I pulled my cock out from between her breasts. She rubbed her tits and her pretty collared throat all over, smearing the jizz over them, then licked her lips and ran her fingers through her come-matted hair. I smiled down at her.

"Very impressive," came Sarah's voice from the doorway, dripping with sarcasm. "A vicious young slut and a dirty old man. Two peas in a pod."

CHAPTER 4

Sarah was standing in the doorway—of course, I had left the door open. "But then, I am such a connoisseur of sluts. As you are. Is she up to measure—so to speak? Or is it *you* who needs to be brought up to measure?"

"She'll do," I said coyly, stroking Shade's matted hair.

"There are so many ways to enjoy a slave when she's properly cooperative. Do you come up with filthy ideas spontaneously, or do you have to work at it? Or did you take some sort of *class* or something? Or was it the little slut's own idea to let you tit-fuck her and come on her face?"

Shade blushed, but she was still breathing heavily from arousal. I could tell that the presence of her

Mistress was at once humiliating and thrilling to her. I wondered what she would like to do right now with that filthy little mouth, given her choice. Lick my cock clean or service her Mistress's doubtlessly wet pussy? Probably she would like to do both, one after the other. But which one first?

"I can't recall. Both of us were so enthusiastic about the filthy act, I've lost track of which one thought of it first."

Sarah looked more beautiful than ever. She had changed into an almost translucent long white robe that plunged low between her breasts and had high slits up each side, showing her wonderful legs up to her hips. I could just faintly see the outline of what little *was* hidden by the robe—particularly, I could tell that Sarah was wearing a very skimpy pair of black panties. Probably more like a G-string, if I knew Sarah. The robe, which appeared to be silk, clung to the outline of her breasts and showed me quite evidently that her nipples were very hard. Her hair was still down, combed out to form a golden mane around her beautiful face.

"Well, no matter. She makes such a pretty picture, on her knees and covered in your semen. I think it's her proper state. You know so many delightful ways to improve the appearances of my slaves."

I laughed. "As many ways as I can think up, my dear. Perhaps you would care to switch places with your slave? Your chance for a full three-minute beauty makeover."

Sarah's lips curled contemptuously. "Oh, dear Carlton! You know how that would delight me—but in my own good time, not yours. And I'm sure it would take no longer than a minute—*if* you could get it up at all. On the other hand, I came to discuss *important matters* —not the all-natural cruelty-free makeup of this horny little bitch of a slave—you do remember *Tina?*"

"How could I forget?" I said. "She's the one you can't seem to control. Well, this one is certainly quite obedient." Shade blushed still deeper. "You're dismissed, Shade. But first, get me a robe."

Shade stood up and quickly retrieved a rich satin robe from the closet. She returned and held it up for me. I slipped into it and turned to look at Shade. Her face, throat, and breasts were still slick with my juice, her hair glistening with it.

"Such a pretty picture!" Sarah echoed my thoughts. "I think your fluids really do improve her appearance. Don't you think so, Carlton?"

I smiled. "She is quite attractive this way."

"Very well," Sarah said. "Shade, don't wipe yourself or wash your hands. Remain this way until I tell you differently. In the meantime, summon Adriana to serve us tea. But you will be attending us at dinner. As you are. And Tina shall be our centerpiece."

Shade blushed a deep red, my semen still dripping

off her breasts. "Yes, Mistress." She hustled off, her pert ass disappearing through the door. I was delighted. Sarah's emotional sadism was enough to stir me once more, even though my soft cock still glowed with the warmth of my recent orgasm. I pulled my robe closed and tied it, seating myself in a chair facing the coffee table and putting my feet up on a velvet ottoman. Sarah sat in the chair opposite me.

"Thank you for the use of your slaves," I told Sarah. "Both Shade and Whisper have proven to be well worth my time."

Sarah shifted, showing me more of her cleavage as the robe parted slightly. "Yes, well. Perhaps you should turn your attention to Tina? After all, we have a wager going here."

"Ah, yes," I said. "I trust your clerk has drawn up the Contract?"

"Yes, we'll have it signed before dinner. Which is at eight. In the meantime, there are a few things I would like to discuss—if you're in the mood for discussion."

"Always in the mood for a discussion," I told her. "Especially when my partner in the discussion is wearing as little as you are."

"Little? I feel I am wearing so much, Carlton." With that, she loosened the tie of her robe and let it fall open a few more inches. Now I could see much of her breasts, and the flimsy fabric threatened to fall completely off her body at any moment. God, how I prayed it would—

THE CONTRACT

already my cock was stiffening by Sarah's presence. If I didn't stop flogging the little yeoman, he was going to jump ship one of these days.

Adriana entered the room, naked except for the black leather collar around her throat. Adriana was a redhead, her long, coarse hair a shimmering rust. She was a bit taller than Shade or Whisper, with medium-sized but very firm breasts and a ripe round ass. Her flesh was very pale, almost glowing white, and bore a liberal smattering of freckles, particularly her face and breasts. But her thighs, belly, and ass also were quite freckled. Adriana's small nipples were a shockingly pale shade of pink and were pierced with thick silver rings. Her cunt, too, was pierced—more times than I could count on such short notice—and a ring went vertically through Adriana's clitoris. Her cuntlips were thick and full, appearing even more so with their many rings. However, the lips of her mouth were somewhat thin, an enticing pale pink accented by the freckles on her face. To my surprise, her pubic hair was not shaved, though it was clipped very short. It was the same lustrous red as on her head. I could see why Sarah allowed Adriana to go without shaving; it presented an aesthetically pleasing picture. In fact, though Sarah usually did not prefer redheads, I could see why she'd made an exception in Adriana's case.

Adriana held a tray with tea and two small bottles of wine—one white and one red—and a small selection of Italian breads with a cruet of olive oil and its accompanying dish for dipping. Adriana said softly, "It pleases you to take refreshment, Mistress?"

"Certainly, Adriana. Tea, Carlton? Italian breads?"

"I'm not hungry just yet, but I would really enjoy a glass of wine."

"Very good," said Sarah. "White or red?"

I looked at Adriana, my hunger for her showing plainly. "Red, of course, my dear."

Adriana blushed a little. With her pale skin, she seemed to blush easily.

"The Chateau Réage, 1953," said Sarah. "I'll have the same." I was impressed.

Adriana poured the wine, bending over so her bottom looked that much more delightful. The lips of her sex were enticingly pale, like the rest of her. But the entrance of her cunt was a radiant shade of pink, just begging to be entered. I could see the appeal of having it framed with her lovely red hair. I wondered whether she had the same oral talents as Whisper, if her pretty mouth could give head as exquisitely as the blonde slave. But I also wondered what the girl was like on the other end. She had a magnificent pair of freckled cheeks, petite but just full enough to frame her pretty asshole when she bent at the right angle. And as she bent just a little farther to pour the wine, I could again see her pink slit. I resolved that I would sample both of those before too much longer had passed, and see if her mouth was indeed as good as Whisper's.

The Contract

I sprawled out on the velvet divan, stretching my legs as Adriana prepared the wine for Sarah to taste. I looked out the window, admiring the setting sun. Sarah certainly knew how to live in luxury, and the view of the bay really was spectacular. It caused me to meditate on the beauty of Shade's, Whisper's, Adriana's—and, most importantly, Tina's Mistress.

Sarah was the most breathtaking creature I could imagine. Her beauty was legendary, of course, but she possessed much more than beauty. Her magnetism drew people to her, made them submit to her will with or without a Contract. Her strength caused people to slide deeper into total submission. And her cultured but primal sexuality made them unable to resist becoming her slaves for delightful eternity.

I felt sure that Tina was different. She had a will that Sarah could not break, or Sarah would not have enlisted me. The mere fact that Sarah agreed to those terms showed me that she was desperate. Sarah had fallen in love with Tina. But Tina resisted her Mistress's charms.

Perhaps it was Tina's unbreakable will that so attracted Sarah. I didn't doubt that she was turned on by a challenge, and she deeply loved to destroy the resistance of a naughty slave, to bring that slave to her knees.

Sarah had long selected more women than men as her submissives, though she had certainly taken her share of both. As I had found out over the many years that Sarah and I had known each other, she dearly loved sex with men, and sought it out every chance she got. She was particularly fond of being fucked, and even enjoyed sucking cock—something she did without the slightest hint of submission. Sarah could drop to her knees before you and swallow your cock till you came in her mouth—but *she* was always in control.

Perhaps that was part of what made Sarah such an incredible fuck—everything she did was done for her own pleasure. Even my own climax was achieved because Sarah wished to feel my seed shooting into her. This love of the male sex allowed her to take male slaves with a profound zest, and I had seen her destroy a male slave's will and seduce him into complete and total submission with a passion that was nothing if not supernatural. I had seen the Mistress minister to the needs of many young men, obviously enjoying every moment of it, every inch of their hard cocks. She borrowed male slaves from many of her friends, enjoying them for as long as it suited her whims to do so. But for full-time slaves, she usually enjoyed women—young women of magnificent beauty and ripe sexuality.

And so it was not surprising that Sarah was in love with Tina. In a way, love was its own form of submission, and it delighted me to imagine the Mistress on her knees before Tina, bound and offering oral servitude. Which was similar to the truth.

For Tina's iron will had brought Mistress Sarah to her knees. She had enlisted my help, already offering me a form of submission, by admitting she was helpless against Tina's resistance. Knowing that fact made my cock stir.

I would seduce Tina, would break her will, would cause her to become the true submissive that Sarah wanted. Tina would give Sarah her soul and become Sarah's slave, like so many before her. She would finally be on her knees, properly dedicated to her Mistress. Sarah would welcome Tina into her vast stable.

And then I would take Sarah's submission for myself. I would see her pierced and shaved, chained for me. I would savor the sight of her on her knees, head bowed, mouth and cunt and ass open for my use. I would take long hours to avail myself of her lush, fragrant body, to feel the warmth of her mouth clutching my organ, knowing that this time her pleasures were offered by a woman in submission.

I could already feel Sarah's attraction toward complete submission. No truly dominant woman—or man—is free from the curiosity of what it must be like to submit. Part of her *wanted* to submit to me. There was a close bond between us. We had known each other for many years, had been friends and lovers, had shared many submissives. I had always sensed in Sarah the faintest echo of a desire to submit herself to a man's ownership.

Given the opportunity, Sarah would find that submission delightful. She would offer herself to me eagerly, even if she hid behind the necessity of the Contract. And after tasting the wonders of life on her knees before me, I believed that Sarah would find herself more fulfilled than she expected by those delights.

Sarah's dominant spirit would crumble. While she felt the thrust of my cock, the slap of my hand on her ass, the weight of my collar around her neck—she would find herself giving up her power and her will in exchange for ecstasy on her knees at my booted feet.

I would not be fully satisfied until I owned Sarah, until she inhabited a tiny cage at the foot of my bed. And I did not doubt that that time would come to pass.

I did not doubt that, when Tina bowed her head and submitted totally to her Mistress, Sarah would happily lower herself to her knees before me, with her passion rising.

Adriana finished with the wine and handed me my glass. It was excellent. She curtsied.

My cock had grown incredibly hard as I imagined Sarah's inevitable submission, despite its recent efforts. I saw Sarah eyeing its shape under the fabric of the robe.

"I wonder what you could be thinking about, Carlton."

"You in chains, my dear. Care to join me in my thoughts?"

The robe, fringed in lace and trimmed with white fur, plunged deep between her ample breasts, showing her milky cleavage. Her nipples were clearly visible through the translucent fabric. They were quite evidently hard, and I wondered if she might be aroused by the thought of herself in chains before me.

Sarah's eyes lazed over my erect cock. She gave me the faintest of smiles.

"That must be a delightful fantasy!" her voice dripped with sarcasm. "But I think I'll leave it for you to enjoy."

I didn't justify that with a reply. I stretched on the divan, letting my robe fall open farther, more completely revealing my erect cock.

Sarah never took her eyes off of my cock as she said to Adriana, "Wait just outside the door in case we should need you. And...well, no reason to waste the time. Summon Eduardo from downstairs and have him fuck you while you wait. On your hands and knees. I want Eduardo to take you from behind. But neither of you is allowed to come. Understood?"

"Yes, Mistress." Adriana didn't miss a beat, but her face was turning red. "Shall I leave the door open or closed?"

"Closed." Sarah sipped at her wine. "And don't make any noise. But his thrusting must be constant. No breaks until I summon you. Eduardo is very good at outlasting frenzied little bitches like you. Isn't he?"

"Yes, Mistress." Adriana curtsied before fluttering off and closing the door behind her.

After a long moment of silence in which we both sipped our wine: "Practicing for Tina?" I asked.

"Not particularly," said Sarah. "Just enjoying myself.

And you?" Her eyes were fixed lustfully on the shape of my erection under the robe. Sarah smiled cruelly as she shifted in her velvet chair across from me.

"Practicing for you." I curved my hand around my hard cock, giving it a single slow stroke through my robe.

Sarah chuckled. "No need to practice. Submission will come naturally to you. Life on your knees pleasuring your Mistress will prove such a delight...simply letting all that control slip away, giving your body over to me for abuse and nurturing...feeling my hand inside you as you give up all your power...to me...."

"I think you have it backward," I said. "For I sense in Tina's Mistress an extreme desire to kneel...."

Sarah yawned. "You *are* quite impressive, Carlton—quite a hard-on you're sporting there. I shouldn't mind falling on it myself—some other time in some other circumstance. But if you think you can conquer Tina by sheer staying power, you're quite wrong. Perhaps a younger man could make a go of it—but as magnificent as your famous staying power might be, it's no match for our little Tina, even on an off day. You understand that she's eighteen?"

This was war.

"I've been practicing my Eastern meditation techniques," I told her. "I can fuck a pretty young woman for six days straight and still not shoot off or lose my woody." I looked Sarah up and down suggestively, particularly focusing on her breasts and then her face. "You, on the other hand...I imagine fifteen minutes would be my limit."

"Ooooh! A tenfold increase!" Sarah made a show of buffing her nails on her silken robe.

"My darling, how sweet of you to say, but you know that fifteen minutes is a hundredfold increase for me—but yes, it seemed much longer to me, as well. It's so hard to judge time's passage when you're having a beastly experience, especially one that's fairly rhythmic in nature."

"Perhaps you ought to look in to getting one of those patches."

I shrugged. "I'll need it only if I have cause to sleep with you again," I said. "And with so many young women to choose from...I doubt that's a possibility." I smiled.

Sarah yawned faintly and stretched, letting the robe shift enough to show me the full length of one gorgeous leg and an ample amount of cleavage. She looked quite fetching stretching out there in her chair. She had grown tired of our verbal sparring; neither of us could win. I knew that she would take each insult personally, and that would fuel our hunger when we finally did fall into bed together—which, from the look in Sarah's eyes and the way her nipples showed through her robe—hard and ready—would most likely be before she left this room.

"Certainly you wouldn't need a patch," she told me,

getting in the last vicious stab. "You would just blindfold your partner and tell her you're still inside long after you've shot off on the bedspread. How would she know any different?"

Ouch! That was a good one. Before I could come up with a suitable reply to dignify Sarah's kidney punch, she fixed my eyes in hers and told me, through her smoldering gaze and nothing more, that she was going to fuck me in half within a matter of minutes. I toyed with the idea of getting out of my chair and rushing over to take my pleasure with the evil bitch right then. But that was exactly what Sarah wanted—to have me come to her, without her asking. I knew that beneath that thin robe she was wetter than a river, and my cock would find her ready. The verbal abuse she had heaped on me had turned her into a ravenous beast. I knew she would not be happy until she had my cock inside her again, clenched in the tight wetness and firm muscles of her pussy—but for the moment, she was too proud to ask for it. And so this was a game we would play. The verbal beating was one of Sarah's favorite types of foreplay, and we had enjoyed it many times together, each session of mutual insult culminating in a fervent passionate fuck. Our little game had done more to turn her on than anything else this afternoon. Ah, what a joy it is to dine at the table of cruelty with a fellow gourmand of sadism.

Sarah's eyes fluttered. With the position of her body, she all but begged me to fuck her silly. But then, her voice breathy and hungry with need, she went on. "I only hope that you can show her the same consideration you've shown Shade." Her eyes lingered over my cock. I let my eyes rove over Sarah and my cock did not dwindle.

I laughed. "Every punishment that I perform on Tina will be performed for your glory, Mistress. It will be your face I see when I administer Tina's discipline."

Sarah looked perturbed at my mocking tone, but then she laughed. The laughter was not arrogant, but friendly, which surprised me. I watched her excitedly as she leaned back into the chair, relaxing for once.

"There's no need for us to fence, Carlton. Your wit is as sharp as ever—but please, let's turn it toward Tina and her deflowering and taming. It is going to be quite a task. Much more a task than taming Shade, who's a horny little slut with an urge for the most extreme degradation possible. Besides, Shade so loves to be fucked, and Tina has never been taken."

"As you told me. And yet Shade was never taken in the way I just took her...." I moved the robe modestly to cover more of myself.

Sarah made a dismissive gesture with her hand. "If I miss a few things here and there...well, then, all the more pleasure for my guests—you included. Now on to Tina."

"No arguments here." I licked my lips hungrily.

Outside, I heard a faint moan, then a louder one—Adriana's voice.

"Sounds like our little bitch is getting fucked properly." said Sarah, licking her lips. I can always count on Eduardo. But Adriana will pay for that later."

"God, I hope so," I said, listening closely and detecting the faint rhythmic panting—almost undetectable—outside the door.

Sarah continued, "Tina is a very rebellious young woman. Of course, that is what attracted me to her in the first place, and her to me. As I said, she is eighteen. That is the time in a woman's life when she asserts her strength and independence, if she is the type who is inclined to do so. I am very lucky that I caught Tina just as she was coming into that period, so that the seeds of her eventual complete submission would be planted early enough. Her sexuality has been awakened, but she hasn't yet released it completely into my control."

I nodded, fascinated by watching Sarah talk. It was plain that Tina affected her deeply. I didn't doubt that the Mistress was becoming aroused just talking about her slave's sexuality. Sarah's need for Tina was extreme.

"You know that I do enjoy virgins, though they are generally less willing or able to sign the Contract. When I discovered her, Tina was the perfect virgin. She had a fire, a raw sexuality, a desperate need to submit and to give and receive pleasure. And she had an incredible hunger for women. I knew these things as soon as I laid eyes on her. She was a virgin because her father was a rich, powerful widower, and he wished to save her for a suitable marriage. It wasn't hard to convince her to come with me; on the contrary, she wanted me as much as I wanted her. The hoax was set up, and her father convinced through some well-forged paperwork that I was the daughter of his mother's long-lost younger sister. I was given charge of Tina's education. Her father was willing to sign her over to me—and Tina was deliriously happy to come."

Sarah's cleavage had flushed deeply as she spoke of Tina. I could see that her nipples were still hard beneath the robe, in fact they were harder than when we'd begun talking. Sarah sat up quickly as she realized how aroused she was becoming. She continued, her voice deep and husky with sexuality.

"Tina was eager to submit, but as she did, her will exerted itself. And her will was incredible. She desperately wanted to please me in every way with her ripe young virgin body, and I allowed her many liberties—far too many. I found myself fond of giving Tina orgasms. I was too lax with her in every way, so that she began to resist my will when it went against hers. And when I finally tried to take control of her rebellious little masturbation games—you know how young women are—and her flirtations with the other slaves, she resisted me powerfully. She still hungers for my love, but she needs severe training."

"But you don't have the heart to give it to her." I laughed softly.

"That is not the case, Carlton." Sarah did not sound defensive—just firm. "I have given her all punishments possible. But she refuses to give her sexuality over to me. I must control every sensation, every emotion, every feeling inside her luscious body if I am to receive her submission. I must know that her *only* desire is to please me, and her physical pleasure is an extension of that."

Sarah was breathing heavily, and her face had grown as flushed as her cleavage. She had let her thighs slip partway open, the robe riding up a bit. My cock was harder than ever, and I watched her with wide-open eyes. The Mistress was the most desirable woman on Earth to me. I looked at the curve of her legs, and I desperately wanted to spread them and climb on top of her...to ram my cock inside her....

"To save both of us time and trouble, I will tell you the secrets that I have discovered about Tina. I have put her to work doing some of the more menial, humiliating jobs in the house, and have received considerable resistance. She enjoys the submission inherent in the work but some part of her thinks she deserves more respect. Imagine! As I said, I believe she needs desperately to be fucked—she wants her virginity to be taken. She is hungry for it. That will be your greatest leverage against her stubbornness.

"She loves to use her mouth, and becomes incredibly aroused when she does so. That is why she must be watched so carefully—she can reach orgasm easily if she receives any stimulation while she is servicing someone. Since her clitoris has been pierced, this has become particularly true. While serving orally, she can climax with the slightest stimulation."

"Men—or women?" I smiled faintly.

"Both. She has showed a particular affinity for pleasuring men with her mouth, and more than once I've caught her climaxing without permission as she pleasured a male guest. The best way to avoid this, of course, is—"

"To use a spreader bar to separate her legs while she is performing her services?"

"Ah, you remember my techniques! If she is allowed to rub her thighs together—even just a little bit—or to receive even a slight stimulation of her clitoris, she will easily climax while satisfying a man orally. She can do the same when servicing a woman, but she seems to be more in control of her arousal at such times. When she's allowed to pleasure a cock, she goes simply mad with sexual excitement. However, she is very orally inclined toward women and certainly has a talent for cunnilingus. Especially if it is 'forced' on her, though of course that's just a game the little bitch plays—she's dying to eat pussy every minute of every day. As I said, her visceral arousal is probably greater when she has a cock in her mouth, but even so, Tina shows an endless fascination with using her mouth on a woman. It's a little easier to keep her from coming when she uses her hands or breasts on a man, but she still approaches orgasm quite easily when she's allowed access to the cock she craves so obviously. And, of course, she has not yet used her hands on me—she is always bound when she's allowed to pleasure my pussy."

"Then you have not taken her to your bed? Unbound, I mean?"

"Most certainly not!" Sarah was nonplused. "Not until the little slut earns it. When she is wholly and totally mine, she will know the pleasure of being received into my bed with both her mouth and her hands free to worship me. And then I will fuck her as she never dreamed she could be fucked."

"Ah, yes...I remember that night in Venice...."

"Don't let your mind wander, Carlton. Tina deserves your attention now."

"Obviously! She sounds like more than a handful."

"She is," Sarah laughed, her eyes fixing mine hungrily. Her thighs had slipped slightly farther apart, and now the robe just barely hid the enticing wisps of her pubic hair, the pink slit of her cunt. I could tell that Sarah's arousal had already turned into undeniable need, and that I could have her anytime I wanted. But to rise and take her would be to give her the upper hand. For now, I preferred to let her stew in her own painful sexual desires—however much I wanted to lean her back in that chair, spread those beautiful thighs, open that robe and slide my cock into her moistened cunt.

"How many men has Tina serviced?" My cock tingled to think of her beautiful lips parted around it, her tongue working the head into a froth.

"Fourteen," Sarah said with some difficulty. "Not including my male slaves, of course. She has pleasured several of the slaves and has shown great pleasure in doing so. But to be specific, those fourteen cocks she pleasured all belonged to guests of mine. Each time, she went mad with hunger for cock. In the last few weeks, I haven't allowed her to pleasure my male slaves, though she certainly has expressed a desire to do so—not verbally, but through her actions."

"What sort of actions?"

"God, Carlton! You would have to see the little bitch—she does everything but trip them! The way her eyes linger on their cocks—when Tina sees an erection, you would think she was being offered the food of the gods! Perhaps you didn't notice it in the drawing room—"

"I did." I smiled.

"—But she was about to struggle over to you and swallow your cock no matter *what* my orders. The fact that I fucked you in front of her and then let Adriana blow you where Tina could see is the most horrible torture for her! I have watched Tina when she sees an erect cock, either a slave's or a guest's—her nipples go from soft to fully hard within five seconds—I am not exaggerating—and if I let her continue to look, within a few minutes she actually begins to *drip on the floor!* I once punished her by giving her to nine of my male slaves and instructing her to pleasure them orally until I returned to fetch her. I left her in there for seven hours, Carlton—and when I returned, she had worn out all the male slaves and there was a *wild* look on her face—her hair was all mussed and her breasts and face slick with come, though, believe me, she had swallowed the great majority of their sperm! She was almost crazed with desire for more cock. She would have gone on pleasuring them enthusiastically until she dropped dead from exhaustion! When I inquired later, I found that each of the slaves had come in Tina's mouth five times, two of them seven times, and one eight! Does that give you an idea of how incomprehensible and unquenchable her desire for male flesh is? I've never seen a girl who wants cock so badly!"

Sarah's voice was rough with arousal; she was having a very hard time speaking. My own cock was throbbing in time with her words, and I almost hauled it out and began stroking it right there. But I managed to restrain myself—pardon the pun.

"But Tina is equally enthralled by pussy?" I was intrigued by the oral tendencies of this young slave, and I imagined she would prove herself quite entertaining when she was finally allowed to get at my own hard prick.

Sarah seemed to be pondering the question. "I believe she is. But she has had so much more of it. Perhaps I was too permissive at first—I always think more is better.

THE CONTRACT

"It generally is, dear," I said wryly.

"Usually, yes. But I may have overdone it in giving Tina unlimited access to cunt. She has serviced almost every female slave in my service many, many times, and you know there are many more female slaves in my house than male slaves."

"That I do," I said with a wink.

Sarah ignored my rejoinder. "She has also serviced many dozens of my female visitors, perhaps hundreds. At one party, at which, of course, no men were invited, I gave Tina to my guests in order to teach her a lesson about submission. My guests were told they could utilize Tina's mouth and face in whatever way they wished, but nothing else—they could not use Tina's hands, nor penetrate her in any orifice. Tina took to her duties with an impressive enthusiasm. By the time morning came, each of the party guests had departed *more* than satisfied—and Tina, though exhausted and filthy, was still available for more." Sarah laughed, remembering fondly. "I took her to bed for the morning and afternoon and gave her more, much more—but even then she satisfied me eagerly."

Sarah continued, "I couldn't begin to count the number of times she has serviced a wet, willing cunt in the last nine months she has spent on her knees—but it is doubtless well into the thousands. I believe she loves pussy as much as cock—but cock is such a novelty in my house."

"No surprise there," I said. "It's such a pleasure to be thought of as a novelty."

Sarah scowled. "You are nothing more, Carlton. Nothing more." I ignored her jab, and Sarah continued, "Tina is quite humiliated, but deliciously so, by physical punishments applied to her cunt and her breasts. To the point of extreme arousal, in fact. I have been very gentle with her cunt, wanting to preserve her virginity for as long as possible. But you won't have to concern yourself with that—I imagine you will want to take her virginity as the first order of business."

"Certainly." I smiled. "As the very first order of business. After some preliminary exploration of her oral abilities…which I imagine will be prodigious…I shall be honored to deflower your slave."

Sarah could hardly contain herself at the thought of watching me take Tina for the first time. "Keep in mind that her ability to climax with ease is rather surprising. Left to her own devices, Tina would come ten or twelve times a day with her hand or by rubbing her thighs together. Her ass is delightful, as you have seen. But I have not penetrated her there."

"Then I am allowed the pleasure of taking both her cunt and her beautiful little ass for the very first time?" I was excited by the prospect.

"Of course." Sarah was visibly aroused by that inevitability. "You are more than allowed. Please do. Just make sure you are very cruel about it."

"Oh yes, I shall. And her breasts?"

"As you saw, they are perhaps her best feature. The nipples are not yet pierced—I have been saving that for after her deflowering. I presume you will want to pierce her nipples soon after you take her."

"Very soon," I said with gusto. "I shall take great delight in piercing her."

"Take care—her nipples are incredibly sensitive, though perhaps not as sensitive as Shade's. But Tina can also climax from having her nipples stimulated even if she receives no clitoral stimulation whatsoever. Rarely, but it can happen. I intend to train her the way I am training Shade to come from only the stimulation of her breasts. But not until after her total submission has been obtained. I intend that she and Shade become lovers and teach each other. But only after Tina's total submission to me."

"How delightful! Tina is a saucy little slut, isn't she?"

"Yes." Sarah was talking very fast, as if trying to communicate all possible information before she lost control and threw herself on me, which from the look on her face, she seemed mere seconds from doing. "Her hunger for punishment is matched only by her hunger for sex. She deeply desires the lash, especially on her ass. But what Tina really enjoys is a good spanking. If you can spank her until she cries, she will do anything you want afterward—up to a point. But she will be so turned on that she may be unable to control herself, or to stop herself from coming while you spank her—if she receives any stimulation at all."

"I shall look forward to that."

"Humiliation also delights Tina, and she is quite an exhibitionist. She has been exhibited extensively, with excellent results. Our little recreation earlier drove her mad with desire. If I know Tina, she is desperate for submission and attention and sex by now.

"The main blockage for Tina's submission is that she thinks submission is a game, and she wants to control it for her own sexual pleasure. Tina doesn't even know that she thinks that, though I have tutored her extensively in the wrongness of her thinking. She must realize that her sexual pleasure belongs to me and the persons I give her to."

Sarah and I were both having difficulty continuing the conversation. I thought that perhaps we should continue it in bed—Sarah was obviously raging with desire. Soon, I knew, she would satisfy herself on my erect pole. But I wanted *her* to make the first move.

"I think your best bet is to play with Tina's desire for punishment and her need for pleasure. Torment her as much as possible and control her completely. Be *extremely* cruel. Teach her the agonies of total submission, along with the pleasures. Do not allow her to make a single decision, unless it is calculated to humiliate her. Take her sexual pleasure from her and manipulate it for my gain."

"Indeed!" I rasped. "I shall tear that sexual pleasure from her and use it mercilessly, use it to control...the little...bitch...."

Sarah and I looked at each other, our sexual hunger overwhelming us.

"Perhaps you would like to continue this conversation in bed?" I panted.

Sarah's hands quickly worked the tie of her robe and swept it open, revealing the full length of her gorgeous body, naked except for her minuscule panties. They plunged low in front, showing me the faint swirl of her pubic hair, and they were thin enough that the lips of her inviting cunt showed around the crotch. Sarah was flushed with desire, her excitement obvious as she looked me up and down, particularly letting her eyes rove over the bulge of my cock.

Sarah said in a snarl: "I don't think I can make it to bed, you bastard. You're going to have to fuck me right here on the couch."

"On the couch?" I asked, feigning horror. "What are we, Americans??"

Her hand rested between her legs, offering her silk-sheened pussy to me in a gesture of abandonment.

"If you like." Her red lips parted.

I could hear the wet thrusting of Eduardo and Adriana, hear the creaking of the floorboards as Eduardo thrust into the young slave. Outside the door, there was a thunderous moan from Adriana's tortured lips.

CHAPTER 5

I upped Sarah's ante by opening my own robe, revealing the length of my erect manhood and lifting it for her to see. "I don't think so, Mistress. If you want satisfaction, you're going to have to come to me."

Sarah was touching her own breasts, pinching the erect nipples, stroking them softly and calling attention to how beautiful and full they were. She pinched hard and pulled the nipples out, lifting her breasts for me to admire. It was like a challenge.

"If I want satisfaction," she said hoarsely, "I have a whole house full of slaves to pleasure me. Perhaps you would prefer that?"

My cock was in my hand, and I stroked it insistently as I spoke. "I would prefer, Mistress, to see you on your knees, begging me to satisfy you with my prick in your hungry cunt."

A shuddering moan came from outside the door.

"Adriana!" Sarah called loudly. "Come here!"

It was several long seconds before the door opened and Adriana came in, walking on shaky legs.

"Yes, Mistress?" she said with some difficulty.

"Service me. Orally." Sarah parted her thighs and leaned back heavily in the velvet chair. "It seems that our guest is unwilling."

Adriana quickly moved to obey, leaving the door wide open. I could see Eduardo in the doorway, on his knees, his cock quite visibly erect and glistening with Adriana's juices. Sarah and I had talked for perhaps thirty minutes; on Sarah's orders, Eduardo had been fucking Adriana that whole time. By now he must have a terrible case of blue balls—from the look on his face, my guess was right. Eduardo was a handsome dark-haired young man with a cock at least as big as mine and a firm, toned body. I didn't doubt that Sarah had enjoyed his cock more than a few times. He looked quite uncomfortable—by the look of his thick, swollen cockhead, he was very close to coming—perhaps he had been that way for some time, and only through sheer will had he prevented himself from shooting off inside Adriana while he'd fucked her from behind.

"Stay, Eduardo!" Sarah ordered. "I would like for you to watch."

Eduardo's face made his torment quite clear.

I turned my attention back to Adriana, leaving Eduardo to suffer alone while he watched. Adriana knelt between Sarah's spread thighs and reached to remove her tiny black panties. Sarah put her legs together just enough to allow Adriana to remove them. "Give them to Carlton," Sarah ordered with a smile. Adriana crawled over to me quickly and offered me Sarah's panties. I accepted them, noting that they were more than just soaked—they were drenched. I lifted them to my face and inhaled deeply of the Mistress's musky cunt. I had been right—her arousal had been great for quite some time. Adriana returned to her place between Sarah's spread legs. Sarah squirmed deftly out of her robe, letting it fall on either side of her now-naked body. Then she relaxed, sighing as she settled into the chair. Adriana's face lowered to Sarah's pussy. I watched her Mistress's back arch as Adriana began to pleasure her. I watched as Adriana eagerly began to eat her Mistress's pussy, bent far forward on her hands and knees between Sarah's legs. Adriana's ass swayed deliciously as I stroked my cock. Her own pussy was pink and open from the lengthy fucking she had just endured in the hall.

"You see, Carlton? I have only to say the word, and I have a harem of young slaves to work their magic on my cunt."

"I see," I said. "But since you're only using one side of her..."

"Be my guest," Sarah said hoarsely, then groaned as Adriana hit some secret, powerful spot in Sarah's private regions.

I wasted no time. Adriana was indeed a delicious slave, and it took me but a moment to cast off my robe and lower myself to my knees behind the young woman. My cock was aching with need. I guided the swollen head to the fully parted lips of Adriana's cunt, which was extremely wet but rough from Eduardo's fucking just outside the door.

"Make sure you fuck her well!" Sarah gasped as she ran her fingers through Adriana's thick red hair. "But don't let the little bitch come. I suspect she's right on the brink, if she hasn't come already."

I moaned as I felt Adriana's welcoming cunt clutch the head of my cock. It seemed she was sucking me in, hungrily seeking the nourishment she craved. I quickly thrust my shaft into her, eliciting a loud groan from the willing slave. She snuggled her beautiful cheeks back against me as I penetrated her with almost the full length of my hard cock. She was not nearly as tall as Sarah, and so her cunt wasn't as deep—it was some effort for her to accept the fullness of my long cock into her pussy. But she adapted admirably, pushing back against me to force it in as deep as she could take it. Adriana was rather tight, but her pussy had been opened up quite admirably by Eduardo's stiff rod. The warmth and wetness of her pussy felt like a salve to my own burning need. I began to fuck her slowly, drawing out our pleasures as I entered her in rhythmic thrusts, feeling her body shudder as I possessed her.

"There are many advantages to slaves," Sarah said as she squirmed in her chair. Adriana was indeed showing herself to be talented. The movements she made against my own movements, meeting each thrust of my cock with her own thrust, told of a young woman who truly loved to be fucked. I leaned heavily against her, feeling the head of my cock grind against her shallow cervix, bringing whimpers from the young woman between her hungry explorations into Sarah's cunt.

"Such a delightful pussy!" I groaned. "It almost seems that she was made for my cock."

"She wasn't!" Sarah rasped as she stroked Adriana's beautiful red hair. The slave, down on her hands and knees, seemed to be in heaven—allowed both her favorite activities at the same time. I began to thrust into her more quickly, and Adriana's whimpers grew louder as she took my cock.

"Don't let her come, Carlton!" Sarah said breathlessly. "She's already so close...."

"Your slave's orgasm is no concern of mine," I said as I fucked Adriana. "That's your problem."

Sarah smiled as she watched my cock ravaging Adriana's willing pussy. Sarah's hands were still on her breasts, stroking their fullness and pinching the nipples. The sight of her doing that was so enticing as to make me want to take my cock out of the slave and press it between Sarah's lovely breasts, as I'd done to Shade earlier. I felt sure that would have pleased the Mistress to no end, to feel my cock thrusting between her tits until I released myself all over her flesh.... Oh, but that would have been admitting defeat!

Adriana's freckled behind wriggled underneath me as I fucked her rapidly. I heard Adriana beginning to moan, and I knew she was going to come, directly disobeying her Mistress's orders. That delighted me so—to be able to unravel Sarah's power over her slaves....

I was still in control enough to prevent my own orgasm. I wanted to see Sarah come first, see her naked body explode.

But even so, part of me wished to uphold the Mistress's wishes, to see this slave writhe on the very brink of orgasm without being able to bring herself over the edge. I wanted to see Adriana suffer.

"Surely she's had her rear taken?" I asked Sarah, my voice hoarse with exertion and pleasure.

A devilish look crossed Sarah's face. "Of course, Carlton. Why, I've had her fucked in her ass many dozens of times. Just because her pussy's so good, that doesn't mean you should limit yourself. Take her ass, too. I'm sure the filthy-minded little slut would enjoy such a thing. Wouldn't you, Adriana? Haven't you been

THE CONTRACT

taken many times in your ass as well as your cunt?"

With some difficulty, Adriana managed to lift her mouth off Sarah's cunt and turn to look at me over her shoulder. She was blushing a deep, beautiful red, and seemed more than a little reluctant. "Yes, my Liege. I've been taken back there many times."

"Well, then…" I said.

Adriana wriggled her butt prettily. Her freckled behind presented itself to me as an invitation, and I saw no reason not to make use of everything delightful about the half of Adriana I'd been loaned. Adriana whimpered as I pulled my cock out of her pussy. I looked down at it, all glistening with her juices. I reached out to the tray of food, where there was a small dish of olive oil—meant for dipping bread in, but perhaps included on the tray by Adriana with more than a single purpose in mind? I poured a liberal amount at the very top of Adriana's crack, letting some dribble over my cock. I stroked the thick, oily fluid over my cock, then used the head of my cock to slather the olive oil between Adriana's cheeks, hearing her groan with pleasure as I spent particular time greasing up her tight little asshole. I positioned it between her delicious cheeks and fitted the head to the opening of her back door.

Adriana let out a long, low groan as I stroked the head of my cock up and down against her rear entrance. She was plainly a willing victim to this spontaneous sodomy. But Adriana didn't let herself cease her ministrations on Sarah's pussy. If anything, from the sounds coming out of Sarah's open mouth, Adriana became more fervent and skillful in her oral services.

Sarah pinched her nipples harder, staring as I jiggled my oiled cock back and forth in Adriana's rear entrance. She was plainly more than a little interested in what I was doing to her slave, and as I found the delicious bud of her asshole, I heard Sarah whisper, "Oh, yes, Carlton …push it into her…."

I worked the head into the entrance of her ass, and Adriana stiffened as she felt me penetrating her in her most private spot. She seemed willing—even eager—to accept me in to her posterior's tight embrace. But her ass itself seemed to have other ideas—it was deliciously tight and unyielding at first. No matter—I was enjoying the slave's discomfort as she felt herself being penetrated in her behind, as she worked to satisfy her Mistress without losing that all-important rhythm. And so I took a long time pressing against that unwilling entrance with my cockhead, letting Adriana feel that she was about to be entered in her darkest place— before I finally worked my thick cockhead into the opening, and felt Adriana's naked body stiffen as my ramrod popped in.

Her head lifted, and her mouth came away from Sarah's pussy. The Mistress stroked Adriana's hair as the girl struggled to accept my cock into her ass.

"Oh, God!" she moaned. "Oh, Master…."

"There, there," Sarah cooed soothingly. "Now's the time. Push it in without mercy, and watch the juicy little bitch squirm."

I thrust forward, feeling the oiled shaft of my cock slide into Adriana's tightest spot. Adriana's back arched and she shuddered against Sarah's naked body as her asshole was filled with my thrust. Then, whimpering, Adriana finally lowered her face to Sarah's pussy again, accepting my cock inside her ass as she began to pleasure her Mistress once again.

Sarah sighed as Adriana's mouth began to service her. "That is a vast improvement," she said. "I must remember to thank you, Carlton."

But I was lost in the intense sensations of having my cock embraced by Adriana's posterior. Her freckled behind looked so beautiful with its full cheeks spread around the shaft of my cock as I thrust down into her; she was unable to keep herself from shuddering and groaning as I fucked her forbidden entrance. Her movements pushing herself back onto me, impaling herself in time with my thrusts, seemed unsure at first—but within a few short minutes of receiving my tool inside her behind, Adriana was moving against me with the skill of a well-trained slave. Soon, I knew, it would be an easy thing for me to release my seed into this delicious derriere. But I took my time enjoying her ass, letting her concentrate on pleasuring her Mistress, which she was doing with newfound gusto.

"Oh, yes, yes, yes!" Sarah groaned, her eyes wide open and fixed on the sight of my cock as it penetrated Adriana's rear. "God...yes...fuck her harder, Carlton—fuck her!"

Suddenly Sarah's back arched as she threw back her head and moaned. Adriana's mouth clamped onto her Mistress's pussy, fervently bringing her off as Sarah's orgasmic wails grew louder. I kept an even rhythm as I penetrated her behind, enjoying the feel of the spasms that went through her as she worked the muscles of her tongue up against Sarah's clit. But I could sense from the tension in Adriana's body that it would not be long before she came. I relished this thought, for it meant that Adriana, through her body's own excitement, would directly disobey the orders of her Mistress —and Sarah's punishment would surely be quite amusing.

Sarah's groans told me that she had finished coming. Adriana accepted this as a sign and let her face rest unmoving against Sarah's pussy. Then I heard Adriana's rhythmic panting, telling me that the unfortunate young woman was going to climax any minute. No concern of mine—I was intent on my own orgasm, which was within my reach. I thrust quickly into Adriana's asshole, hearing her moans as she mounted toward orgasm. Cruelly, I reached down and pressed my right hand against Adriana's slit, feeling the full lips of her sex with their many shimmering rings, and the firm, pierced bud of her clitoris. As I began to stroke her clit, working its ring around in small circles, Adriana realized she was beyond the point of no return. She was about to disobey her Mistress and have a thundering orgasm. To be doubly evil, I let my left hand join my right, slipping between her pierced sexlips and penetrating her cunt with two fingers as I continued working on her clit. I felt sure that Adriana had been fighting to prevent herself from coming; she had not wished to defy her beloved Mistress. But my fingers reached their deepest point inside her cunt, and it was matched by my deepest thrust into her asshole. Adriana lost control of her orgasm. Her climax exploded through her helpless, naked body.

"Oh, God!..." she moaned as she came. "Forgive me, Mistress—ohhhhhhhhhhhhh!"

Her cunt and asshole spasmed simultaneously, clutching my fingers and cock eagerly. I continued fucking Adriana and thrusting my fingers into her cunt as she rode her climax to its peak and then shuddered to its conclusion. I would have sworn she was weeping.

Now that I had achieved my goal of humiliating the delectable Adriana before her Mistress, of making her climax without permission, I turned my attention to my own pleasure. I eased my fingers out of Adriana's cunt and put my hands on her beautiful asscheeks, thrusting into her with the precise rhythm that would bring me off inside her ass. Sarah was watching with wide eyes, an eager expression on her face. But I was quite unprepared for her reaction to my impending orgasm.

"Pull out of her, Carlton. Pull out of Adriana's ass!"

I held deep inside of Adriana, resisting the urge to thrust for a moment.

"Mistress," I grunted. "In case you're slow on the uptake, I'm about an inch from the best come of the afternoon. Do you really want me to pull out?"

Sarah climbed out of her chair and towered over me, her naked body flushed with desire. "Yes. Her strained voice was evidence of her desperation. "Please. For me."

With some difficulty, I pulled my hard cock slowly out from between Adriana's cheeks. She gasped as the head popped out of her asshole and slumped forward against the chair.

"Roll over, Adriana!" Sarah ordered breathlessly.

Adriana rolled onto her back obediently, stretching out on the floor so that her legs were parted very wide and she could snuggle down until her belly and breasts were underneath my cock.

Sarah leaned forward, wrapping her fingers around my erect prick, which still glistened with olive oil. The coolness of her hand was a bit of a shock after the warmth of Adriana's asshole. But Sarah was as expert with her hands as she was with her mouth. She bent low and began to stroke me, lavishing affection on my cock. She took it in both hands so she could work her fingers around the head with one hand while she pumped the shaft with the other. I had forgotten how incredible Sarah could be with her hands when she wanted to. In fact, she gave hand jobs better than any well-trained slave I had experienced. And Sarah obviously was enjoying this, knowing that I was completely at her mercy, as I gave control of my orgasm over to her. Even so, I was delighted that she had lunged forward to grasp my cock—it meant she couldn't hold herself back any longer; she had to see my orgasm with my hard cock spasming in her hands. In a sense, both of us were victorious—and besides, Sarah's firm grasp made me groan with pleasure. I heard her moaning softly, "Yes... oh, yes...."

Adriana squirmed underneath me, her eyes glazed with sexual excitement, looking up in anticipation as Sarah brought me off. I surrendered my sperm as my cock began to spasm in Sarah's hands. Her pumping grew to a frenzy as the first stream shot out from the head of my prick. Adriana wriggled her beautiful naked body as a stream of semen splattered across her breasts. Sarah stroked me eagerly, cooing in delight as another spasm went through me and a stream of jizz hit one of Adriana's upturned tits. Adriana's small, delicate freckled hands began to stroke her breasts, rubbing my fluids into her delicious tits, smearing it all over as I came again, this time on her belly. She reached down with one hand to rub my come into her pubic hair while she lathered up one breast with her other hand. Then she lifted her hand, cupping it just in time to catch the next stream. She brought her hand up to her face and smeared my semen across her lips, then her cheeks, then into her long red hair as I came my last, one final spurt drizzling into her pubic hair. She massaged that in as she lay looking eager, waiting obediently for my next spurt—but there were only tiny droplets to be milked out by Sarah's firm, insistent hand, the final spasms of my cock forcing those drops out to drizzle over Sarah's hand, mingling with the expensive olive oil.

I was spent, but still Sarah's hand worked me. She squeezed out another few drops of semen, letting the thick fluid coat her finger, until a few droplets splashed across Adriana's spread thighs. After four orgasms in a single afternoon, my cock felt exquisitely sensitive, much more so than usual. Sarah's skillful hands made my oversensitive cock explode in sensations that took over my body and made me gasp. I put down my hand to stop her as the sensations grew suddenly too intense for my tortured member.

My head spun from all this exertion. I crawled to my chair, sat in it, and put my legs up. I was exhausted. Sarah looked at me, her eyes afire with lust as she lifted her hand, slick with oil and my semen, to her face. She began to lick her fingers sensually, her eyes locked in mine. She started with her middle finger, which glistened with my juice; Sarah slipped it in between her lips and then took it in to her mouth, licking off my semen. She let her finger slip in and out of her mouth several times while we locked eyes. She knew damn well that she was imitating the thrusting motion I would love to be making into her cunt. But alas, as Sarah well knew, my cock had shot its last for several hours.

But Sarah loved to torture me. She reached down to touch her breasts with her free hand as she suckled on the come-slick middle finger of her other hand. Then, slipping her finger out of her mouth, she smeared her palm over her mouth and face until her lips and cheeks glistened with my fluid. She could see the obvious effect this was having on me. Her slick hand traveled down to her breasts, and she began to smear the spittle and sperm over her breasts and neck, loving the sight of the torment she detected in my eyes. The Mistress was obviously very pleased with herself and was enjoying seeing me suffer. I could feel the ache increasing in my cock as I saw Sarah slide her glistening hand down between her spread legs, stroking her slit with her middle finger as she watched me. Adriana still lay on her back, rubbing my juice into her breasts and face and belly as she watched Sarah's display. The two of them made an unbelievably pretty pair.

I felt a curious kind of victory; Sarah had been unable to stop herself from handling my cock, and now she was very much enjoying the fruits of her labor—or, rather, mine. In a sense, she had surrendered. But I was beginning to wish that I had just fucked her when she'd asked me to, instead of playing this game. I should have just spread her out in the easy chair and fitted my thick cockhead to her willing pussy, entering her and feeling her strain up against me as she took my cock inside her. God, that would have been exquisite! Even though Adriana had proved herself a wonderful fuck, I still longed for Sarah's ripe pussy. God, to think how she would have moaned as I penetrated her. To imagine her back arching as I drove my shaft into her. To feel her shuddering as my cock spasmed and filled her cunt with my seed. How I wished I had just given in to her and savaged the beautiful Mistress with my rod. I could almost feel the grip of her wet pussy around my cock.

Sarah curled up on the floor next to Adriana and began to kiss her hungrily, their tongues tangling as Sarah reached down to stroke Adriana's well-fucked pussy.

Sarah kissed Adriana more deeply, moving to crouch over her slave, getting on her hands and knees. Sarah leaned over and rubbed her face against Adriana's breasts as the two women squirmed together on the floor.

There was a faint male groan from the corridor.

"Oh, goodness," Sarah said after a while. "Poor Eduardo!"

I looked up to see Eduardo still kneeling in the doorway, having obediently remained to watch Adriana being shared by Sarah and me. His face was filled with a look of extreme discomfort, and his cock was still as hard as ever, full and swollen, twitching and throbbing as he watched the two women kissing. It was crusted with the white residue of Adriana's abundant juices, which had long since dried. He must be in agony by now.

Sarah rolled off of Adriana and lay on the floor, her arms and legs spread eagerly.

"Oh, Eduardo!" Sarah cooed. "Come in the room and relieve yourself. Poor thing. You must be suffering horribly."

Eduardo crawled over to Adriana obediently and took his place between her splayed thighs. He grabbed his cock readying himself to fuck her. Adriana whimpered and squirmed underneath him, clearly overjoyed that she was about to be fucked again.

"Don't be silly, Eduardo!" Sarah reached down to steady his cock, to prevent him from penetrating Adriana. "She's had more than enough attention already."

Eduardo looked slightly surprised, but I realized at once what Sarah was up to. She propped herself up on her knees, legs spread, presenting her inviting backside to Eduardo.

Eduardo hesitated for a moment as Adriana looked up at him with desperate disappointment. She obviously had been anticipating her next fuck with more than a little excitement. But Eduardo showed a certain arousal when it became clear that he was to fuck the Mistress—more, even, than he had when it had been Adriana's sweet pussy he was to plug. Sarah's ass swayed back and forth as Eduardo moved off Adriana and crossed over to his Mistress. Adriana pouted fetchingly, still spread out on the floor. Eduardo slid up behind his Mistress as her ass danced back and forth, luring Eduardo's erect manhood to her pussy.

Eduardo's cock was engorged and painfully swollen, thick with blood. As he fitted the head of his prick between Sarah's swollen lips, he first let out a gasp, then a sigh of pleasure.

"Slowly now," Sarah said as Eduardo rubbed his thick head against her opening. "No reason to rush yourself, sweet Eduardo.... You've got all night to savor my pussy if you wish...." And Eduardo, obedient as ever, took his time entering, rubbing his cock up and down in the Mistress's slit. His cockhead fitted in to Sarah's tight entrance. As he groaned suddenly, it popped into Sarah's snug opening, bringing a gasp of surprise and then a deep moan from her lips.

From my spot in the easy chair, I was blessed with the perfect angle to witness the penetration, and also to see Adriana as she stroked her own pussy and let her eyes drift from Eduardo's attractive buns back to me—making it very clear from the licking of her lips what she was hoping for.

THE CONTRACT

"No reason to lie there bored, you little slut," Sarah sighed as she wriggled her ass back and forth, enjoying the feel of having the most sensitive part of her cunt filled with the thickest part of Eduardo's cock. Still, she was interested in torturing me with my own pleasure. "See if you can get Carlton hard again and make him come in your mouth. I know how you love to swallow it." She laughed cruelly. I had to admire the way she pushed my limits—even as it annoyed me. And Adriana was such a fetching dish, if anyone could do it, she was certainly the one. The flush that came over her face—pure lust and enthusiasm—made her look that much more beautiful. When she rolled over, I saw the enticing picture of her ass, its entrance all open and slick from the fucking I'd given it earlier. She seemed to be quite aware of my hungry eyes on it, and she wiggled it back and forth, as if trying to entice me in again. Then she lifted herself to her hands and knees.

My cock was spent, depleted, helpless—but the ache just grew as I saw Adriana crawling toward me, her face overcome with the hunger for sex. As she lowered her face into my lap, her lips parting, I heard Sarah moaning louder as Eduardo worked his cockhead back and forth inside her, taking his time penetrating her. He was enjoying the slowness with which he penetrated Sarah as much as she did—from what I'd seen, he was a true artist. Then, as Adriana dropped low—so as not to block my view—and fitted her lips around the head of my soft cock, Eduardo succumbed to his own urgency and penetrated his Mistress in a rough, unforgiving thrust—the whole shaft into her in one movement—that brought a sudden wail from Sarah's lips—part surprise, part delight.

Her whole body convulsed as she took his shaft into her. Then, without pausing, Eduardo began to pump into his Mistress, rutting crazily into her as his own moans of pleasure grew louder and louder. His hands gripped Sarah's beautiful asscheeks as he pounded into her, thrusting again and again into her tight pussy.

Sarah shuddered and pumped back against Eduardo, meeting each of his thrusts with one of her own, forcing his cock harder into her pussy. Eduardo was obviously not wasting time—he was going to come at any second, and as he pounded into Sarah, it was clear that her pleasure was not on his agenda—or, rather, she was deriving her own pleasure from the incredible lust Eduardo was expressing. As dominant as she was, Sarah could take cock more eagerly than the most devoted slave. She showed herself quite talented as she moved with and against Eduardo, pounding his shaft deep into her softness again and again, working him into a frenzy, ready to milk every drop of semen from the young man's cock. God, she was lovely! I wished again that I had merely pushed her back into her chair and worshiped her with the full length of my shaft, penetrating her slowly—oh!

Adriana's mouth slid up and down on my cock eagerly. I looked down to find—to my astonishment—

that I was hard again, as hard as I had been. I couldn't remember the last time I'd gone this long in a single afternoon, but I was gripped by the urgency of my need. And Adriana was gripping eagerly as well, covering my cock with affection, savoring the head and the underside.

As Eduardo picked up speed, Adriana took my cockhead between her lips and then took me slowly into her mouth. When my head reached the entrance of her throat, she rubbed it deliciously, then took a deep breath before swallowing the rest of my shaft, forcing my cockhead in to the tightness of her throat. She whimpered and moaned as she began to pump my cock, working her hands under my body to grip my buttocks and pull me harder against her face. I let out a string of expletives at the delirious pleasure I was feeling, and they mingled with Sarah's as Eduardo rammed into her. The young man's asscheeks were clenched tight as he pumped, and his whole body gleamed with sweat. Sarah had long since abandoned moving against him and was just resting there on her hands and knees, hunkered down low to give Eduardo the best possible leverage to thrust into her pussy, taking everything he had to give her.

Suddenly I heard the Mistress's groan, and knew she was very close. I didn't doubt that Sarah had intended a quick fuck, just to get Eduardo off and feel the pleasure of his thick cock shooting inside her. But once his skilled thrusts had aroused her desire, Sarah had mounted toward orgasm quickly. Now, Eduardo was well aware that his mistress was about to climax, and even the worst case of blue balls couldn't keep him from holding back his own orgasm until he brought off his demanding Mistress.

Luckily for him, there wasn't long to wait. As Eduardo struggled with his own orgasm, Sarah let out a wail of ecstasy and began to thrust back against Eduardo, taking his cock into her pussy. It was clear from the volume of her cries that Sarah was climaxing fervently. Eduardo began to fuck her rapidly, meeting each of her thrusts with one of his own, and then he let out a deep-throated groan as he let himself go inside her pussy. His whole body shuddered as he came, and he leaned forward to embrace his mistress from behind as he humped into her.

Eduardo's climax seemed to last for thirty or more thrusts into Sarah's pussy. As Adriana heard him come, her own ministrations on my cock became much more insistent. She knew that I wasn't far off—to my own amazement, I was going to come again! Adriana clamped her lips around the head of my cock and began to pump my shaft with her hand until I arched my back and thrust my hips up to meet her. My cock spasmed in ejaculation. Adriana swallowed my semen eagerly as I shot into her—she didn't miss a drop. Finally, as my pleasure bottomed out into a delicious void, I slumped into the chair and let Adriana lick my cock clean.

Sarah was still on her knees, her legs spread as Eduardo bent down behind her obediently. He began to lick her pussy, drawing sighs from Sarah's lips as Eduardo lapped at his own thick fluid that filled her cunt. I had seen Sarah demand this of her male slaves before—to pleasure her with their mouths mere seconds after they had ejaculated into her. She moaned softly as Eduardo suckled on her come-filled pussy. Then, slowly, he began to lick Sarah's beautiful buttocks. His tongue slipped between her full cheeks, and Eduardo spent some time kissing his Mistress's ass in the most literal sense of the term. This was the form of submission Sarah most loved from her male slaves—each was expected to show his absolute worship of her in the moments after she climaxed on his stiff pole. Eduardo did so enthusiastically, rimming Sarah and eliciting approving sighs from her lips.

When the ritual was finally completed, Eduardo helped Sarah to stand. Adriana's hand curled around my soft cock as Eduardo kissed Sarah's feet reverently. Then Adriana crawled over to do the same, making for quite a pretty picture as the two of them ingratiated themselves before their Mistress.

Sarah smiled at me evilly, knowing how much I had enjoyed the sight of Eduardo fucking her. No doubt she also knew how much I wished it had been me thrusting into her willing pussy, and that the next time she demanded that I fuck her, I wouldn't hesitate following her orders. That caused me some chagrin, but I knew there was nothing I could do about it—the Mistress had bewitched me.

"No doubt you would like a nap before dinner—after all this exertion," said Sarah, reaching down to stroke Eduardo's and Adriana's heads. "Shall I send in a fresh slave to keep you company while you relax?"

I chuckled. I knew as well as Sarah that there was no chance I could perform sexually for the remainder of the evening—the Mistress had found my limits, had pressed me to the very end of my endurance. But I wasn't about to admit that to her. "Please do, Mistress, one would help very much in my relaxation—in fact, if you could spare two, it would be most appreciated."

Sarah looked a little surprised, but she immediately recognized what kind of game I was playing.

"Certainly, two slaves won't be a problem—would you like three, perhaps, Carlton?"

She had met my challenge and raised the stakes. "If it wouldn't be an imposition," I answered calmly.

"No imposition at all. Adriana, do fetch them, won't you? You know the three I mean."

"Yes, Mistress." Adriana crawled off obediently.

"I'm sure they'll serve you quite well," said Sarah, eyeing my soft and reddened prick. "Eduardo—my robe."

Eduardo quickly fetched the Mistress's robe from where she'd left it in the chair. He helped her on with it, belting the flimsy garment around her waist. Sarah gave me one last supercilious look as she moved toward the door, Eduardo crawling after her.

"Dinner is at eight," she told me. "That should give you enough time for a nap and some...recreation. I'll see you in the main dining room. Oh...and don't dress."

I watched Sarah, with her male slave in tow, as she left the room, ever the victor in our contest of wills. Exhausted, I almost had to crawl to the bed and sink between the covers. A nap would be most welcome right now....

CHAPTER 6

As I relaxed into the softness of the bed, Sarah's next weapons in our war of wills came into the room. As she had promised, there were three of them. They introduced themselves as Alana, Benicia, and Cynthia. All three were as delectable as any of Sarah's slaves, and naked but for their collars. Each had pierced nipples and genitals, indicating that they had been with Sarah long enough to be fully and completely dedicated by their piercings. All three women were blondes, Sarah's preference—Sarah was a blonde—with shoulder-length hair and smooth-shaven pussies. I threw back the covers, and all three young women joined me in the warmth of the bed.

"How shall we service you, Master?" asked Cynthia, or perhaps it was Alana, rubbing her naked body against mine. "We are here to offer you service."

I cleared my throat. "You shall serve me by entertaining each other on *that* side of the bed," I ordered. "And making as much noise as you possibly can in doing so, while I take a much-deserved nap. And please—no matter how many times you climax, don't stop until dinnertime."

All three slaves seemed rather taken aback by this. "Entertain yourselves," I growled, rolling over. Obediently, they crawled into each others arms and began first to kiss, then to pleasure each other with eager hands and mouths, squirming and thrashing and moaning louder and louder as their pleasure mounted. I took vague notice of the postures of the women as they satisfied each other with their mouths and hands. Clearly, my gamble had paid off—these women knew each others' bodies quite well, and took great delight in exploring further as they lay entwined in my bed. If Sarah was listening—and I was quite sure that she was—she would be treated to the enthusiastic sounds of lovemaking, perhaps assuming that I was one of the participants—while I rested myself for this evening's proceedings.

In other contexts, perhaps, it would be thought difficult to sleep while three submissive and very fetching women are making passionate love in your bed—but for me, it was barely an effort. I fell into beloved slumber while listening to Alana—or perhaps it was Cynthia—come for the second time.

I awakened slowly, aware of the sound of the dinner bell downstairs. The exhausted moans and whimpers of the three slaves were not quite loud enough to drown it out. I looked up at the three of them, their bodies glistening with sweat and their faces slick with each other's juices. Plainly, the three women were more than just exhausted, they were utterly spent. Exactly as I had hoped; they were clearly having a great deal of difficulty keeping themselves going despite their great interest in each other's bodies. I propped myself up on one hand and watched as Alana pleasured Benicia's cunt fervently as Benicia struggled toward another orgasm. Meanwhile, Cynthia was frigging herself hungrily with both hands, one hand's middle finger thrusting into her cunt while her other hand worked her clitoris. Her face was buried in Alana's cunt as Alana crouched low on top of Cynthia. All three women were gasping and panting with exhaustion. But it was clear that Cynthia and Benicia, at least, were very close to climaxing, and certainly Alana could be very close as well.

So help me, as I watched them, I felt my cock stirring yet again, swelling until it was full and ready.

"Enough," I said. All three slaves looked at me. Benicia, in particular, looked somewhat nonplused that I had called a halt to their play just when she was so close to orgasm.

"Dinnertime," I said. "We don't want me to be late. Benicia, fetch my robe."

Benicia had some trouble walking, which was exactly what delighted me so. But she managed to retrieve my robe from where I'd left it on the chair and to return to the bed on unsteady legs to help me on with my robe. She took note of my erect cock, obvious lust in her eyes as she looked it up and down. But I wasn't about to bring myself off when there was another, even more sumptuous, meal downstairs.

"If anyone asks," I told the three of them, "I fucked each of you with an amazing fervor. I took my time bringing all three of you off and utilized several of your delightful attributes to climax. I was just getting started on another round when the dinner bell rang. Do you understand?"

"Yes, Master," they said in unison.

"If *anyone* should ask—this includes your Mistress. Do you understand that?"

All three looked uncomfortable, and I laughed.

"We cannot lie to our Mistress." Tears formed in Benicia's eyes.

"Did she not order you in here to pleasure and serve me in whatever way I demanded?"

"Yes, Master," said Alana. Or maybe it was Cynthia.

"Then this is what I demand. This is what brings me

pleasure. This is your way to offer me service. *Lie.* Now finish what you're doing and be gone by the time I come back from dinner. But finish what you're doing *silently.*"

Hearing the dinner bell chime once more, I got out of bed quickly and belted the robe. On the bed, all three slaves returned to their fervent entanglements, and I glanced back just in time to see Benicia's mouth opening wide in a silent scream of orgasm. Ah, the delights of the flesh!

Despite the fact that three vixens had just spent several hours entertaining themselves in my bed, I felt well rested. I found Shade waiting just outside the entrance to the dining room, her face and breasts still crusted with my ejaculate from earlier. She blushed and looked down as I passed her.

Sarah entered the dining room just as I did. She looked as ravishing as ever, but despite the fact that she wore the fetching transparent silk robe trimmed in white fur, it was not Sarah that made me stop and stare wide-eyed.

Rather, it was the delectable feast which was spread before my eyes.

Tina had been bound to the table, naked, faceup, her arms and legs spread and her body used as the setting for our meal. Between her legs was a candle in a silver holder, and several other candles lined her body on either side of it. Grape stems formed a wreath around her pussy, hooked through the rings of her cunt, and more grapes, mixed with other fruits, had been laced through Tina's lovely blonde locks. Her nipples were capped with dollops of what appeared to be cheese dip, with crackers assembled neatly on the inside of each breast. Her white belly was graced with an arrangement of fruit as well, and down each of her spread thighs was the main course: slices of roast turkey.

Sarah threw her head back and smiled at me. It was then that I realized just how gorgeous Sarah looked in the opulent robe with its white fur trim framing her half-exposed breasts. Sarah was most beautiful, totally in her element, when she had achieved the creative and complete degradation of one of her beloved slaves.

"Does the feast appeal to you?" Sarah asked me.

"It does," I said, shifting my robe so that it was evident to Sarah that I was erect and more than a little interested in what I saw, both on the table and at its head. "I fear I shall have to join it on the table."

"Please do," she said. "I'm sure our little centerpiece is quite wet from all this attention. You'll have to squash a few grapes, though, to truly take advantage of that delicious main course."

"Or perhaps I'll wait and savor the leftovers—many dishes are better when they've had some time to ripen."

Tina was doing a very good job of holding still, but that comment caused her to move just a little, sending an attractive jiggle through the oranges and sliced pineapple on her belly.

I walked to the table and plucked a grape from Tina's nether feast. "I hope you don't mind if I nibble." I popped it into my mouth.

"I was hoping you would," said Sarah. "I'm famished." She bent forward from her place at the head of the table to suck a succulent cherry into her mouth from Tina's stomach. To do so, she had to lean over Tina, pulling her robe open to prevent its being soiled by the cheese dip. This put her bare breasts right into Tina's face, well within my grasp. After all I had been through this afternoon, the sight of those lovely breasts still sent a surge through my expectant cock. Sarah took a brief moment to slide her hard nipples across Tina's parted lips, drawing a murmur from the centerpiece and another jiggle that sent fruit dribbling off of her stomach.

Sarah left the robe partway open, her breasts now revealed and caressed by the soft white fur. "Don't hesitate," she said. "After all, this is a casual meal. Dig in."

With those words, Sarah bent forward and began to kiss Tina. Obviously overcome by the situation, Tina responded enthusiastically to her Mistress's kiss. "Poor thing!" Sarah breathed when she pulled back. "She hasn't had a thing to eat all day. Isn't that right, Tina?"

"Yes, Mistress," Tina said softly.

"Well...no reason for us to suffer." Sarah crawled up onto the table as she reached down to pluck a thick slice of turkey from Tina's thigh. She unfastened the robe all the way as she ate the turkey. Seeing her do that created the rumblings of two kinds of hunger. I reached out and seized several slices myself, allowing my hands to take their time to do it, even though that just increased both kinds of hunger.

Similarly adorned with more carnal fruits, Shade appeared beside me. "Wine, Master?" It was white, evidently chilled.

"Of course." I indicated Tina's belly. "But just a taste."

Shade obediently tipped the bottle over Tina's pale stomach. Tina gasped as the cold liquid hit her flesh, and fruit and meat both went shuddering off her body. Sarah was entertaining herself by sucking up a trail of fruit morsels across Tina's body, placing herself just above her squirming slave. The feast was in an increasingly precarious position, even more so as I bent forward to lick the wine from Tina's navel. I declared the wine excellent and indicated that Shade should pour more. Shade obeyed. Tina gasped and shuddered as the wine trickled down her belly to drizzle into her cunt. She gasped as I guided Shade down to pour the wine directly onto Tina's virgin pussy.

"That's good wine." Sarah was distracted by the taste of Tina's nipples with their cheesy cargo. "Don't waste it."

"You call this a waste?" I asked, bending forward to lick Tina's flesh and savor the wine. I let my tongue graze the pierced bud of Tina's chilled clitoris and

THE CONTRACT

found it quite firm. I licked just low enough, with the mere tip of my tongue, and found her taste tangy and sharp—Tina was very wet.

"Tina is enjoying the meal as much as we are," I said as I slipped my tongue between Tina's pierced lips, tasting more of her delicious pussyjuice. When I did not receive a reply, I looked up to see that Sarah had lifted her robe and settled down with her legs spread on top of Tina's face, and was whimpering softly as she bobbed up and down, reacting to Tina's tongue working its magic. I felt the hardness of my own prick and was tempted to take Tina's virginity right there on the table amid the food and wine. What a mess that would make! My hard cock burned for the feel of Tina's inviolate hole opening before it, embracing my flesh. But that would be much too easy—and too rushed. I wanted to take my time with Tina; I wanted her to enjoy all the sensual delights of her first time being taken in that way. Delightful as these sensual delights were, they weren't quite enough; so I set out to entertain myself at Tina's lower half while her top half was quite occupied with Sarah's pussy. Sarah was rocking back and forth now, squirming and shaking the table so that bits of cheese, crackers, slices of fruit and meat all slipped onto the ground. Sarah threw back her head and came loudly, her unmistakable moan of orgasm filling the dining room, so loud that Shade blushed. Sarah seized the bottle of white wine out of Shade's hand and took a long slug from it, gulping the wine to refresh herself. White wine dribbled down over her face and splashed across her breasts, which already glistened with the sweat of her arousal and exertion. Sarah cast off the expensive robe, tossing it to the floor carelessly, rising and falling astride Tina's face.

Sarah looked directly at me, the enormity of her lust made obvious. Then she laughed, as if she and I had shared a private joke. How gorgeous Sarah looked, nude and riding her slave, taking all the pleasure that eager little mouth could give. I desperately wanted a sample myself—a sample of Tina's hungry mouth and of Sarah's equally hungry cunt. But both were quite occupied at the moment.

Sarah began to wriggle on top of Tina again. Her hips started to pump, making it very clear that her slave was going to bring her off not once but *twice*, and that the second time was going to be as good as the first. From the sounds that issued from Sarah's mouth, it was clear that Tina was quite willing to service her Mistress for a second orgasm. And that her skill did not diminish with time—or, at least, she was not tiring just yet.

With that in mind, I set about to break Tina's concentration and thus confound her Mistress.

But first, I took the time to slake some of my hunger by sucking morsels of turkey off Tina's spread thighs and to pluck grapes out of her pubic grapevine, tickling the poor slave and making her jerk from time to time as I ate. I looked up just long enough to accept a mouthful of wine from a very attentive Shade, before lowering my mouth once more to Tina's delicious feast.

My tongue snaked between Tina's lips again, licking gently her entrance. Tina shuddered as I teased each of her rings and licked my way up to her pierced clitoris. I felt Tina's whole body squirm in time with the strokes of my tongue as I chose a rhythm that seemed to match the movements of Tina's body. I heard her muffled groan of pleasure as I descended upon the ring in her clitoris and began to work it rhythmically back and forth. Her ass lifted off the table as she arched her back, pressing her cunt more firmly against my mouth.

"Carlton!" Sarah laughed. "You're much too kind to my slaves. The little slut doesn't deserve that kind of treatment. I haven't let her have it yet—I don't know why tonight should be any different."

"Let me be the judge of that," I deadpanned, panting between strokes and flicks of my tongue around Tina's clit. I hadn't shown Sarah my surprise or delight—Tina hadn't been satisfied orally! No wonder she was reacting with such extreme pleasure! I knew that I was causing her greater discomfort with this distraction as she sought to pleasure her Mistress than even a severe whipping would have caused.

I glanced up to see Sarah watching me hungrily.

"You *do* show a knack!" Sarah said. "I can tell the girl isn't concentrating—she's much more interested in what you're doing to her."

I chuckled with pleasure, then launched myself into the task of pleasuring Tina with a newfound eagerness. But hearing Sarah's cautioning tone, Tina began to concentrate more on what she was doing with her mouth, and I heard a surprised gasp from Sarah as the eager mouth on her pussy grew that much more eager.

The rhythm of Sarah's moans began to match that of my own tongue on Tina's pussy, and I imagined that the lucky slave had discovered the secret of getting while you gave—to let one feed the other. I slipped my hands under Tina's gorgeous ass and held onto her cheeks while her muscles tensed. I heard Sarah's cries growing louder, louder—then Sarah was coming, and just after she started to come, I felt the shudder go through Tina's body. If anything, her tongue must have become more insistent on Sarah's pussy and clit, for Sarah all but went mad with ecstasy, shaking the table and threatening to make it collapse. I rode Tina's clit, working it rapidly, listening to her muffled groans and feeling the spasms go through her body as the pleasure exploded through her. When she finally settled down, her pistoning hips lowering so that her ass rested amid the smashed food and spilled wine, I saw Sarah staring down at me, an unreadable but undeniably devious look on her face.

"Dinner is such a festive meal around here," she said breathlessly. "Would you care to retire to the parlor for a drink?"

I chuckled, lifting my face and licking my lips, which were slick with Tina's juice. "I believe I've had quite enough to drink, my dear."

"*Other* refreshment, then?" She winked.

"I could be persuaded."

"Very well, then. Shade, bring Carlton a fresh robe."

"Thank you." I looked down. My robe had become soaked with the juices of smashed fruit and turkey, and with the spilled wine.

"Then have Tina washed and brought to the parlor —collared and leashed, otherwise free. Be quick about it!"

"Yes, Mistress." Shade rushed off while Sarah descended from the table.

CHAPTER 7

I retired to the parlor with great pleasure, Sarah at my side. Whisper had been called to bring Sarah a clean robe; Sarah belted the translucent white garment loosely, so that it hung well open between her breasts. Once we had settled ourselves in the parlor, Whisper appeared with brandy and after-dinner treats —a Gauloise in a cigarette holder for Sarah, a cigar for me. Sarah reclined fetchingly on the black velvet divan; I rested in a leather armchair with my feet on its matching ottoman. The brandy and cigar both proved to be of excellent quality, which didn't surprise me. After a short time of Sarah and my making light conversation, a freshly washed Tina was led into the room, collared and leashed, but otherwise unbound. Her arms rested submissively at her sides. Her blonde hair was beautifully mussed around her face, and her downcast eyes told me that she was in the proper frame of mind to receive my attentions. Apparently, Sarah found Tina pleasing, as well. I beckoned Tina over to where I was sitting.

"You know, Tina, at dinner I didn't really pay proper attention to your tits. They are quite large, aren't they? Very nice. Bend forward, Tina, so I can see them better."

Tina obeyed, leaning over me just enough so that her breasts hung down enticingly, their ripe nipples beckoning me, begging to be plucked. Sarah was obviously pleased too. Her eyes were fixed on the sight of Tina's ass and her upper thighs as she bent forward, her legs spread only slightly.

"Doesn't she look delightful, Carlton?" Sarah asked breathlessly, her desire for Tina obviously rising as she taunted the juicy little slave. "Especially those ripe tits and that curvy little ass of hers. When she bends over like that, I can see her pussy from behind. It's a treasure. Almost good enough to take right here, don't you think? Bent over the ottoman? Or perhaps spread out on the sofa?"

I felt my cock rising at the prospect, and I could see Tina blushing as she felt Sarah's burning eyes all over her. She knew just how momentous an occasion her deflowering was to be, and that I was to be the one to grace her virgin pussy with my hard shaft. Just thinking about it made me almost lose control, almost grab Tina and bend her over to penetrate her pretty pussy from behind. But I managed to hold myself back without showing the extent of my arousal.

"Good enough to take right here, yes," I said. "But that would be such a waste. I plan to make the poor girl beg for hours before I finally pop her little cherry. Perhaps tomorrow night, or the next."

That statement brought a noticeable reaction from Tina. A tiny whimper escaped her lips, barely audible. She shifted uncomfortably as her unpierced nipples stiffened visibly. From the deeper reddening of her face, it was clear that she knew I had noticed the rising of her desire.

"Nothing to be ashamed of, Tina," I said, amusement in my voice. "I'm quite aware you're becoming aroused—your nipples are so inviting when they get hard like that. And your pussy must be getting quite wet. Is it thinking about being taken that affects you so? Thinking about what it will feel like when I spread your lips and penetrate you for the very first time?"

Tina's breathing came heavier, and now her nipples were quite obviously at their full erection. She was still leaning forward a little. I could see her breasts quite close to my face, could smell the sweet aroma of her skin. Behind Tina, Sarah was given quite a nice view of the girl's ass as the slave bent forward to let me see her tits.

Setting the cigar in an ashtray, I reached up and began to touch Tina's firm breasts, teasing them and stroking the nipples, pinching lightly as she began to whimper.

"Carlton, what did I tell you? The poor girl's going to get so turned on, we'll hardly be able to stop her from throwing herself onto your shaft."

"Oh, I'm sure I can resist her," I said as Tina began to squirm in my grasp. I pinched her nipples more firmly, and her lips parted in a gasp of mounting lust. "No matter how badly she might want it, she'll not lose her precious virginity tonight. But if she's very good, she might get a mouthful of my come."

Tina's eyes widened and she began to tremble. I caught her glancing down to see the visible bulge of my cock, fully hard, under the thin fabric of the robe. As I teased her nipples, she kept glancing down—she was plainly having some trouble looking away.

"She seems to want exactly that," Sarah noted. "The little bitch is really getting worked up. Whisper!"

"Yes, Mistress," said the redheaded slave, appearing beside Sarah.

"Tell me if this little bitch is getting wet. Careful not to slip your finger inside—remember, she's a bud, not yet a blossom. Just feel her slit."

"Yes, Mistress. I won't forget."

Whisper moved up behind Tina quickly and eased her hand between Tina's slightly spread thighs. Tina gave a little gasp as Whisper's hand explored her slit.

"Well? Is she?"

"Yes, Mistress. She's quite wet. She's even starting to drip a little."

"Well." Sarah smiled faintly. "It's your choice, Carlton. Give her what she wants if you think she's worth it."

I was having quite a time with Tina's breasts. Their texture was delightful, firm yet yielding, and her nipples were deliciously sensitive. My pinches and proddings brought gasps and whimpers from Tina's parted lips, as I teased her into a frenzy of arousal. My own cock was throbbing, ready for release.

"All right," I said matter-of-factly. "Whisper, open my robe."

"Yes, Master." Whisper took her hand away from Tina's pussy and moved around the side of the chair to untie my robe and pull it open. Her hand grazed the hardness of my shaft, and I let out a grunt of anticipation.

Tina's eyes were riveted on my hardness. She was obviously fascinated with it, hungry to taste and feel it. I teased her for a time, glancing over to Sarah now and then to find that she was plainly enjoying the show. In fact, her posture suggested that she was quite eager to see it progress. Her legs were spread slightly and the robe had fallen awry, showing me the curve of Sarah's breasts and the pink furrow of her pussy. I felt a surge of lust for Sarah as well as for Tina, and resolved to bed

Sarah as soon as possible. But for now, my pleasure was reserved for Tina. In fact, my need was overwhelming me, my lust filling my body.

"All right," I said hoarsely. "On your knees, Tina, and let's see what you can do with that pretty mouth of yours. But don't forget to use your hands, too. *And* those big tits."

Tina lowered herself to her knees before me and took my cock in her hands eagerly. She lifted the hardness and ran her fingertips over it, guiding the thick head to her lips. She took long moments to pay homage to my prick before she serviced it with her mouth. She used her hands to rub the head across her cheeks, smearing my glistening precome over her skin. She rubbed the shaft up and down on her face, sliding my prick into her soft hair as she licked my balls. Then she rose and, following my instructions, slipped my cock between her breasts obediently. She moved against me, stroking my shaft into the deep furrow of her cleavage, pressing her breasts together to encircle my prick. She whimpered as she worked my hard shaft in and out between her breasts, so that I could feel the hardness of her nipples grazing my belly. As she slid her body down and my cockhead emerged from between her milk white tits, Tina let her tongue laze downward and swirl around the head of my cock. Then she pressed her tits together more firmly and worked her body up and down, caressing me with her gorgeous breasts. She slid my cock all over her most beautiful possessions, teasing her nipples with the head so that she whimpered in pleasure. She wrapped her slender fingers around the shaft of my cock and brought the head to her parted lips, easing her tongue out to tease the underside of my prick. Then she licked her way down to my balls, her tongue tracing wet circles around my flesh. She spent some time caressing my balls with her tongue, eliciting gentle moans from my lips as I stroked her hair. Tina licked her way back up to my head and took its thickness between her wet lips, her tongue slicking it up for the passage into her mouth.

I relaxed into the chair as Tina wrapped her lips around my cockhead, whimpering softly as she worked the shaft into her mouth. Then, hungrily, Tina took my shaft down smoothly, pressing the head against the back of her throat.

"She shows quite a talent, doesn't she?" Sarah said breathlessly.

"I'm sure that more than a little of it is your admirable training skills," I sighed as Tina swallowed my cock, working it into her mouth and pressing the head against the entrance to her throat. "But yes, she does seem to show a natural talent for being a cocksucker."

At that, Tina's eagerness seemed to grow. She pressed my shaft down her throat, swallowing all of me, savoring the feel of my hardness thrust into her. Then she began to work her head up and down, swallowing my cock in a perfect rhythm. I groaned softly as I ran my fingers through Tina's blonde hair.

"Whisper," Sarah ordered, "seeing that little bitch go to town on Carlton's prick is making me more than a little wet. Get over here and see to my needs."

"Right away, Mistress." Whisper hurried over to Sarah and lowered herself to her knees beside the divan. Sarah spread her legs as Whisper's face settled into her Mistress's pussy. Sarah's hand came to rest gently on Whisper's head, but her eyes were still fixed firmly on Tina as she sucked me. Tina circled her tongue around my cockhead and then swallowed me again, thrusting my prick all the way down her throat. She pumped me in and out, each long thrust ending with a quick, eager pleasuring of my cockhead with Tina's tongue before melding into a delicious thrust into Tina's mouth and down her throat.

She began to squirm as she pleasured me.

"Very nice, Whisper," Sarah cooed. "But do you think Tina could do better?"

Whisper didn't answer; her mouth was quite busy, and she knew better than to stop her work on Sarah's pussy. Sarah writhed, her legs spread around Whisper's face as the slave did as she had been bidden, pleasuring her Mistress with her mouth. Meanwhile, Tina's cocksucking was picking up speed. She plainly meant to make me come—and I knew it wouldn't be long. I merely had to decide whether Tina would be graced

THE CONTRACT

with a mouthful of my seed, or if I should reserve it for other, more visible, parts of her—this latter case would certainly please her Mistress.

But Tina knew better than to bring me off right away —for then her own pleasure in sucking me would be lost quickly. She slipped my cock out of her mouth. It glistened with her saliva and the juice of my precome. Tina began to rub my shaft over her face, smearing her cheeks with her own saliva. Then she slipped it between her breasts again, working them together with her hands to form a luscious tunnel, and bobbed up and down on me slowly, pushing my cock in and out of her now-tight cleavage. She looked up at me eagerly, her blonde hair mussed even more now, a look of expectant pleasure on her face.

"Am I pleasing you, Master?"

"I haven't decided yet," I rasped. "Keep trying."

Tina obediently continued stroking my cock with the tunnel of her breasts, dipping down occasionally to suckle on the head of my cock. She knew I was very close, but that my pleasure would be that much more if she teased me for a long while. I smiled as I saw that Sarah had trained Tina quite well. I sighed with pleasure as Tina went back to working my cock with her mouth, this time concentrating on the head. She wrapped her hand around the lower part of my shaft and sucked and licked at the head and upper shaft with her eager mouth. Soon I was going to shoot off in her mouth—but Tina sensed this, and her pleasuring slowed.

"She's not going to get you off already, is she?" Sarah's face was red, her voice rough from the pleasures of Whisper's mouth. "That would be such a waste...."

"Of course not," I said. "Tina knows she must pleasure me for a long time before she'll be granted the privilege of receiving my seed in her mouth. Does she swallow?"

Sarah flashed me an amused look. "Carlton, how could you?"

"Just curious." Then I lost myself in the sensations as Tina's mouth became an eager whirlwind on my prick. Plainly, hearing herself spoken about in the third person aroused Tina tremendously. Her hands teased my balls, which had ridden up tightly into my scrotum in preparation for my orgasm. Tina felt the first tiny spasm of my cock and sensed that I was going to shoot. She slowed her movements and eagerly swallowed the first tiny spurt of my come. But I was pleased to feel my orgasm dissipating before it arrived, and sensed that Tina's pleasure was increased, too.

"That was close," Sarah mumbled, sensing the tension of my body as she watched.

"She's got quite an eager mouth. Eager to taste my come. But I think she'd be better utilized between *your* legs, my dear. Why don't we trade?"

"Of course!" Sarah was delighted with my suggestion. "Whisper, your services are needed by our guest."

"Tina," I said, "finish what Whisper has begun."

Tina slipped my glistening cock out of her mouth obediently and crawled over to Sarah as Whisper moved onto me.

"Just your hand," I ordered Whisper. "Be cautious. You're fluff, girl. Just enough to keep me interested."

"Yes, Master," said the redheaded Whisper as she curled her fingers around my shaft and began to do her work—stroking me very, very slowly. My cock, so close to exploding in orgasm, gradually returned to a semiflaccid state by a sheer act of my will as I watched Tina lowering her face between Sarah's spread thighs. As she began to worship Sarah with her mouth, Tina became more and more enthusiastic, her pretty ass wriggling back and forth as her tongue slicked up and down in Sarah's pussy. Meanwhile, Whisper's gentle caresses quickly brought my cock to full erection again. She seemed to sense my arousal and slowed her hand enough to keep me from coming, while retaining my hard-on—and my interest in the scene of Tina pleasuring her Mistress. Sarah began to moan softly, clearly approaching her orgasm. She looked at me hungrily, a smile on her face.

"You're sure you don't want to take the little bitch right now?" Sarah taunted me. "With her face in my cunt?"

Tina's ass swayed back and forth invitingly as she serviced Sarah. Her legs were spread just enough to show me her pretty little cunt between her creamy thighs, and it *did* look wonderfully tempting. But I would not gobble this morsel—Tina's virginity was to be savored. I winked at Sarah, and a shudder went through her body, as she lost herself in the sensations Tina's tongue was eliciting in her pussy. Sarah grasped Tina's head, stroking the girl's hair as she brought her Mistress to orgasm. Sarah snuggled down into the divan, pressing her cunt against Tina's seeking mouth. Then Sarah threw back her head, moaning loudly as she came. Whisper watched, enraptured, her hand tightening on my prick. I was quite close to coming myself, but Whisper's touch was too expert to allow that—she held her ground, keeping me on the brink as Sarah thrashed back and forth, climaxing loudly on Tina's skillful mouth.

"Oh, yes!" Sarah sighed. "You *do* know how to torture a woman, Carlton. Making me wait to see my pretty little slave impaled.... *Oh!*" Sarah's final spasms convulsed her body as she finished her climax. Tina continued working until Sarah's fingertips on her face told her it was time to ease off.

"Now, why don't you be a good girl and finish off Carlton," said Sarah. "I think she should swallow your come, don't you? She seems so eager for it."

"Definitely," I said as Tina turned and crawled toward me obediently, her face slick with Sarah's juices. Her hunger was evident as she took her place between my spread legs again. Whisper relinquished her grip on my cock, guiding the head between Tina's eager lips and stroking Tina's hair as my cock disappeared into her willing mouth. Tina gulped down my prick, holding herself down on me, holding my cock with the muscles of her throat for as long as she could manage it. Then she returned to pleasuring my cockhead, while Whisper held my shaft with her hand and guided my cockhead in and out of Tina's mouth. Soon Tina was moaning softly as she licked and sucked my shaft. Then she swallowed me again, all the way, squirming that lovely naked ass up and down as she sated her hunger.

"Whisper," Sarah said, "I think our little slave is badly in need of some services herself. Do provide them, won't you?"

"Yes, Mistress." Whisper left her place at my side and settled down between Tina's spread thighs, propping herself up to get at Tina's luscious virgin pussy. Tina snuggled down onto Whisper's eagerly slurping mouth, and I felt the shudders of pleasure going through Tina's nude body as Whisper began to lick her. Whisper's tongue on Tina's clit made Tina suck me with ever-increasing hunger, and soon Tina's hips were pistoning as Whisper rode her. Whisper's body moved with Tina's so that the suckling mouth never left Tina's pussy, and Tina paused in her ministrations to my cock just long enough to let out a long, tortured, shuddering groan of orgasm. Then, as she continued coming, Tina settled back down on my cock, pumping my shaft as she worked her lips and tongue around the head.

I was very close, but Tina managed to hold me off for another minute. As she came, Tina moved her breasts back over my cock, pressing them together to thrust my shaft back and forth between them. Then Whisper finished her off, and Tina took my cock back into her mouth as I moaned my approaching orgasm. Tina's sucking mouth and insistently stroking hand brought me quickly to the brink. And then I came, my cock spasming as I shot my semen into Tina's mouth. Tina swallowed eagerly, and as I spasmed again and again, she gulped down each mouthful of my come. She continued sucking me until I had finished. Then both she and Whisper ground to a halt until Tina's face rested against my softening prick, offering it a reverent kiss.

I looked up at Sarah to see her flushed and red with arousal, obviously still hungry. She smiled at me.

"Tina shows a great deal of talent, does she not?"

My only answer was a rueful chuckle.

"I imagine you would like her in your bed tonight, then?" Sarah asked with a wink.

I shrugged. "She's been used quite sufficiently for the moment. I would prefer to wait until tomorrow to explore her talents further."

Sarah's pleasure was obvious. "Then she'll spend the night in my bed, if you have no objections. There are quite a few of her little tricks I wouldn't mind enjoying tonight. Shall I send the three slaves back to your bed in case you should need…something in the night?"

"One will be sufficient. I shall take Whisper with me—just in case I should need services while in my bed. If you have no objections."

"None." Sarah smiled. "I'll try not to wear this little bitch out too much—I imagine you'll be needing her tomorrow."

"I certainly will." I stroked Tina's face fondly. "Tina, service your Mistress well tonight. As well as you serviced me."

"Yes, Master." Tina crawled over to Sarah's side obediently. Flushed and red with excitement, but clearly not satisfied from the evening's activities, Whisper took her place beside me. My cock was sore from its frequent use—but I imagined it would be prudent to utilize Whisper for at least a little while.

CHAPTER 8

As soon as we were upstairs, I turned my full attention to Whisper. Even after my workout in the parlor, I wanted to explore all the other delights that Whisper had to offer, all the pleasures her body could give me.

I came up behind her quickly and pushed her down onto the sofa; she yelped as she lost her balance and fell across the big padded back of the sofa, her front half lost in the softness of the pillows, her ass in the air and her legs flailing wildly. It was a rather large sofa, so her feet dangled just off the ground. I could see the pretty slit of her clean-shaven pussy as she put one leg up on the back of the sofa and tried to crawl over. But I was behind her in an instant, holding her down as she tried to swing her other leg around. I pressed against her body, pulling open my robe and slipping my quickly hardening cock between her asscheeks. I reached down and placed my hand between her thighs, stroking her pussy as she squirmed to get free.

"Not so quick, Whisper. Your Mistress sent you upstairs with me for a reason, don't you think?"

Whisper knew her place well enough to stop struggling. She knew that she was to serve me, and it was her place to receive whatever cruel punishments I devised, or to provide for me sexually in whatever fashion I wished—no matter how degrading she might find them. She remained there, bent over the sofa, one leg up, exposed for me. As I began to fondle her pussy, I found the lips swollen and the bud of her entrance quite moist—she had been as excited by Tina's little display as I had. My cock stiffened quickly as I rubbed it between Whisper's glorious mounds. I could feel the slick bud of her asshole between her spread cheeks. Certainly, I would take Whisper there, too. But for now, I kept my attention on her shaved pussy, stroking its softness and feeling how full and ready the lips were. Ready to be parted, which is what I did with my fingers, exposing her tight little entrance.

"Don't you think your Mistress left you here because she wished you to be taken by me? Certainly that's what she intended."

"I—I couldn't suppose, Master," she said breathlessly. "I can't pretend to know the Mistress's desires—oh!"

Whisper gasped as I began to stroke the tight little entrance to her cunt. Good—a sensitive girl. Now she was squirming on the velvet couch, her naked body splayed out for me to enjoy from behind before turning her over to savor her front. Whisper was plainly a little shy, as she'd shown herself to be earlier. But I didn't doubt that she would show herself to be as horny a vixen as her sister Shade. I spread Whisper's lips a little more and watched her writhe on the couch as I teased her opening. She clawed at the velvet pillows with her hands, moaning softly.

Even as I played with the entrance to her pussy, I began to stroke my cock—which was now fully hard at the sight of the naked and helpless slave bent over for me—back and forth between her asscheeks, teasing the ripe entrance to her netherhole. Whisper moaned softly as I did so, and I imagined I had discovered a particularly sensitive spot of her anatomy. Not wanting to take the time to provide a more proper lubricant, I let spittle collect in my mouth, then let it dribble down between Whisper's cheeks, running down into her crack, slicking up the tight hole. Then I began to work my finger in. Whisper yelped, her ass working back and forth enticingly as her whole body squirmed.

She looked over her shoulder at me, breathing heavily. "Please, Master...I'm so tight back there...."

"Deliciously so, my dear." I had gotten the very first part of my pinkie into Whisper's bottom, and had discovered her hole to be even tighter than I had expected. Then the thought occurred to me. "You're not...a virgin too, are you?"

Whisper looked at me helplessly, her cheeks turning bright red. "Only back there, my Liege."

I was stunned. "Sarah never had you taken back there? Not even by her cock? She's so fond of such things...."

Whisper's discomfort was increasing rapidly as I wriggled my little finger farther into the tightness of her bum. "No, Master," she breathed. "I've never been taken back there—Oh!"

I let another drizzle of spit fall between Whisper's cheeks, working my little finger out just enough to let the saliva lubricate it as I slid it back in. Whisper's pretty butt moved back and forth as I penetrated her; all the while, I was slowly stroking her wet slit with my fingers, teasing her clit, feeling her lubricate more and more as I played with her pussy.

I could hardly believe it—a virgin in her most private spot! But the answer was obvious: Sarah had saved her for me. Oh, perhaps not for me specifically, but for a fortunate guest. Sarah loved to penetrate all parts of her slaves, and it seemed strange that she would have let any part of a delicious creature like Whisper go unexplored. But, then again, Sarah's extreme

THE CONTRACT

fondness for anal penetration was largely reserved for her male partners, as I had found out firsthand more than a few times. So it would have been fairly easy for Sarah to restrain herself in Whisper's case, on that small matter of her inviolate asshole, with the full knowledge that some lucky guest would find himself even more in Sarah's debt.

Well, I didn't intend to let such a sublime gift go wasted. Whisper was about to find herself buggered.

I could still see the discomfort on Whisper's beautiful face, but it looked as if she was beginning to surrender to my insistent touch. In fact, as I slid my fingertips up and down in her wet slit, I felt it moistening further, felt Whisper's clitoris grow fully erect under its hood. I played with that for a while, smearing the juice of Whisper's pussy over her firm clitoris, teasing it back and forth. Sarah had left Whisper's genitals unpierced—why, I couldn't imagine, when almost all of her other slaves had received as many as ten rings through their lips and clitoris.

But I was not the least bit disappointed—from the enthusiastic noises she was starting to make, Whisper was proving her clitoris to be extraordinarily sensitive. She still had one leg up on the back of the sofa, and she squirmed against me as I teased her pussy open and worked her clit back and forth. The tightness of her asshole had begun to yield slightly, and I could feel her relaxing, beginning to accept the intrusion into her darkest and most private spot. I let another thick drop of spit fall between her asscheeks and began to penetrate her with my ring finger, knowing that the increasing thickness might cause her a little discomfort. But take it she would—and on and on, until she took my cock.

Whisper's back arched. She hauled herself up onto her arms, pushing back against me, obviously fighting a strong impulse to get away. But she managed to hold there as I entered her with my second finger. She looked so enticing there with her back arched, her small but firm breasts hanging invitingly down with their large, pierced nipples all erect and ready, the rings glinting in the candlelight. Then Whisper looked back at me, her gorgeous face sheened with sweat, her pale hair beginning to dampen with the exertion of taking my finger into her ass. She had a look of delightful shame and embarrassment on her face, mixed with a hunger I loved to see in my submissives. If anything needed to tell me that Whisper was ready for my cock, that would have done it—though her dripping cunt had already communicated that.

I eased my finger out of Whisper's asshole. She gasped to feel the sudden vacancy. Her leg came down, and with a slight adjustment of her lower body, she was able to stand on tiptoe, bent over the sofa. Looking back over her shoulder, her face was filled with a mixture of disappointment, fear, and anticipation—

disappointment that I hadn't gone farther into her ass, and fear that I might now penetrate her there with my cock, which—she was sure—would prove much too big for her rear hole. And anticipation that I might do something even more devious and filthy to her.

I took my hand away from her pussy. It was very wet with her juices, and I rubbed them over the head of my cock, slicking it up for the penetration.

"Reach back," I told Whisper. "Pull apart your asscheeks for me."

I saw a look of fear come over Whisper's face, saw her redden as she realized that she was about to be used in that most secret place. Surely she had to know it would happen, but the terror on her face gave away the sudden shock that it was happening *now*, and there was nothing she could do to stop it short of disobeying her Mistress and resisting me. All that showed on Whisper's face. But mixed in with her fear, I was sure I saw the faintest hint of delight, excitement, arousal— that her last virginity was about to be taken, that she was going to be used where no man or woman had ever used her.

"Reach back," I growled, more firmly this time. "Show me where I am going to take you. Open up your asscheeks for me."

Her hands shaking, her face still showing her fear despite the resignation in her movements, Whisper reached back and slipped her slender fingers between her asscheeks, parting them gently for me. I received a much better view of her inviting little inviolate asshole.

"More!" I ordered her.

Whisper obeyed, tugging her cheeks further apart to give me better access to her netherhole.

"Hold them there until I'm finished taking you!"

Whisper was now in a very uncomfortable position, her waist bent over the side of the sofa and her upper body pointing down, making her helpless. With her hands behind her, she could do nothing but lie there. The blood must be pounding in her head, I thought with delight. Whisper obediently kept her asscheeks parted for me as I prepared to enter her ass.

I let a thick gob of spittle fall from my mouth to Whisper's crack, dribbling down between her cheeks. Whisper gasped as the warm fluid hit her and slowly drizzled in to her private place. Now she knew she was to be taken in the one spot she'd never been taken. She moaned softly in a combination of excitement and terror. Then I added more spit to the head of my cock, rubbing it over, mingling it with Whisper's juices until the head glistened.

Finally, it was time for me to savor the feeling of Whisper's ass opening up for the first time.

I guided my slick cock up between her cheeks. Whisper moaned softly, squirming on the back of the couch, as she awaited the penetration. She kept her cheeks spread wide as I pressed the thick head up against her tight hole. Whisper gasped, then wriggled her ass back against me. It was impossible to tell if she was merely acceding to her Master's wishes to take her, or if she was truly eager to be entered there. I would never really know the truth, but I fancied that, more than a little bit, Whisper was as excited by her deflowering as I was.

I felt her muscles tightening around the very head of my cock as I moved my hips around, entering her slowly. She struggled to accept my cock into her, but her ass struggled involuntarily to prevent the violation. Then Whisper let out a groan of exertion as I forced my cock into her ass, feeling the head pop in and rest just inside the entrance to her netherhole, gripped by the tightness of the young slave's virgin bottom.

"Oh, God!" she moaned. "It's so big...please, Master, it's so enormous...."

I am blessed with a rather impressive endowment—about which I do not mean to brag. It's often proven more of a hindrance than a help, though at times, size queens like Sarah make me thank my good fortune. But in this case, though it made it that much more difficult for Whisper to accept my cock into her ass as her very first, the feeling of this petite slave squirming against me, thrashing and moaning as I took her slowly, drove me mad with desire. I had to fight to keep myself from throwing her down and ravaging her brutally. But I managed to keep my sanity, so that I could savor every minute, taking Whisper as slowly as I could stand, making her feel every inch of my penetration into her.

"Please...oh, God, Master!... Please..."

Despite her protests, Whisper kept her slender fingers on her cheeks, prying them open to reveal her hole for my taking. Just as I had ordered her. My hands came to rest on her waist, and I felt the tension in her body as she fought to accept my shaft into her behind. Holding her close, I began to press in, feeling the tightness of her ass fight against me with every inch.

"Oh—oh—oh—please, Master!..." Tears were forming in her eyes and splashing down to stain the velvet sofa. I towered above her and pressed into her tight hole more deeply, giving her every inch slowly. She gasped with the exertion of taking my cock, but she kept her fingers on her cheeks obediently, offering her last hole to me. I pushed in farther. Whisper's face turned to look up at me from over her shoulder, her eyes sheened with tears. Then I thrust in deeper, and Whisper's tear-filled eyes went wider, wider, wider, wider, as her mouth opened in a soundless moan.

I grinned down at her, overwhelmed with the magnitude of my achievement. I had taken her all the way. The entire length of my cock was thrust into Whisper's asshole!

"Feel it," I told her. "Feel the shaft."

Still looking up at me in a silent plea for mercy, Whisper obeyed, her slender fingers sliding between our bodies. She reached for the shaft of my cock and felt that it was inside her, her tight asshole stretched impossibly around the very base of my penis. I felt the tips of her fingers and her sharp fingernails grazing my balls, which hung heavy against Whisper's hairless pussy. I saw the shock on her face as she realized that she had been taken all the way, that my entire cock was inside her ass.

"Oh, Master!" she whimpered. "Please, have mercy...."

"Never," I told her as I began to ease my cock back and forth inside her. The fear and sensation overwhelmed her face; she began to moan uncontrollably. Fear mixed with ecstasy, pain mixed with pleasure. I fucked her ass very gently, and as I eased it a bit further out, Whisper's fingers curved around the base of my cock, gripping it tightly so that she could feel the place where it entered her.

"Oh...please, Master—"

I grasped her hand and guided it away from the shaft of my cock, since it was preventing me from entering her all the way again. I placed her hands back on her asscheeks and ordered her, "Part them again as wide as you can."

With some effort, Whisper obeyed, tugging her stretched cheeks open for me. She let out a whimper as I pushed my cock to the hilt inside her ass once more, then began to fuck her in little inch-long thrusts, filling her deeply with my flesh. I rested deep inside her.

"Put one leg up on the back of the sofa," I ordered her. "Like you had it before."

Whisper was having trouble moving, but she managed to get one beautiful leg stretched up on to the back of the sofa, exposing her ass still more to my thrusts. This also left her pussy quite exposed, and as I toyed with her clitoris, I felt Whisper's ass muscles clenching.

"Keep them parted!" But now she needed no coaxing. Her ass had received my shaft, and her body was adjusting to accommodate its new invader. She snuggled her ass back against me, impaling herself on my cock. Slowly, her groans of pain had turned to pleasure without my even realizing it.

I slid two fingers into her pussy and felt the thick shaft of my cock pressing through Whisper's flesh to stimulate her pussy. Some women are built that way—a good hard cock thrust inside her asshole will strike just the right spot inside her pussy, so that she'll come faster than she would if you were making love to her in the conventional way. In fact, in some extreme cases, the woman doesn't even have to have her clit touched while you're doing it. As I coaxed Whisper's cunt open with my two fingers, and stroked the underside of my shaft through Whisper's internal flesh, I sensed that she might be one of these women.

In fact, I could feel the tightness of Whisper's asshole loosening up for me. I could sense that somehow the penetration in her asshole, which she had never felt before, was stimulating her in a way she'd never experienced. I felt sure that she was going to come if she was allowed to take the lead. In fact, I was determined to make her do exactly that. If it could be done.

"Make yourself come," I ordered her.

"But Master..." she whimpered, plainly excited by the prospect but unable to see how it would be done.

"Without using your hand. Fuck yourself on my cock until you climax. You can do it."

"But Master..." she protested. "With your cock inside my ass..."

"You don't feel it?" I pressed in with my two fingers again, and Whisper gasped as my fingertips worked against her sensitive spot inside, the spot that Sarah so loved to have stroked with the head of my cock. Then I thrust slightly against my fingers, and felt that the head of my cock was stimulating almost the identical spot. I eased my fingers out and began working my cock at an angle that pressed the head against that very place.

Whisper gasped, louder—then moaned. Suddenly she seemed confused at the sensations enveloping her. Then her mind seemed to lose grasp of what was happening, and her overwhelming desire to come took over.

"You do it," I ordered her. "Put your hands in front of you. Push yourself onto my cock.

Whisper obeyed as I put my hands on her waist and

pulled back just enough to give her room to work. She gasped to feel my cock leaving her, even by the few inches necessary. Then I first sensed her hunger to have my cock inside her ass. Soon her actions caught up with her desires, and she pushed herself back against me, forcing my cock up into her again. Her feet just barely touched the ground as she stood on tiptoe, so to pull herself up, she had to lean forward and use her arms. But months of service to Sarah had given her the strength to do just that, and she worked her body back up, pulling my cock out of her ass by perhaps four inches, then thrusting her body back down until her tiptoes reached the floor. As she did, she let out a wild moan like I had not yet heard from this demure slave, and repeated the thrust with sudden eagerness. Her whole body twisted and squirmed as she lifted herself and forced her lower body onto my cock, impaling herself again and again, moving faster as she became used to the action and as her asshole opened up still farther to accept the hard rod inside it. Whisper moaned louder and louder as she fucked herself onto my cock, ramming her body down, forcing it harder and harder into her ass. I could sense from the way she was losing control that she was indeed going to make herself come—in fact, she was going to come hard, impaled on my prick.

"Yes, Master...yes, Master...oh, God! Oh, God! OH GOD OH GOD OH GOD—"

I felt the muscles of her tight ass clenching as she

rammed her body down onto my cock one last time. Her whole body began to spasm as she moaned her orgasm. But she was unable to keep fucking her body up and down on my cock while she came—the sensations were too overwhelming. So, taking that as my cue, I began to fuck her even harder than she had been fucking me, ramming my cock fully and rhythmically into her asshole.

"Oh, yes, oh, yes, oh, yes," Whisper wailed as I fucked her ass, shoving it in with increasing urgency as my own climax approached. I held her down against the back of the sofa, directing her orgasm with my own, as I pounded into her and took every inch of her nether opening gleefully.

Then the pleasure exploded from my cock, radiating through my whole body. Whisper's naked body grew taut as she felt the pulsing of my cock inside her ass. She could feel herself being injected with my seed, her ass filled up with my thick fluid, and the new sensation aroused her even now. "Yes...yes, Master.... Fill me up...." I pumped until the last spurts of my seed had infused Whisper's asshole. I pulled my cock out of her, finding it slick with come. Whisper collapsed over the back of the couch, her asscheeks turned temptingly upward, her newly receptive hole presented as an invitation to further buggery. Whisper was panting heavily, her excitement and exhaustion mixing in that naked, vulnerable body. Her ass, pink from the violation of my cock, was slick with my semen, which greased her entrance and dribbled a drop at a time down the backs of her thighs.

I slapped her ass once, playfully, bringing a slight yelp and a wriggle of her hips from the deflowered slave.

I was struck by a delicious thought. Like all the furniture in Sarah's house, the sofa was constructed with more than a single purpose. In fact, its alternate function was clear from the thick rings which graced its legs and arms. Similarly, each room in Sarah's mansion—and especially the bedrooms—had at least one drawer which offered bondage equipment, so that at any moment, an unruly slave could be trussed and shackled.

Whisper had hardly been unruly, but what a delight it would be to see her pretty body restrained over that sofa, rather than just exhausted.

Before the girl was able to move, I had turned and retrieved four sets of shackles from the drawer near the bed, then quickly circled an ankle with one set, locking the other set to one side of the sofa back.

"Master—what are you—" Whisper began to get down from the back of the sofa.

"Don't move!" I ordered her, pushing her back into position with more roughness than probably was necessary. "You will remain in that position all night, so I can savor the way I took you. And you can savor it, too, and remember how you came on my cock."

The Contract

"But Master..." She wrestled me slightly, trying to get free.

"Silence!" I barked, holding her down over the couch, pinning her arms. She writhed and struggled for another moment, until the strength finally went out of her. When I felt her body relaxing and sensed that she had given herself over to her punishment and had resigned herself to her fate, I locked her other ankle to the sofa and climbed over the back quickly, pinning one wrist so I could shackle that and fix it to the arm of the sofa. I was careful to pull her naked body forward so that she was lifted almost off the ground, forcing her to stand on her very tiptoes.

Whisper began to struggle again. I felt my cock hardening rapidly as she whimpered and squirmed against her imprisonment. I wrestled her into position, pulling her still farther forward; then I grasped her other wrist as she began to struggle again, and locked it with the last shackle to the remaining arm of the sofa. It was only after I had her locked that Whisper really began to struggle in earnest, and whether she was testing the bounds of her imprisonment or deriving arousal from resisting the shackles, I couldn't know. Either way, she was bound quite effectively—her newly deflowered ass thrust high in the air, legs spread wide and her toes barely touching the ground, arms stretched out to either side, head hanging down so that her face was just visible in the tangle of her straight blonde hair. And either way, her struggling against my shackles was making my prick very, very hard.

"But Master," she whimpered, struggling against the bonds. "I have to stand on my tiptoes." She was on the verge of tears. "Please don't make me stay like this...."

"That's what you get for showing reluctance, for protesting when I told you how I was going to take you. Some reluctance can be accepted in a virgin, particularly in the case of her pretty bottom being taken. But what a delight it is to punish you, you little slut. We'll see if next time I tell you to spread your cheeks, you display even the slightest hesitation."

Tears flowed down Whisper's cheeks and onto the sofa. I realized I couldn't wait another instant. Despite the wonderful fucking I'd just given her, my cock was rock hard at the sight of the shackled naked slave weeping in degradation. I simply couldn't wait until morning to take her again, and it wouldn't have been the same to have another slave see to my erection. I wanted to increase Whisper's humiliation, to make her understand just how submissive she was meant to be, just how completely I owned her. I lowered myself to one knee, which put the hardening shaft of my cock almost level with Whisper's face.

"See what you've done?" I told her. "All that squirming of yours has given me another hard-on. Now let's see if you show a little reluctance now...or are you eager to obey me?"

Whisper's face was crossed by a look of disgust, presumably at orally servicing a cock that so recently had been inside her behind. She looked up at me with horror in her tear-filled eyes and sobbed once as I guided my cock closer to her mouth.

"Please, Master...I can't.... That would be..."

"Come on," I coaxed her. "Certainly you're not going to resist your Master's wishes again, are you?"

Whisper buried her face in the soft velvet of the sofa, struggling and pulling against the shackles. I grasped her hair and lifted her head, exposing her face to the head of my cock.

"Come, now," I told her. "You did such an admirable job that first night. You're a woman with a gift. Now use it!"

"Please...please, Master...."

I fed my cock to her, pressing it between her lips. I knew well that a particularly vicious slave might attempt to bite me. That excitement—that thrill of knowing that Whisper could either succumb to my desires or truly rebel—made my cock surge harder into her mouth.

"No...no...no..." she whimpered as I fed my hard cock into her mouth and guided it to the entrance to her throat. She gagged on the taste, but as I worked it in and leaned against her, I felt her relaxing slightly, felt her resistance fleeing. I sensed that she was resigned to having to give me a blowjob, to taste the shaft that had just deflowered her anus. Her warm tears splashed into my pubic hair.

"Do what you did the other night," I ordered her. "I'm *not* going to take your ass again until you do. And something tells me you're eager to have me do that to you again."

The choking sob that came from Whisper's throat told me I had hit the right spot. Despite her initial reluctance to give herself to me in that way, she had quickly learned to love the sensation of being impaled on my cock, her ass filled with my shaft. By the time I had finished with her ass, her reluctance had turned to eagerness. She had climaxed while I plumbed her nether regions, and she knew that she would climax again if I were to take her ass again the way I just had. She had enjoyed it as much as I thought she would.

"Use your mouth on my cock. Follow my orders. I have no desire to punish you. I only want you to see to this need you've awakened in me. Satisfy me with your mouth."

Whisper whimpered and finally gave up. She began to suckle on my cock, working the shaft in and out of her mouth. She gagged again on the taste as she took the shaft into her mouth, but this time she didn't try to stop. Instead, she lifted her head and ran her tongue around the tip of my cock, making me moan faintly with pleasure.

"All of it! Swallow it down."

Whisper went down again, taking my shaft into her mouth until the thick head pressed against the entrance to her throat. In this position it wasn't going to be easy, but an accomplished cocksucker like I'd seen the other night could deep-throat even in this position. Whisper hesitated, working her head around as she found the proper angle—and then she swallowed.

I leaned forward, pushing my cockshaft into her, filling her throat. I held it there, letting Whisper savor the feeling of my cock thrust down her throat; then I eased back and Whisper gulped air, readying herself for my next thrust. I pushed down her throat again, holding it longer this time, until she began to squirm a little bit.

"Very good," I said. "You're a gifted woman."

I began to thrust my hips rhythmically, pushing my cock down Whisper's throat. She opened her throat wide and accepted it, letting me use her mouth. She developed a rhythm to her breathing as I plumbed her mouth and throat. Her body had relaxed. Her hips were moving in time with my thrusts. I leaned forward just enough to slip my hand between her spread thighs. Not only was her pussy wet—it might have been wet from our previous lovemaking—it was positively dripping, leaking new juice. As I began to touch it, a loud moan came from Whisper's throat, and her whole body began to wriggle in pleasure.

Her ass, wide open like that with my semen greasing it, looked so inviting that I almost came around to her backside and took that again. But she was giving me such royal treatment with her mouth, that I didn't want to give it up—not for an instant.

I kept thrusting into Whisper's throat, taking her again and again with each long stroke of my shaft into her. As I did, I teased her clit, working it quickly back and forth, then up and down. I could sense by the moans low in her throat and the gyrations of her hips that she was already very close, so I worked my rhythm into hers, thrusting into her throat with the same rhythm required to bring her off. The result was overwhelming—Whisper's throat opened wide for my cock and she swallowed eagerly as I stimulated her clitoris. Then she was coming, moaning wildly, so that I felt the vibrations on the head of my cock when I thrust into her throat. Then I was thrusting faster, even as I brought her off with my hand. My cock spasmed as Whisper clamped her lips around the halfway mark of my cock, milking my head with hungry motions of her lips and tongue. I came in her mouth, as she guided me through every sensation of my orgasm with her skillful tongue. She swallowed hungrily, thick streams of my semen shooting into her. I released my hold on her pussy and clit, and Whisper's naked shackled body lay spread-eagled and bent over the back of the sofa.

"You see? I can be a kind Master. But you'll still spend the night this way for your earlier reluctance. In fact...I think it might be pleasurable to let some of the other slaves see how you've just been taken...see my sperm leaking out of your private hole. Don't you think that would be wonderful?"

Whisper looked up at me almost crying, and I felt a wave of lust for her as she nodded tearfully. I sent her off to display herself to the other slaves, while I got some much needed sleep; I instructed her to return to my bed when she had finished showing herself—just on the off chance I might need something during the night. This done, I wrapped myself in the covers and dropped into much-needed slumber.

CHAPTER 9

I have been blessed—if you can call it a blessing—with an overactive sex drive. It has been my further good fortune in life to have the means to exercise this trait of mine.

As well, I can be said to have rather...esoteric tastes in women, by which I mean that the most delightful sight to me is the sight of a woman on her knees, bound and pierced and in total submission, servicing her male or female owner. While I can certainly appreciate the aesthetic attraction of forced submission, it does not excite me the way willing submission does. What I seek is the experience of seeing a woman, particularly a young woman (though older women certainly have their unique charms) being subjected to extreme treatment, with the knowledge that this woman, even while being totally humiliated and used sexually—in whatever degrading fashion her Master or Mistress deems appropriate—*wants* that humiliation and degradation, that she not only submits willingly to this treatment, but that she *seeks it out* for her own pleasure, for the pleasure of absolute submission and service to her owner.

I have seen many women subject themselves to this treatment, and I know that for a woman so inclined, there is no greater ecstasy than that of her total service to an unforgiving and demanding owner and, if it pleases her Master or Mistress, her total humiliation. I have been lucky enough to witness and participate in a great many such humiliations, and to see the flush of pleasure in the slave's face, the spasms of orgasm shuddering through her body as she achieves physical release at the moment of her greatest submission. These have been the sweetest moments of my life.

Of course, once a submissive woman has been properly tamed, correctly subjugated, her own pleasure becomes merely an outgrowth of the dominant's, a tool to bring him amusement and to cause suffering for the slave. For what better way is there to torment someone than with her or his own sexual desires? A kind Master will torment his slave with her own pleasure, will force her to confront her own physical need every moment

The Contract

of every day, will force her to become one with that lust and to have her own personality snuffed out by it. She will be trained to be always ready and eager for sex, to think of virtually nothing else, to offer service at the Master's whim, and when ordered to service, to continue service until the Master allows her to stop. Certainly a slave can be used for domestic tasks—in fact, this increases her submission and her usefulness. But her primary purpose in life, when she is treated properly, remains to suffer at the Master's pleasure and to service others sexually.

To be sure, I had taken many other virgins—and certainly, this was one of the sweetest pleasures possible. There had been Maria, the sweet Portuguese submissive given to me that summer in Lisbon as a gift from one of my lovers. She had never been with a man—not even for oral service. At first, Maria had been nervous, but by the time I took her she was eager to receive my cock inside her.

Then there was the succulent blonde Olga, the prize slave of one of my Swedish friends. Much to my friend's chagrin, I had won the right to take Olga's virginity in a card game. But Olga had proven to be even more eager than Maria, and before she left my bed she had been taken a dozen times in a wide variety of interesting positions.

There was Christine, whose virginity was shared by me and my lover Annalise, who brought Christine to our bed and enticed her to give herself to us. Christine had spent a long week in our hotel room, learning to service Annalise and receive my cock in every way I could think of—and several that Christine came up with on her own.

There were others, for the world is full of virgins eager to lose themselves in the tender love of their chosen gender—or genders, in the case of Maria and Christine. Each of these young women had found in themselves an intense desire for sex, and whether or not they thought of themselves as "submissive," soon they were eager to receive the thrust of my cock into their succulent and willing bodies.

This was the fate that awaited Tina, and I could see from her behavior in the parlor that she was well on her way. I would become an instrument of her submission, taking Tina's virginity from her and helping to prepare her for a life spent on her knees, a life of sexual servitude, so that she could service a Mistress more completely. Clearly Tina would become an exceptional slave, one so completely available for sexual use that she would receive any erotic attentions the Mistress wished her to receive enthusiastically. Thinking of all the sexual humiliations to which Tina would gladly submit in her lifetime of submission was particularly erotic to me. I thought of the many orgasms Tina would have on her hands and knees, being fucked by huge numbers of slaves or submitting to the thrust of the

Mistress's strap-on dildo. I imagined the many moans of pleasure that would come from Tina's mouth as she was penetrated in her cunt and ass.

I didn't doubt that Sarah had already caused Tina to submit to a vast number of sexual situations, to receive attentions whenever it pleased Sarah to watch her submit. But she had not yet had Tina taken in that one important way, and it would be my great pleasure to experience the feel of a virgin Tina yielding hungrily to my thrust. I would feel the writhing of her body underneath me as I eased my cock forward to taste the sweet honey of her inviolate virgin cunt. I would feel her tense under the slight pain as I entered her, tearing her maidenhead from her, and then feel her flooding with release and excitement as my shaft settled easily into her newly opened cunt. I would be Tina's first true male lover, but she would, shortly thereafter, have so very, very many. So *very* many. I, for one, would see to that.

I have also been blessed in that I always wake up with a hard-on. Every day of my life. But the fact that I woke up with an erection that morning, after the severe flogging my cock had taken the previous night, was a testament to just how long I had slept.

I lay wrapped up in the satin sheets, feeling the throbbing hardness of my cock against the soft fabric. I had slept deeply, my mind filled with images of Tina's ultimate submission. I woke sheened with sweat, my body aching from yesterday's workout but feeling filled with energy for a repeat performance today. My cock felt as ready as ever as I opened my eyes to experience the new day.

I was greeted by the image of a very naked Tina, holding a silver tray with a large array of juice, fruit, breads, and coffee. It was a stunning display, but I took little notice of it as I looked Tina up and down. She looked none the worse for wear after her night in Sarah's bed; in fact, with my raging hard-on, I found her naked body to be of even greater interest than it had been the previous night.

"Good morning," I said.

Tina curtsied without tilting the tray. "I have brought you breakfast, Master." she said. "Whisper sensed that you would awake soon, and came and got me to serve you your morning meal."

I looked out the window, where the sun seemed to be high in the heavens. "Morning? What time is it, anyway?"

"Just before noon, Master."

"Noon! Damn, I've slept twelve hours!"

"Yes, Master," Tina gave me a naughty look. "It was my greatest pleasure to exhaust you last night."

I laughed contemptuously. "That's delightful, my dear, but please don't think for a second that *you* exhausted me. You were merely the dessert to a delicious meal. I had savored the bodies of two female slaves, as well as that of your Mistress, before you were allowed to service me."

Tina's face reddened, her embarrassment clearly showing. I continued to tease her, taking great pleasure at her shyness.

"Before long, I hope you can truly see the error of your ways in thinking that a quaint little blowjob like that could exhaust me. I imagine there will be some evening soon—who knows, perhaps even tonight?—when you will find out just how much effort it will take you to exhaust me. Then perhaps you will understand that your greatest pleasure is not to exhaust me—but to exhaust *yourself.*"

Tina's eyes were downcast, and the flush of her face deepened. I took pleasure in noticing that her nipples had begun to harden. Already our game had begun. And I hadn't even had breakfast yet!

"I'm sorry, Master. It would be a great honor to have you exhaust me completely with your attentions, though I'm sure I am not worthy of this."

"We'll see if you are," I said. "A little later. In the meantime, I've half a mind to deny you access to this hard-on I've waked up with. I should make you watch while I bring Whisper back in here and fuck her soundly like I did last night after you got your mouthful. Would that disappoint you?"

Tina was shifting uncomfortably; her eyes floated over the visible bulge my hard-on was tenting in the bedcovers. Her breathing seemed to be quickening. My harsh words were plainly having the desired effect on her. "Yes, Master. But if you should desire it, it would be my pleasure to watch."

"I'm sure it would," I said. "But I'm too fucking hungry right now. Bring the food here."

Tina relaxed visibly and brought the tray to the side of the bed. It fitted just over my lap, placing undue pressure on my erection through the covers, and causing me more than a little sexual discomfort. Well, no matter—soon my hard-on would be taken care of by that pert little mouth or maybe those juicy tits—or possibly that tight little ass? Should I take that before I relieved Tina of her troublesome virginity?

Tina stood obediently at my bedside, her naked body displayed to me as I ate. It was quite a bit more entertaining than reading the paper, and it didn't do anything to diminish the size or hardness of my erection. I took great pleasure in inspecting her, looking her over, admiring the size of her breasts, the hardness of her pink nipples, the inviting shape of her legs (I imagined they would be even more inviting when spread wide), and the smoothness of her shaved crotch. She remained standing as I demolished the entire tray of food. Mostly for her benefit, I demanded more.

"This meal you brought me is fit for a lesser man, perhaps, but I'm still hungry."

"Yes, Master," Tina hurried away to get more food.

She returned with another tray, and this time I sated myself with slightly over half the offering. Tina watched in astonishment as I ate.

"You are a man of great hungers," she said softly, her voice breathy.

"Not until after breakfast," I said sternly, looking her over with my passion evident in my eyes. "Then you shall see just how great my hungers are. And we'll see what you offer me for a second course."

Tina shifted nervously, her nipples hardening further, until they stood out quite erect from her large pale breasts.

Finally, I motioned for Tina to take the tray. As she removed it and went to leave the room, I called to her.

"Leave the tray on the floor," I said harshly. "There are many things I require in the morning, other than food."

"Yes, Master." Tina returned to my side quickly, an expectant look on her face.

She stood beside the bed as I looked her over, admiring the nervousness she displayed. She had no doubt that I was to use her most enthusiastically, and I could tell how much the prospect excited her.

"Draw back the covers. See what you find."

Tina leaned forward to obey, and as she drew back the covers I grabbed her and pulled her off balance, causing her to fall across my lap.

Without warning, I clutched her slender waist to my

body with one hand, and with the other, began to give the little bitch a sound spanking.

Tina gasped and then moaned in shock, as my hand came down on her firm behind. She squirmed a little as I spanked her again and again, picking up speed and hitting her harder as I felt the tension in her body flowing away and the pleasure begin to fill her. Within seconds, she was flushed, her face hot with desire. Her bottom, too, was beginning to redden.

"A good long spanking always helps me get going in the morning," I said. "You don't mind, do you?"

"No, Master." I could tell from the huskiness of her voice that she didn't mind at all.

"Spread your legs," I growled, for she had kept her thighs pressed together as I spanked her. But now, obediently, she parted her thighs, exposing her virgin cunt. Her feet dangled a few inches off the ground. I could feel the softness of her belly pressing against my hard-on, and I was quite aware from the way she was reacting that she could feel it as well. Now that her cunt was available to me, I took my time administering her spanking, and caressed the twin globes of her ass, slowly feeling their texture before I launched into another volley of slaps against her buttocks. Tina squealed and squirmed in my lap, her squirming sending waves of pleasure through me as her belly stroked against my hard cock.

"Hold still!" I snarled. "You're going to make me

shoot off all over your tits if you keep squirming like that! Or would you like that, you little slut?"

"I'll try to hold still, Master," Tina whimpered. I began spanking her again, harder than ever, taking great pleasure at the way she bit her lip and tried to keep herself from squirming and struggling, but was unable to do so. Soon I had to stop spanking because it was *I* getting flushed. Her squirming threatened to bring me off.

Now Tina seemed ecstatic, bent over my lap and helpless to resist the cruel spanking I was giving her. Her asscheeks, bright red with my many blows, were spread just slightly, letting me see the tempting bud of her inviolate asshole. To keep her from squirming and bringing me off just like that, I slid my thumb down into her crack, savoring the cleft between her luscious globes. I began to stroke her most private entrance, teasing her. Certainly, that didn't stop her from squirming, but it kept me distracted enough so that I could savor my arousal without getting myself off. In fact, Tina's squirming increased as I played with her nether opening. Then I began to explore her pussy, teasing open the full, pierced lips of her sex and feeling just how wet her slit had become during our spanking.

"How delightful," I said. "Two holes on you that have never been taken. I think I shall enjoy both of them before long."

"Yes, Master," she panted. I reached down and teased

her clit, playing with the ring pierced through it. Tina began to groan and hump against me.

"Hold still!" I spat. "Or do you think Whisper could better follow my orders...while you watch?"

"No, Master," Tina sighed, obviously afraid that I would desert her for the ministrations of the red-haired slave. I pinched her clit roughly and felt a spasm go through Tina's body. I stroked the smooth-shaved mound of her pubis and teased the very entrance to her cunt. The tension in Tina's vulnerable, naked body increased as she felt my fingers at her opening.

Unable to hold back anymore, I launched a new spanking, this time concentrating fully on slapping her furrow, bringing moans from her lips. Then I spent a long time spanking her upper thighs, reddening these until Tina's pussy had juiced considerably. God, she was lovely, bent over my lap like that with her legs spread and her ass offered eagerly for my punishment. Before I knew what I was doing, I had lifted Tina in my arms and all but thrown her onto the bed, faceup, as I climbed on top of her. Tina's face was filled with shock and confusion; but as I mounted her, I saw her fear change to excitement, her shock to eager supplication. Her legs were parted wide, her virgin cunt displayed for my use. I settled down on top of her, the shaft of my cock hard and ready to penetrate her, the thick, throbbing head just inches from her opening.

I grasped Tina's wrists and forced them over her

head. Her back arched and I felt her lovely tits pressing up against my chest, her nipples hard and sensitive. Her thighs spread around my hips as my cock neared her maidenhead. She whimpered, "Oh, Master…yes, Master…" as my cockhead slipped between her cuntlips. I moved my hips gently, teasing her opening with the hard head of my prick. Tina looked up at me, eagerly offering her succulent virginity to me.

"Yes…Master…please take me.…" she begged.

I brought my hips around in tiny circles, feeling the full, spread thickness of her pierced lips and the wetness of her opening. Tina's eyes fluttered closed, and she whimpered rhythmically in submission as she realized she was about to be taken. She snuggled her ass just a bit deeper into the softness of the bed, spreading her legs a little farther to give me better access to her. I still held her wrists above her head, but this was clearly an appropriate position for her to be fucked. And Tina clearly liked it; she was ready to give herself to me. And God, I was ready to take her!

"Please, Master…" she whimpered.

I pressed my cock into her opening, feeling her tightness against my head. Tina arched her back, pressing her body against me, as I entered her slowly. She let out a wild groan of ecstasy as she felt my thick cockhead slipping into her; then I felt the resistance of her maidenhead and heard Tina gasp in surprise. Her eyes opened wide and she looked up at me in desire, making it quite clear that she was ready to receive my cock inside her, ready to feel her maidenhead rending as she gave herself to me. I rested my body fully on Tina's, holding her down as I pressed forward, struggling with the unwilling entrance. Tina's mouth opened wide in a soundless wail as I bore down on her hymen, thrusting rhythmically against it. I pressed in and felt Tina's virginity holding against my thrust, felt her body tense as the struggle continued. Then I pressed into her with all my might, and Tina strained upward to meet me. She gave a loud groan of pain and release as her maidenhead was broken, as the thin wall of flesh gave way to my thrust and was pierced, torn open to admit my hard cock against the last resistance of her virginity. Her breath came in shuddering gasps as her tight cunt accepted me, her flesh finally giving way under my pressure.

I sank my cock into Tina, savoring the feel of that first entrance. I released her wrists and propped myself up so I could place my hands on her hips, giving me more leverage to enter her more completely. Tina groaned as I penetrated her fully, until the length of my cock was thrust into her and her pierced cuntlips parted around my shaft.

Tina's hands lay above her head, limp, inert, as I savored the feeling of taking her completely. But then she reached down with one hand as I pulled out slightly and wrapped her fingers around the base of my cock, feeling the place where I entered her. The look on her face was one of absolute rapture, as she stroked the shaft that had pierced her. Droplets of blood had formed on Tina's cuntlips, dribbling onto the lower part of my shaft. I thrust into her again, all the way, and her hand pressed against my lower belly, feeling the strength of my thrust and our desire. Tina put her arms around me, holding me close as I began to take her.

I fucked her slowly in rhythmic thrusts, taking my time bringing myself to a climax. Of course, her pleasure was inconsequential to me, but it was clear that even through the pain of her lost virginity, she was overwhelmed with pleasure. There are some women who are lucky enough to be—to put it kindly—*made* to be fucked. And judging from her whimpers and groans, Tina seemed to be one of those lucky women. I felt her hands gripping the cheeks of my ass as they went taut with each thrust into her. I pumped more rapidly as my pleasure mounted, and I could tell from the writhing and squirming of Tina's luscious body that she was going to come quite soon.

I leaned back, getting on my knees and lifting Tina's ass off the bed with the thrust of my cock. She let go of my ass and dropped her hands to her side, giving her the look of a woman who has given herself wholly over to the desires of her partner. Now my prick pressed upward inside her pussy, hitting the spot that, in Sarah, made her so deliciously likely to spurt her fluid. Tina clearly received similar pleasure from having that spot stimulated, and she began to shudder and moan as I thrust into her. Now I could see her better, could see the submissive posture she assumed with her legs spread wide and her hands limp at her side, the look of absolute pleasure on her face. My thrusts quickened, and I heard Tina wailing her approaching orgasm. She reached down to feel the shaft of my cock thrusting into her, cleaving her furrow; then she arched her back higher than before and her head thrashed back and forth on the pillows. Shudders and spasms went through her body as she came with an intensity that would have made Sarah jealous. I thrust faster and faster, my own climax moments away. I let out a groan of release as my cock spasmed inside Tina's cunt, and she whimpered, "Yes…yes…oh, yes, Master…come inside me…."

I came hard, shooting stream after stream of come into Tina's newly opened cunt. Tears formed in her eyes as she received my seed, and I watched them trickle deliciously down her cheeks. I leaned forward again, lying on top of her so I could lick the salty droplets from her cheeks. She put her arms around me again and held me close as I came my last into her receptive cunt. I clutched Tina as my cock softened and slipped out of her, dripping with her juices and with the blood of her torn hymen. But Tina's discomfort had not diminished her desire, and as she lay underneath me, I felt her still-hard nipples. Soon Tina would be ready for more.

The Contract

"Thank you, Master," she whispered into my ear. "I am privileged to have given myself to you."

"You've a lot more to give," I sighed. "I don't intend to get out of bed today. By the time you get off this bed, you're going to find many more ways to take my cock."

Tina's back arched the promise. "Thank you, Master," she said softly. "I won't disappoint you."

I laughed cruelly. "You most certainly won't. I'll see to that."

CHAPTER 10

It was a great pleasure to have taken Tina's virginity, but there were many other ways I wanted to enjoy her body. After we had spent some time cuddling, the squirming of her body causing my cock to stiffen again, I took a long while exploring Tina's body with my hands. I started by caressing her lovely breasts, pinching her nipples and feeling the enthusiastic reaction that brought.

"I'm going to have you pierced there," I told her. "A proper submissive should have her nipples pierced, just like her cunt. You'll like that, won't you?"

Tina squirmed as I played with her hard nipples. "Yes, Master," she said breathlessly, "if you should desire it. But I'm already so sensitive there—I fear if I've got rings through them I'll never be able to take my mind off my breasts." She giggled a little, and I pinched harder, drawing a gasp from her full, parted lips.

"Oh, I'm sure we can take your mind off of them now and then," I growled. "Certainly having your pussy and clit pierced, you still think of your other body parts sometimes, don't you?"

"Yes, Master," Tina said softly as she relaxed into the sensations I was causing in her breasts. I moved my attention to her spread thighs, exploring their contours and the lovely way they curved together to frame her pierced cunt. Now that she had been taken, her cunt opened up for my fingers quite easily. She was lubricated with my semen and with the juices of her own intense arousal. I fingered her slowly, fucking her first with one and then with two fingers. She accepted my fingers eagerly, though I could feel the stirrings of resistance as I slowly worked two fingers into her slick hole. I felt the contours of her newly opened channel, stroking the remnants of her hymen listening to Tina gasp as I penetrated her with my fingers.

My cock was quite hard by now, but I wasn't yet ready to fuck Tina again. Instead, I curled up in her embrace and ran my fingertips down her back, making her shiver. I let my hands rest on her glorious ass, gently prying open her cheeks and letting my finger graze her asshole.

THE CONTRACT

"You know, of course, that I'm going to take you here, too. Before the day is out. Before you are allowed off this bed."

"Yes, Master," Tina said nervously. It brought me some pleasure to know that she was a little afraid of having her ass taken—it would make it that much more delightful when I penetrated her there. I held her close, my hard cock pressing against her belly as I kissed her deeply.

I had decided to take Tina's mouth again, to give her the pleasure of orally servicing a cock that had just fucked her pussy. There would be a delicious sense of servitude about that act, of worshiping the shaft which had just taken her. Tina seemed to sense this instinctively. As I caressed her, she reached down and wrapped her fingers around my shaft. Whether she was able to intuit my desires, or whether she was simply prone to absolute oral submission, made little difference. What mattered was that Tina slowly slid herself down my body as I lay on my back. Her mouth hovered over my prick.

"Please, Master," she whispered. "If I may be allowed to service you orally.... I want to taste you now that you've taken me."

"Be my guest," I said. Tina lowered her mouth to my cock, licking the head and slipping it between her lips as she whimpered in pleasure. There were traces of blood and the residue of Tina's cuntjuices on my cock, but she showed no reluctance as she swallowed my shaft, gulping it easily down her throat. She eased it back out and worked it all over, licking it clean and then rubbing the shaft against her face and between her breasts. She hoisted herself onto her hands and knees to give herself greater access as she leaned down and took my cock into her mouth and throat again. She took a long time savoring the feeling of it thrusting into her, then began to pump it in and out of her mouth insistently, steadying it with her hand as she swallowed me. If anything, her services were more enthusiastic this time, as she gave herself over wholly to pleasuring my cock. I ran my fingers through her tangled hair as she swallowed me rhythmically. Groans escaped from my lips as I mounted quickly toward my orgasm. Tina sensed my impending climax and clamped her lips tightly around the head, working the shaft with her hand so that she wouldn't miss a drop of my issue. Then my back arched and I moaned loudly as spasms went through my cock, spurting my seed into Tina's eagerly waiting mouth.

She swallowed obediently, then hungrily licked the last remnants of my sperm from the head. She curled up with her head in my lap, her cheek against my softening cock, as I stroked her hair and contemplated what other delicious things I could do to her. But to my pleasure, both of us dropped into a light slumber for a time.

My sleep was filled with pleasant dreams.

* * *

I awakened slowly as I became aware of Tina's squirming body against me. I'm not even sure whether she was fully awake as we started to make love, but it was clear that her lust transcended consciousness. I felt her against me, her limbs wrapped around mine, as she rubbed her belly against my hard cock. I pressed Tina onto her back gently, climbing on top of her as she spread her legs and opened her eyes slowly. "Yes!" she moaned. "Oh, yes...."

My hard cock hovered at her entrance, stroking between the slick lips of her pussy. Tina lay underneath me and ran her hands down my back, then gripped my cheeks and tried to pull me forward into her. We were both groggy with sleep, but as desperately as I wanted to fuck her again, I knew that now was the time to take her further.

"Roll over," I growled. "On your belly."

Tina rolled obediently onto her stomach, spreading her legs around my knees. She lifted herself up just enough to show me the enticing bud of her asshole between her luscious cheeks. I guided my cock to Tina's cunt, sliding it in easily and feeling how wet she was. Good—that was exactly what I needed. I heard her moaning wildly and felt my own pleasure mounting as I fucked her slowly. But as much as I would have liked to fuck her until I came inside her pussy again, I had other, more devious things in mind.

I let a ball of saliva form in my mouth, then let it

splash into the furrow between Tina's cheeks. She gasped as she felt it, and the three more that followed it. By then she understood what I had in mind for her, but I took great pleasure in telling her at length just what I was going to do to her.

"I am going to take your ass," I told her cruelly. "I'm going to enjoy that cute bottom of yours. I'm going to open you up in a new place. Reach back and part your cheeks for me."

Tina's hands were trembling; plainly, she was nervous at the prospect of giving herself to me in that way. But now—now that I had taken her virginity and was enjoying her body—this was when I should take everything she had to give.

She reached back obediently and parted her cheeks, revealing her asshole to me more completely. I let three more drops of spit fall into her crack, and massaged them in with my fingers. Then I eased my cock out of her, and Tina gasped as it left her pussy.

I slid the head of my cock up and down in her crack, slicking up her rear entrance. Tina groaned at the sensations that flooded her body as I teased her asshole open. Then I pressed in. I felt her trembling as I began to enter her. She groaned as her tight bottom fought the intrusion of my large cock. But with a firm thrust, my cockhead, lubricated with her cuntjuices and my spittle, slipped in to her tightest entrance.

"Oh!" she gasped as she felt it going in. Then she

moaned softly and gave herself over to be used by me. I slid my cock into her slowly, feeling her asshole tighten around my shaft. Tina's moans grew louder, and when she felt that I was inside her all the way, she reached back and stroked her buttocks with her fingers, feeling the place where I had penetrated her. Her breath was coming short, and it was clear from the way she whimpered with my every movement that the sensations were intense and difficult for her—at first painful, but, as I moved my cock slowly inside her, growing more and more pleasurable. Tina lifted her body off the bed slightly and snuggled back against me, wriggling her ass to tell me she wanted more.

"Oh…Master…I'm so tight back there…. Oh!…"

Savoring the feel of her submission to me, I began to fuck Tina's ass, slowly at first, then faster as my own pleasure mounted and Tina surrendered to the sensations flooding her naked and vulnerable body. I looked down to admire the way her pale asscheeks spread around my thrusting shaft, the way her hole stretched to accept my cock. Soon Tina was moaning and bucking back against me like a cat in heat.

"Oh, Master…it feels wonderful!…"

I reached down to feel the erect bud of Tina's pierced clitoris. She gasped as I touched her there. As I began to stroke it roughly, in time with my hard thrusts into her ass, I heard her moans rising in pitch. I knew she was going to come, and I felt her ass tightening around my thrusts as she neared. I kept working her clit as she mounted toward orgasm, thrusting back against me and thrashing her head back and forth in time with my fucking. Then she lifted her head, and an inhuman wail escaped her lips. I felt spasms going through her ass as I plunged into her. I held onto her clit until I felt her orgasm riding up out of my control; then I held her down and started fucking her ass rapidly. Tina went wild underneath me, pressing up into my thrusts and taking each one with a newfound vigor. Then I, too, was coming, my cock jerking inside her, filling her with my thick jism. I groaned and let out my last spurt inside her ass as I slumped, exhausted, on top of her. I felt her ass wriggling back and forth as my dwindling cock eased out of her sperm-filled hole.

"Oh, Master!" she moaned softly. "Oh, thank you, Master. Thank you for taking me that way."

I remained on top of Tina for some time, stroking her hair as I savored the feel of her body underneath me. She turned her head to let me kiss her, my tongue exploring her mouth eagerly, tasting the sharpness of my sperm.

"Time for a bath," I said. "Or are you hungry enough for lunch?"

"Only if it should please you, Master." The submissive tone in her voice had a newfound passion to it.

I summoned Adriana to bring us lunch and draw us a bath. But by the time lunch arrived, I had already lost myself in the pleasures of Tina's body, and so lunch had to wait.

Tina remained in my room for the rest of the day, each hour bringing delightful new ways for her to submit to me sexually. After lunch, we had a long, luxurious bath, with a naked and beautiful Adriana soaping and scrubbing Tina's body, paying particular attention to the places where she had just been taken. Adriana brought us wine, which we enjoyed in the bath. Tina was more than a little drunk by the time I began to caress her body, and she had gotten very turned on as Adriana had soaped her. So I took a long time exploring her body under the warm water. By the time I bent her over the side of the tub and penetrated her cunt from behind, she was almost delirious with desire. She came three times as I fucked her and eagerly accepted the jet of my sperm over her steam-reddened buns.

Adriana rinsed us and we returned to bed, where I utilized Tina's eager, seeking mouth for a long time before mounting her and fucking her fervently. It took at least half an hour of fucking before I was ready to come, and this time I slid my cunt-slick cock between Tina's glorious breasts and pressed them together, fucking her in that way until I came all over her tits. She rubbed my seed over her breasts and throat, licking her fingers when she was done. By this time it was late in the afternoon, and it was clear to me that there was no way I was going to wear out this little vixen. I was badly in need of a rest, so I summoned Adriana and told her to bring Eduardo. I could tell by the way Tina's face brightened that she was acquainted with Eduardo, and knew full well what I had in store for her. I rested while Eduardo fucked Tina in three different positions, climaxing inside her each time.

Finally, Tina's boundless enthusiasm seemed marred by exhaustion. This excited me enough to get me hard again, and this time I started with Tina's lovely mouth, proceeding to her cunt and getting her off twice, before rolling her over and utilizing her ass until I came inside that inviting orifice. She participated eagerly, but it was clear that she was beginning to get worn out. Knowing this, I took great pleasure in calling in two more male slaves to take their turns with Tina, fucking her several times each.

By the time they had each had her, Tina's exhaustion was apparent. She dozed off in the bath we took afterward, and it gave me great pleasure to lift her and take her to bed, fucking her while she slept until she wakened to the thrusting of my body and moaned in overwrought pleasure. I took my time fucking the very sleepy Tina, and by the time I came inside her, it was clear that I had won our little battle of wills. I had exhausted the little slut, and perhaps now she had reached the threshold of her submission. Now that she knew the lengths I would go to see her used sexually, perhaps she would begin to give herself to me wholly. It was such a delight to have her sleeping in my bed, fully exhausted from the long day of sex. But tomorrow she would serve me breakfast again—an even more carnal breakfast this time—and that would be just the start of another long day for Tina. I caressed her sleeping body and cuddled up beside her, dropping off to sleep with her limbs wrapped around me. Tomorrow, I knew, would be an even more trying day for Tina.

CHAPTER 11

The next morning, my first awareness—before I had a conscious thought, and certainly before I was even slightly awake—was of the painful hard-on throbbing between my legs. My fervent lovemaking with Tina had only served to heighten my desire for her, to increase my lust for her sensual, nubile young body. Though I had come many times the previous day, I woke with as powerful a desire as if I had not come for weeks. My morning erection was as demanding and insistent as ever.

I reached out for Tina before I even opened my eyes, without looking out from under the silken pillow. My erection ached between my legs, stiff and straight and ready for the morning's release. I had already formed the idea to climb on top of Tina and take her quickly, fucking her delicious pussy as a way of greeting the day. I reached for her, but I found her side of the bed empty, though warm.

I opened my eyes, feeling around for Tina, experiencing a wave of righteous anger. Where had that horny little bitch gone? How dare she leave the bed without my permission! The thought occurred to me that perhaps the slut had awakened before me and, being overwhelmed with sexual need now that she was no longer a virgin, had gone off in search of a partner to fuck her—perhaps one of the male slaves. If that was the case, I would make that slut sorry she had given in so easily to her physical lusts, in the meantime denying her Master his rightful morning services. I would certainly punish her most severely for this lapse in judgment—but thinking about doing just that increased the ache in my crotch.

So I sat up, and it was only then that I saw Sarah, standing nonchalantly beside the bed. She was not yet dressed for the day, but wore a very short peach silk nightgown—so short I could see that she wore matching panties—and a loose, transparent white robe that hung open, so that very little of her lovely body was hidden from me. Plainly, that was the idea, as Sarah had already applied her makeup for the day—even though she hadn't gotten dressed yet. I looked Sarah up and down hungrily.

THE CONTRACT

"What, no breakfast?" Sarcasm dripped from my voice. "The last slave who woke me up brought food. And even so, she found herself getting more than she bargained for."

Sarah smiled condescendingly, humoring me. She tugged her robe farther open so that it fell off her shoulder. The nightgown's strap fell with it, letting the rich silky lace inch down—not quite far enough to reveal Sarah's breast, but very close to it. The nightgown was very low-cut, and the V-neck was of lace, so that I could already see most of her prodigious breasts. Her nipples were already visible through the thin fabric—and were becoming more visible as they hardened. Arching her back so that her breasts pressed invitingly through the fabric, which was growing damp with Sarah's sweat, Sarah tossed back the robe so that it hung off of both of her shoulders, leaving it wide open so that the full length of her body was revealed to me in the barely-there nightgown and panties.

"I've brought breakfast." Sarah's voice was husky. She moved closer to me and put one knee up on the bed. This meant that she parted her legs just enough for me to see the thin crotch of her peach silk panties tugging tightly between her cuntlips. I knew that she must be very wet, for her to be this forward with me.

"Good, because I'm hungry." I reached up for her. My arms went around her waist and I pulled her down onto the bed. She gasped as she tumbled on top of me, her breasts just before my face. With one arm I circled her waist and pulled her close to me; with the other, I yanked down the covers to reveal my erect cock. Sarah now straddled my belly so that her cunt was just out of reach of my cock. As she leaned forward, moving slightly back and forth so that her breasts swayed just in front of my hungry mouth, Sarah slipped off the robe and reached behind her ass to take my cock in her hand, wrapping the diaphanous fabric around my hard pole. She stroked the soft, smooth silk up and down over my shaft, letting her slender fingers guide and encircle it. I groaned softly as she touched me. Still clutching her tightly with one arm, I reached up with my free hand and pulled the nightie down roughly to reveal one lovely pink-tipped breast. Perhaps I was too eager, for as I pulled, I heard the lace ripping a little. Sarah's eyes went wide as she heard that, and she smiled down at me. "Yes," she said, in a tone that made it clear this wasn't open for discussion. *"Yes!!"*

I stroked her exposed breast with my hand and pinched her nipple. She gasped in pleasure and her grip tightened on my cock. I moved my hand over to caress her other breast, and as she looked down at me I grasped the peach-colored lace and pulled down, hard.

"Yes!" moaned Sarah as she felt the thin material pulling against her flesh. I wrestled with it for just a second before I heard the nightie ripping loudly. I tore a jagged slash down the middle, exposing both of Sarah's

lovely tits. Then, with both my hands, I took hold of the nightie and ripped it open, revealing her completely. Sarah moaned and rubbed my cock harder as I tore the ruined garment off her and tossed it on the bed beside us. I lifted my head and took one of Sarah's nipples into my mouth, sucking hard and then biting as I heard her panting with pleasure.

Sarah clutched my cock as she rocked up and down on top of me. I worked her other nipple with my thumb and forefinger, pinching it roughly as she inched down my body until she had the head of my cock positioned just under her pussy. Guiding my shaft with her hand, she pressed it against the thin crotch of her panties; I could feel that her panties were more than merely soaked, they were all but dripping. Sarah squirmed on top of me, moving up and down, teasing her entrance with the head of my cock through the thin silk panties, driving me mad with desire. I knew that it would be a small matter to pull the crotch of Sarah's panties aside and drive up into her pussy, but I was enjoying being tormented like this, and I could see from the pleasure in Sarah's eyes that it was exciting her for us to tease each other in this way. I arched my back and thrust my hips up, stroking my cock against Sarah's wet crotch as I suckled her breasts. Then, desiring a quick change to the game we were playing, I drove up against her with all my might, throwing her off balance.

Sarah's surprise was evident on her face for the split second I watched her. Then I moved quickly, leveraging Sarah's body until she tottered and fell off me, landing facedown amid the tangled, musky sheets, her face pressed against the nightie I had just torn off her. I came up behind her, leaning on her body, pressing her into the bed as I got on top of her, straddling her. Sarah moaned softly in surprise and excitement, and as I guided my cock between her asscheeks, I could feel from the way she pressed back against me that she was more than excited by this new turn of events.

Sarah's panties were little more than a G-string, really. Only a thin silk band ran between her cheeks. I could feel the silky softness of her bare asscheeks against my cock, and I desperately wanted to take her that way. I knew that if I did take her in her back door, she would let me, for Sarah was as receptive there as in her hungry pussy. But the thought that it might surprise her—even shock her—that I would do so, excited me. Even so, I was overwhelmed with lust for the Mistress's pussy, ever since I had seen Eduardo fuck her two nights ago on her hands and knees. Now I wanted to feel her sweet, wet cunt opening around my shaft. Perhaps later I would hold her down and savor her ass. I wedged Sarah's legs open with my own and reached down to take hold of her flimsy panties. Sarah gasped in surprise as I yanked up, pulling them firmly against her cunt so she could feel the pressure as I tore her panties off of her. Then another yank—and I felt the material rending, heard the sound of the silk ripping as I tore the crotch. Sarah lifted her ass invitingly as I tossed the ruined panties onto the floor. Then, leaning forward heavily, I guided my prick up to the entrance to her pussy.

Normally, I would have teased the Mistress for long minutes before taking her. But this time, I was so desperate to fuck her, I pressed my cockhead right up between her lips and felt her hungry entrance, wet and ready for me. I drove forward and heard Sarah groaning as I penetrated her, felt her body stiffening as she took my rod. Her cunt was so wet that it accepted me without a hint of resistance; and as Sarah lifted herself onto her hands and knees to give me better access, I sighed at how delicious it felt. I started fucking her from behind as Sarah humped back against me, moaning her arousal. I knew that she was already very close to coming—she had already been incredibly turned on when I'd thrown her facedown on the bed. Knowing that she was very close, I wasted no time, but fucked her as hard as I could, driving my cock deep into her, holding her waist with my hands and pumping back and forth, thrusting faster and harder as I mounted toward my own orgasm.

I heard Sarah groaning, "Yes…yes…oh, yes…" then heard her wailing as she climaxed. I felt her cunt tightening and then spasming around my cock as I plunged rhythmically into her, filling her cunt with each lunge. She humped against me faster as she took my cock into her spasming cunt, and I felt myself closing in on an incredible orgasm.

But Sarah was even quicker than I was. She came again as I fucked her on her knees, and I felt her writhing underneath me in ecstasy just before my own cock spasmed and I felt enormous pleasure exploding through me. Streams of semen shot into Sarah's cunt as I lay on top of her and fucked her rapidly. When I finally let out a great sigh of release and relaxed on top of Sarah's nude body, she wriggled her pretty little ass against me flirtatiously. She laughed as I kissed the back of her neck; and something about the tone of her laughter told me that, as always, I had been used sexually by her. While it may have looked as if I just threw her down on the bed and fucked her from behind— roughly, viciously, without mercy—in fact, that is exactly what Sarah had planned for me to do.

"Wonderful!" she sighed. "Carlton, sometimes I think you can read my mind."

That moment of understanding Sarah's need for total dominance, even as she appeared to submit, somehow excited me more than if she had merely given herself to me. I was quite surprised at myself. In my lovers, even apart from my slaves and submissives, I like a very submissive streak, a desire to be dominated and controlled sexually, to give control over to the other partner even if that does not include the usual trappings of "submission." Sarah had always been different—sometimes she performed acts which in another woman might have appeared submissive, but always it became clear to me by the end of the coupling that Sarah did these things for her pleasu`re alone. It was clear that even a blowjob was an act of domination when Sarah was giving it. Perhaps it was something about the way she seemed to take mercilessly from her lovers, in much the same way as she did from her submissives.

Perhaps I had thought for a moment that I was truly dominating the Mistress. Of course, I realized as I lay atop her what a ridiculous assumption that had been. Sarah was a very powerful woman, tall and strong. How had I thrown her so easily off balance and wrestled her to the bed if she hadn't wanted me to do that all along?

I felt more than a little self-induced embarrassment as I realized that Sarah had engineered this fuck. Even as I did, I felt my cock filling with blood, my desire swelling as Sarah wriggled her ass against me.

"Oh, Master!" she said mockingly. "Not again, Master...."

This battle of wills brought a sudden hard-on like none I had ever had. My cock throbbed hard between Sarah's cheeks, still glistening with the copious juices of her pussy. As she rubbed back against me, it became clear what she wanted—and what she was going to get.

I lunged forward and pushed my cock more firmly between Sarah's cheeks, growling into her ear.

"Reach back," I ordered her. "Spread your cheeks for me."

"No!" she whimpered, her voice still carrying that tone of mockery. "I'm so tight back there!"

Exactly the same words Tina had used when I took her in that way. God, had Sarah been watching us the whole time? Clearly, she was enjoying tormenting me by manipulating me into fucking her exactly the way she wanted. But at that moment, I was so overcome with lust that I just didn't care.

"Do it!" I snarled. "Reach back and spread them!"

Whimpering, Sarah reached back and parted her cheeks with her slender fingers, opening herself to me gently. I rubbed my cock against her asshole, feeling that it was indeed tight.

"Put it inside you!" I growled. "Guide it in with your hand."

Sarah's whimpers grew louder, her mock fear serving to further humiliate me. But she took my cock in her hand obediently and guided the head to her rear entrance, pushing back against me. She groaned as she worked my cockhead back and forth, slowly opening up her ass for me.

Then she pushed back harder, making me feel just how tight she really was. The pressure increased. Then, with a groan, Sarah took my cockhead into her ass, the head slipping into the tight orifice as Sarah whimpered and wriggled her bum back and forth. I was inside her, and now, as she pressed up against me rhythmically, my shaft sank deeper into her. I could feel that she was as tight as I remembered from years ago. But from the way she took the first few inches of my cock so easily, it was quite evident that Sarah had lubricated herself anally before she ever came in here.

She really *had* planned everything. But at that moment, I was beyond caring.

Sarah pushed up against me, taking the first few inches and gradually thrusting me deeper. But I had had enough of this game. I wanted to fuck Sarah hard in the ass—whether or not she wanted it. I lunged forward and held her down, forcing her body to a fully prone position. I lifted myself on one knee to give myself the best angle for rapid thrusts into Sarah's ass, and drove into her all the way, bringing a startled groan from the Mistress's lips. She lay on the bed as I worked my cock around inside her, then drew back and began to pump, thrusting into her faster and faster as I felt her asshole opening up for me. Her initial groan of surprise gave way to louder and louder moans as I fucked her.

I wanted to get myself off as quickly as possible, to feel my cock shooting in Sarah's ass and to know that she hadn't come. But as I neared my climax, getting ready to spurt inside her, I realized that one of Sarah's hands had disappeared and was even now rubbing her clit fervently. I was about to grab her wrists and force her to stop when I heard Sarah's moans rise in volume and pitch and felt her naked body shuddering as she thrust up against me, taking my cock into her ass eagerly. The contractions of her ass and cunt seemed monumental as my cock thrust into that tight, gripping orifice of hers. I realized that it was a lost cause—the Mistress had already gotten herself off. I cursed her as I pumped her ass rapidly, feeling her climax finishing. My thrusts took on all the frustration and anger that Sarah's clever manipulation of me had caused. Sarah lay there with her cheeks spread, accepting my cock into her ass even with progressively harder and deeper thrusts—and as she squirmed underneath me, I heard her laughing.

"Yes, Carlton," she whimpered in a sex-kitten voice. "Yes, *Master*. Dominate me. Just like you did poor Tina. Punish me. Humiliate me. Use me. Fuck my ass. Dominate me. Or is it you that's being dominated—oh!"

I groaned loudly as I began to come inside the Mistress's ass. I pulled out and my warm streams shot all over her, covering her ass and thighs as she laughed. As I finished coming, Sarah's laughter dwindled, and I collapsed beside her, my eyes still roving over the inviting posture of her spread legs and her opened, freshly fucked ass. I marveled at how this clever bitch could stir desire inside me to the point of madness.

"No hard feelings?" She sighed. "I trust my ass

pleased you, Master?" Her sarcasm was so obvious it didn't require a response.

"Go to hell," I said as good-naturedly as I could. But Sarah knew that she had won this round—that by lunging onto her to "dominate" her, I had shown how easily I could be tempted and manipulated with the promise of sex. I have always been a pushover, but it was never quite as obvious as it was in that moment. Sarah rolled over, showing me her lovely breasts as she reached back to rub her hands over her come-slick asscheeks. She smiled at me.

"You took Tina," she said. "I had thought perhaps you would take much longer in deflowering her."

"I decided that time was better served in fucking her properly *after* she had been deflowered. She proved most willing, once the deed had been done. Where has the little slut gone now?"

"I've sent her off to be fucked by several of my male slaves. I so dearly loved the performance you put on with her yesterday. I thought we should build her stamina so she can do it more often. By the time you finished with her, she was asleep."

"So I assume you watched the whole thing?"

Sarah smiled, reaching out to caress the mirrored headboard. "Did you think I was a refugee from the 1970s? Swing parties, and that sort of thing? Surely you had to guess that this might be a two-way mirror."

I chuckled. "Always in control, Mistress."

"I try to be. She did prove herself to be as much a little slut as I thought she would. Did you find her satisfactory?"

"She'll do, once she's been trained," I said. "Once she's been fucked enough times, I'm sure she'll fall right into line."

Sarah moved closer to me. "And me—Master? Was I satisfactory?"

"You will make a great submissive, when I win the wager and put my collar on you," I said contemptuously.

"Ooooh, I'll look forward to that!" Once again her words held obvious sarcasm. "Will you humiliate and degrade me utterly?"

"I love it when you talk dirty, Mistress," was the only reply I could manage. A cold fear had started to grow in my balls and travel up into my throat. For the first time, it occurred to me that it was ever so slightly possible that I might lose this wager. It was obvious that Tina was going to make a wonderful submissive, was going to finally give up her rebellion and give herself wholly to her owner. That meant that I should have been confident, that I should have known that Sarah was going to be on her knees soon, serving me per our agreement. But I didn't—I didn't know that. Instead, I felt the cold terror that made me feel as vulnerable as I had ever felt. Sarah seemed so in control. Could it be possible that she was going to beat me at my own game? That *I* would be the one who found myself on my knees, naked and collared, offering service to the Mistress?

Sarah's hand curled around the shaft of my cock. As she looked into my eyes I felt my cock stirring, hardening.

"There are so many possibilities," she said enigmatically and leaned forward, parting her lips.

CHAPTER 12

Now that Tina had been fucked, there was no reason to preserve even the barest hint of her innocence. It had been a truly pleasing innocence, to be sure—Tina had worn her virginity very well. But all things must come to an end, and so her innocence had finally ended. Now, Tina was to be turned into the slut she so desperately wanted to be. The challenge was to see if she could be made still *more* of a slut than she had ever dreamed of being—even with her filthy mind working overtime. And Tina rose to the challenge beautifully.

I had taken not only her cunt but her ass, so all of her luscious young body was now open for depravity.

And I fully intended to see every part of that body used for corrupt purposes, to bring pleasure to every man in a ten-mile radius.

As the weeks rolled on, Tina was debauched so completely that she became almost a whole new person. Her personality slowly dissolved into the intense passions and lusts she felt as she gave of herself again and again.

My stay at Sarah's mansion grew more and more pleasant as I watched Tina's descent into depravity and total submission. The changes were visible in Tina's eyes daily, as she became—with every sexual performance, with every deviant act, with every thrust into her willing body—a complete and total chattel of her owners. I had rarely taken such pleasure in seeing the transformation of a beautiful young woman. And Tina's desire to be corrupted further seemed endless. Each time she was humiliated or degraded sexually at Sarah's hands or my own, she accepted her fate eagerly and begged for more. Her descent into her own private world of lust and depravity matched her desires completely. She was receiving what she had always craved.

And Sarah and I grew to be lovers, too, as we trained and transformed Tina.

Our mutual enjoyment at Tina's humiliation and manipulation brought Sarah and me as close as two humans can be. Our passion for each other became

THE CONTRACT

evident as we watched Tina's ordeals at the hands of Sarah's male and female slaves, as we witnessed her being fucked and tormented endlessly. We were comrades in arms in the war to subjugate Tina's will totally. In fact, Sarah and I took to sleeping together, and many times we would find ourselves making fervent love after witnessing or performing a particularly humiliating sexual experience on Tina. I grew to know Sarah's body quite well in those months, exploring every delicious corner of her. I even came to think of her as a lover. Truly, I must admit that I fell in love with Sarah. I no longer resisted her tendency to be in charge in bed, but it was incredibly erotic for both of us to feel the tension between us, our war of wills in its current state of not-quite truce.

It was obvious that Tina would extend the contract indefinitely when her time came. It was clear that Tina was being completely subjugated, that her only desire would soon be to serve the Mistress.

And of course, that made our sexual trysts even more intense. For it meant that soon Sarah would lose the wager and would be forced to lower herself to her knees and offer me her services. It was the most humiliating thing I could imagine for Sarah—the eternal dominant brought to her knees as a slave to service me. Even for one night. And I was certain that that one night would be a night of unspeakable cruelty. I would take great pleasure at making the Mistress suffer at my hands, at watching Sarah's will crumble. I imagined that once Sarah had tasted submission, she would no longer be the dominant she thought she was and would find herself longing to submit to me full time. Oh, and I would so dearly love to extend Sarah's contract forever....

But that was for the future. For now, we were lovers with a passion for each other that was matched only by our desire to see Tina subjugated.

The specifics of Tina's submission are as delicious for me to recount as they were for me to witness and orchestrate.

Tina was rarely allowed even a few hours' rest, for it was important that she be overloaded with stimulus, to lose whatever resistance to total submission she might once have possessed. Both Sarah and I took great pleasure in having Tina fucked constantly, in a wide variety of ways. Since Tina had shown such a proclivity for male flesh, we focused on having her used by Sarah's male slaves, though of course she was also utilized by the female slaves. Sarah had more than enough male slaves to keep Tina constantly occupied; the slaves were young and virile and extremely well endowed, with libidos that approached my own. These libidos were used to keep Tina quite occupied and keep her days filled with a wide variety of penetrative activities.

Tina's sleep periods were reduced to give her more time on her knees and her belly and her back.

Strangely, even her ensuing exhaustion from lack of sleep couldn't decrease Tina's desire to be fucked—quite the contrary, it increased it vastly. Soon she was sleeping only a few hours a night. Most of the rest of the time, she was pleasuring her sister or brother slaves in large numbers. Sometimes Tina would sleep her few hours in Sarah's and my bed—for Sarah and I had taken to sleeping together constantly. This gave us a particularly intimate space in which to enjoy Tina and to enjoy the tender act of sharing her.

Tina loved this and gave herself eagerly to her Master and Mistress, both before sleeping and upon awakening. This was something we took great delight in. We would sleep in shifts so that Tina could be fucked all night long by us, used to the point of exhaustion. I would doze off to the silhouetted sight of Tina shuddering and squirming under the merciless thrusts of Sarah's strap-on. I would awaken hours later in the middle of the night, my hard-on throbbing, to find Tina whimpering with pleasure as Sarah took her from behind or commanded her to offer her oral services.

As Sarah dozed off, I would take over, often mounting Tina in the same position Sarah had just left her, so that her ordeal would be seamless. I would fuck her until my lusts were wholly depleted, and then I would summon one of the other slaves and have Tina led off, already well-fucked, to be entertained by a group of slaves in the parlor. Even when my lusts had been quite sated by using Tina, I never failed to feel an overwhelming desire and love for Sarah, which found me climbing atop her and waking her with passionate kisses. We would then fuck crazily, my cock still moist with Tina's juices as it slid into Sarah's pussy. I was quite sure that I had fallen madly in love with the Mistress, and that she was equally in love with me. That would make it so much sweeter when she was forced to concede her defeat and lower herself to the status of my slave. Oh, how I would delight in penetrating Sarah with the full knowledge that I owned her—even if only for a single night....

When Sarah and I didn't feel like receiving Tina into our bed, we would have her fucked by a dozen male slaves through the night, her nubile form penetrated and utilized in every way possible. She would be returned to us first thing in the morning well-fucked and -used, her hair matted with the fluids of her partners, her face and breasts slick with their come, her cunt and ass filled with it. Sarah and I took great delight at the sight of her beautiful face and sensual lips glistening with the slaves' semen, her body corrupted and defiled in every delightful way possible. Her exhaustion would be evident in the bleary look in her eyes and the slump of her shoulders—she would have had quite a busy night.

But Tina was never sated, not even after taking on

twelve slaves for the whole night. When Sarah and I welcomed her into our bed, taking her filthy body in our arms and fucking her insistently, Tina's passion always rose quickly. Soon she was eager for more sex, begging us to fuck her harder, deeper, faster, again, again, again. I would slide on top of her, my body becoming slick with the seed of the many slaves who had ejaculated on her, caressing Tina's come-greased breasts and smearing the juices all over both of us. Once I had fucked Tina several times, she would be made to fetch Sarah's strap-on and buckle it onto the Mistress's body. Sarah would then fuck Tina as roughly as I had, bringing the slave great pleasure. Tina grew more and more eager as her exhaustion increased. She would service us with her young body until both Sarah and I were quite satisfied; and then, to our surprise, without exception, the little slut would beg us for more. Tina would keep going until she literally passed out from exhaustion.

Tina was almost supernatural in her desire to be fucked and used. She was truly a treasure in this regard. Most slaves, upon being used so consistently in such extreme fashions, every day and every night, would lose interest after a short while. Sex would become boring or commonplace to them. But not Tina. She became hornier and hornier as sex became a constant stimulus for her. Each time she was penetrated or allowed access to hard cock or wet pussy, the wonder began anew for her. She climaxed more times than she or I could count when she was fucked. Her ripe body was always ready for sex, and her stamina grew until she was only getting four hours of sleep on a typical night. All the physical activity built Tina's muscle tone beautifully, until her beautiful body was hard and disciplined, lithe and toned so that she could assume the most demanding positions for sex, could continue fucking fervently for many hours. Soon I was all but convinced that Tina had made a pact with the devil, that she was a supernatural beast, one who existed only to give and receive sexual pleasure. But in reality, Tina was all too human, and that's what made her tight pussy and sweet little ass so delightful.

When Tina's nipples were pierced, I knew that her fate had been sealed. It was a lovely spectacle which Sarah and I orchestrated.

First Tina was brought naked into the parlor, where the piercing would be performed. Then she was bound hand and foot, her wrists and ankles lashed together. She was placed on her knees; the tight bonds around her ankles meant that she had to lean back slightly in order to keep her balance. She also had to keep her legs well apart in order not to fall, which meant that Tina's lovely pierced pussy was quite revealed and defenseless. It was evident from early on that Tina knew she was to be pierced today, and her level of arousal was high. Her

THE CONTRACT

shaved pubis already glistened with the moisture of her sexual excitement.

At that time, Sarah's household had about two dozen male slaves and approximately three times that many female slaves. All offer absolute obedience to the Mistress, and all have been properly trained. It is an admirable collection of submissives, for the Mistress is very choosy about who she allows to go to their knees before her.

Sarah had summoned all two dozen of her male slaves. They were lined up in two rows along the wall. They made a stirring display of young male flesh, all of them naked, muscled, and extremely well-hung. Sarah chooses only the most virile and endowed young men to become her male submissives.

Many of them were already becoming erect as they looked at the young woman kneeling in the middle of the room. They had been trained to become erect when sexual service was demanded of them, and all twenty-four male slaves had been instructed to use Tina before the piercing was performed.

But today, the manner of Tina's usefulness was determined by the ritual that was about to be performed on her breasts. And so, when I gave the signal, the first male slave came forward.

His cock was not yet entirely hard, but it was well on its way. He slipped it between Tina's lips, and she whimpered softly as she began to service him. With her wrists bound, she had to rely on her exceptional oral skills—which she did, bringing the slave to full erection with her mouth. His cock grew to be nearly ten inches long. But once the slave was fully hard, he did not use Tina's mouth, much as she might have liked him to. Instead, he took her large, firm breasts in his hands and lay his spit-slick rod between Tina's tits.

Tina moaned as the slave began to tit-fuck her. He teased her nipples into hardness with his thumbs as his hips worked his cock back and forth between her breasts. He took a long time savoring Tina's breasts, enjoying the feel of her full, firm flesh caressing his rod. Then, he picked up speed. Soon he cried out, his cock spasming and shooting out great streams of semen over Tina's breasts and face. The slick fluid covered her breasts and splashed across her face, dribbling down onto her belly. From Tina's moans and the look on her face, it was evident that she was quite happy on her knees, being used like this. The slave finished with her and then stepped aside for the next man in line to take his place.

Thus the ritual continued, with each male slave using Tina's breasts and anointing them with his seed. But these men were as talented as Sarah demanded, so one orgasm wasn't all that could be squeezed out of their large cocks. And so once the end of the line had been reached, they started all over again.

Sarah and I watched with great interest. Sarah was

serviced while she watched Tina experiencing her degradation. But I preferred to save my climax to join the others. Sarah received almost unremitting oral attention from Shade, who knelt between the Mistress's open legs. Sarah had hiked up her skirt, revealing her luscious thighs with the very attractive Shade buried between them, seeking fervently to satisfy her Mistress.

To my great pleasure, Tina made her way through the line of male slaves three times, receiving more seed sprayed across her breasts than one would have thought possible. Never for a second did Tina show anything but desperate hunger to take the next hard shaft between her breasts. She did not cease her moans of pleasure as she was used by cock after cock after cock. But despite her obvious enthusiasm for being used like this, by the time she took on the last slave for the third time and received the thick spray of his semen across her breasts, Tina was clearly exhausted.

Now it was finally my turn. I got out of my chair and laid my hard cock between Tina's breasts, amid the thick fluid smeared over there. Tina was all but covered in semen now, her hair matted and her belly and breasts thick with it, great gobs of it across her face and lips. It ran down her thighs and pooled on the floor underneath her. But through the humiliation and exhaustion on her face, I saw exactly what I wanted: absolute submission.

I forced Tina's breasts together and began to slide my

cock in and out, lubricated as that pretty flesh was by so many ejaculations. I took my time enjoying Tina's breasts, savoring the feel of her flesh encompassing my cock. And when I finally cried out and came on Tina's luscious tits, she whispered, "Thank you, Master. Thank you." Sarah moaned loudly in orgasm at almost exactly this moment. Now that I had climaxed, I knew that Tina was ready.

She was untied and laid out on a platform which had been brought into the parlor. She was bound spread-eagled, helpless and exposed. Then Whisper and Adriana cleansed her breasts with antiseptic, cleaning off the seed of the many slaves. When she had been sterilized properly, Adriana removed the cover from a small table near the platform.

Tina moaned when she saw the bright silver implements that would pierce her flesh. She squirmed and whimpered a little when her nipples were clamped painfully. Then the needle was readied by Adriana, who was to perform the piercing.

I bent low over Tina and kissed her, tasting the seed of the slaves which still graced her lips and chin. "You will now offer me your absolute submission," I whispered.

"I do, Master," she answered in a hoarse breath. "You own me. Completely."

I nodded to Adriana. Tina let out a great shuddering moan of pain as her nipple was pierced with the thick needle.

Tina wept softly as the ring was placed into her nipple. Then I bent and kissed her for a long time, savoring the taste of submission on her lips before the needle was forced through her other nipple. When she had both her rings in place through the pink caps of her glorious breasts, Tina looked up with her eyes glazed with exhaustion.

"Th-Thank you, Master," she gasped.

"You're welcome," I said. Then, to Adriana: "Have her brought up to the master bedroom. I want to use her while the pain in her nipples is still fresh."

I walked over to Sarah, who had finished with Shade. "Are you coming upstairs, Mistress?"

Sarah answered with the faintest inclination of her head. Together, we walked toward the staircase.

CHAPTER 13

Sarah and I took a brief detour to a small extra guest room to give the slaves time to lay Tina out on the bed. Besides, both of us were so turned on from watching Tina's tortures that we could hardly wait for her to be properly prepared for us. I thrust my body against Sarah and pulled her into my arms, kissing her desperately. She rubbed her body against mine, reaching down to feel my hard cock through my pants. I was throbbing with need. I wanted to save my desire for Tina; but to my surprise, Sarah dropped to her knees and got my pants open almost before I knew what was happening.

I moaned as Sarah swallowed my cock, thrusting it

down her throat and gulping my hard flesh. She pulled up her blouse—she wore nothing underneath—and hungrily rubbed my cock between her magnificent breasts, imprisoning me in her smooth flesh.

"God, I loved seeing you use her like that!" Sarah said. "I want you to use *me* like that...."

"Today's the day," I said hoarsely. "Tina's last night of servitude. She will extend the contract, Mistress, and you will have lost the wager."

Sarah looked up at me, her breasts pressed around my hard shaft, her face plainly showing the excitement she felt at the prospect of becoming my slave. Oh, this was going to be lovely when I subjugated the fabled Mistress!

"Fuck me!" she panted. "Fuck me before we go in there." Sarah stood and turned around, bending over the side of the bed and hiking her skirt up. Her gorgeous ass was laid out for me, her thighs spread and her pink slit, glistening and ready, begging for my shaft. I came up behind her, my cock still slick with her spittle and sweat. Sarah moaned as I fitted the head between her cuntlips and drove into her, penetrating her mercilessly. Sarah groaned and thrashed as I fucked her from behind, and I held her tight as I felt her coming once, then twice, then a third time as I entered her again and again. Finally I groaned and let my load shoot inside her, fucking her as she whimpered, begging me for my come. When I had finished, I slipped my cock out of her and tucked it away, amazed at the qualities of submission I had found in the Mistress. She would make a truly wonderful slave when I saw her drop to her knees to worship me.

Or was it possible that she had a trick up her sleeve? Clearly, Tina would extend the contract indefinitely... but would Sarah admit defeat and become my servant for a night?

I shuddered as I thought of the alternative.

A very exhausted Tina was laid out on the bed with her nipples red and sore from their recent piercing, making the sight of her naked body that much more beautiful to both Sarah and me. We undressed quickly, then joined Tina on the bed, kissing her softly and caressing her everywhere except her nipples. The occasional brush of a hand against her new nipple-rings sent a jolt of pain through the unfortunate slave— enough to keep her wholly present, and very awake. Sarah and I kissed her tenderly and stroked the folds of her pierced pussy, which was quite wet from her ordeal. Soon Tina was moaning in pleasure as I slid two fingers inside her and teased her pierced clit with my thumb. Sarah mounted Tina's face, careful not to lean back against her breasts, and Tina took eagerly to servicing her Mistress orally. It excited me to no end to know that Sarah was filled to the brim with my semen, that even now my fluids were leaking from the Mistress's pussy into Tina's mouth.

Meanwhile, my hard cock demanded relief. I positioned Tina's body so that her knees hung over my shoulders, pulling her ass up to a level with my crotch and placing her body at the perfect angle for me to fuck her. I penetrated Tina quickly, driving into her as Sarah moaned with her first orgasm. I took my time fucking the slave, savoring the feel of her cunt all wet from her torments and her body taut and willing underneath me. I slid my hands around the undersides of her breasts, being careful not to disturb the peace of her nipples. But I wanted to hold those beautiful tits, to know that I owned them the way I owned the rest of her.

When Sarah had satisfied herself on Tina's mouth, I removed my cock from the slave and rolled her onto her side, turning her head so that I could kiss her mouth, which was slick and filled with my come and Sarah's juices. Sarah lowered herself between Tina's legs so she could feel my cock as it penetrated Tina. When I was finally ready to come, she eased me out of Tina's body so that I could spurt my seed across Tina's thighs and her hand. Sarah licked my juices from Tina's body eagerly, then cuddled up with us as we all kissed tenderly. There was a feeling of overwhelming warmth between the three of us, knowing that the contract would be indefinitely extended—and Tina would belong to us for all eternity.

"You know it's time," I said to Tina softly as I kissed her.

"Yes," she said in response. "I know it's my last day of servitude."

"That is why you were pierced. So you could know that you belonged to us on your last day. You must make a decision. Extend the contract indefinitely, or leave tonight. You must know that both of us eagerly await your decision."

A look of pain crossed Tina's face.

"I know, Master."

"Then what is your choice?" Sarah asked softly, rubbing her thigh between Tina's.

Tears formed in Tina's eyes and began to stream down her cheeks, leaving streaks in the dried semen there. She wept bitterly as I began to kiss her. Finally, I sensed she was ready to speak, to offer us her undying devotion and eternal servitude.

There was no doubt in my mind. My victory would be complete.

"I do not wish to stay, Mistress, Master. I want my freedom."

A shock ran down my spine.

"What?"

"You heard me," Tina said.

Sarah smiled up at me. "Tina, whatever makes you want freedom? I sense a reluctance in you. Surely you'll agree to remain if we…persuade you a little…." Sarah seemed remarkably calm.

"No, Mistress," Tina wept. "I wish to leave tonight."

"There must be some mistake," I said. "You couldn't possibly wish to leave this house of pleasure. Could you?"

"I'm afraid so," the slave sobbed.

"No. That's impossible! I order you to submit—"

"Oh, Carlton!" Sarah sighed. "Don't be ridiculous. You can't order a slave to sign a contract. Poor Tina must be cast out into the world…to make her fortune."

I all but leaped off the bed. "This is a trick! It's not possible!"

Sarah smiled at me. She sat up on the bed, her legs spread, revealing her inviting slit. Cold sweat ran down my back.

"Get on your knees, Carlton. You belong to me."

"No! I won't stand for it! I've been tricked!"

"I don't think so," she said coolly. "You know as well as I do that the contract has been fulfilled. I won. Now get on your knees. Your ass is mine for the next three months. And I intend to use it handily."

"No!" I shouted and turned to go to my chambers. This had to be some kind of trick. Didn't it?

"Carlton!" Sarah called after me. I looked back and saw her standing, looking radiantly beautiful in her rage.

"If you leave, you will be an outcast. No one will socialize with a man who has broken a contract!"

I halted. I knew she was right. My choices were equally terrifying. Fear filled my body as I realized that I was backed into a corner.

Tina wept openly on the bed.

"Now, Carlton." Sarah's voice was imperious and commanding. She stood tall, her posture that of a goddess.

"Yes?" I said softly.
"Get on your knees. *On your knees!*"
Reluctantly, I found myself moving to obey her.

CHAPTER 14

And so did I, Carlton Payne, who had for as long as memory serves been called a dominant, come to be on my knees before the glory of the Mistress Sarah. I came to be her slave and to worship her. If I were a dispassionate observer, I might think that my submission was achieved well before that fateful night when Tina made her choice. Sarah was in control all along, and I was destined to kneel before her.

She is a most cruel Mistress. And yet, her cruelty is something to which one can become accustomed. And even begin to like it.

It is possible that the dominant and the submissive are

two sides of the same coin, that in my years desiring and loving the submission of women, I planted the seeds for my own eventual submission. Certainly, my excitement at receiving the punishments and sexual humiliations that my Mistress inflicts upon me bring me as much joy now—now that I have been properly conditioned—as the punishments and humiliations I inflicted on so many willing and eager female submissives over the years. In fact, I have found a curious sort of freedom on my knees.

The fact that Sarah must have set me up has become less important than the fact that my submission to her was inevitable. It seems clear to me that Tina, owing her first obligation to her Mistress and only a secondary obligation to me, obeyed an order from Tina to refuse the Contract and demand her freedom. This could be considered cheating—in fact, I am quite sure it is. But those sorts of things don't concern me much anymore.

What made it clear that I had been had was the sight of Mistress Tina, wearing high boots like Sarah's and carrying a stiff riding crop, who appeared before me for a long session of punishment. "She's elected to become a dominant," Sarah told me. "And returned to the house asking me to train her. So you see, you still have access to this lovely body of hers—admittedly, in a very different way."

Tina was even more glorious as a Mistress than she had been as a submissive. Her legendary sex drive had, if anything, grown stronger when she picked up the riding crop. She could wear me out many times over before she showed the barest hint of weariness. I learned to compensate by working very hard to please her. At Tina's hands, I found my capabilities as a sexual tool to be far greater than I had originally thought.

Of course, Sarah takes great pleasure in using me as well. She and Tina often share me, in fact, for they have become lovers and often sleep in the same bed, keeping me bound at the foot of the bed for midnight services in case either of them should happen to wake up horny. I am often called upon by Tina—often many times over in one night. She shows favor to me by demanding my services.

This plotting against me, and the fact that I was tricked, should anger me. But it doesn't. After three months in Sarah's shackles, receiving the cruel punishments that so delighted her, I elected to extend my Contract. I never would have dreamed it possible, but I became Sarah's eternal slave.

And so the years have rolled on with my submission growing greater with each act the Mistresses demand of me. I have taken my place at Sarah's knees, and I have finally found my situation—the Contract that *I* crave. Not Sarah's submission—far from it. But her ownership of me, and the knowledge that she will always be there, towering over me, offering me the chance to service her, should she desire it.

Servicing her is a source of eternal delight for me. Perhaps someday I will grow dominant once more, will tire of my life of submission. Perhaps then I will seek to find life on my feet again rather than on my knees. But I certainly hope it isn't anytime soon.

MASQUERADE

AMERICA'S FASTEST GROWING EROTIC MAGAZINE

SPECIAL OFFER
RECEIVE THE NEXT TWO ISSUES FOR ONLY $5.00—A 50% SAVINGS!

A bimonthly magazine packed with the very best the world of erotica has to offer. Each issue of *Masquerade* contains today's most provocative, cutting-edge fiction, sizzling pictorials from the masters of modern fetish photography, scintillating and illuminating exposés of the worldwide sex-biz written by longtime industry insiders, and probing reviews of the many books and videos that cater specifically to your lifestyle.

Masquerade presents radical sex uncensored—from homegrown American kink to the fantastical fashions of Europe. Never before have the many permutations of the erotic imagination been represented in one publication.

THE ONLY MAGAZINE THAT CATERS TO YOUR LIFESTYLE

Masquerade/Direct • 801 Second Avenue • New York, NY 10017 • FAX: 212.986.7355
E-Mail: MasqBks @aol.com • MC/VISA orders can be placed by calling our toll-free number: 800.375.2356

☐ 2 ISSUES ~~$10~~ *SPECIAL* $5!

☐ 6 ISSUES (1 YEAR) FOR ~~$30~~ *SPECIAL* $15!

☐ 12 ISSUES (2 YEARS) FOR ~~$60~~ *SPECIAL* $25!

NAME _____

ADDRESS _____

CITY _____ STATE _____ ZIP _____

E-MAIL _____

PAYMENT: ☐ CHECK ☐ MONEY ORDER ☐ VISA ☐ MC

CARD # _____ EXP. DATE _____

No C.O.D. orders. Please make all checks payable to Masquerade/Direct. Payable in U.S. currency only.

MASQUERADE BOOKS

MASQUERADE

S. CRABB
CHATS ON OLD PEWTER
$6.95/611-1
A compendium of tales dedicated to dominant women. From domineering check-out girls to merciless flirts on the prowl, these women know what men like—and are highly skilled at reducing any man to putty in their hands.

PAT CALIFIA
SENSUOUS MAGIC
$7.95/610-3
"*Sensuous Magic* is clear, succinct and engaging.... Califia is the Dr. Ruth of the alternative sexuality set....".
—*Lambda Book Report*

Erotic pioneer Pat Califia provides this unpretentious peek behind the mask of dominant/submissive sexuality. With her trademark wit and insight, Califia demystifies "the scene" for the novice, explaining the terms and techniques behind many misunderstood sexual practices.

ANAÏS NIN AND FRIENDS
WHITE STAINS
$6.95/609-X
A lost classic of 1940s erotica returns! Written by Anaïs Nin, Virginia Admiral, Caresse Crosby, and others for a dollar per page, this breathtakingly sensual volume was printed privately and soon became an underground legend. After more than fifty years, this priceless collection of explicit but sophisticated musings is back in print—and available to the contemporary connoisseur of erotica.

DENISE HALL
JUDGMENT
$6.95/590-5
Judgment—a forbidding edifice where unfortunate young women find themselves degraded and abandoned to the wiles of their cruel masters. Callie MacGuire descends into the depths of this prison, discovering a capacity for sensual torment she never dreamed existed.

CLAIRE WILLOWS
PRESENTED IN LEATHER
$6.95/576-X
The story of poor Flora Price and the stunning punishments she suffered at the hands of her cruel captors. At the age of nineteen, Flora is whisked to the south of France, where she is imprisoned in Villa Close, an institution devoted to the ways of the lash—not to mention the paddle, the strap, the rod...

ALISON TYLER & DANTE DAVIDSON
BONDAGE ON A BUDGET
$6.95/570-0
Filled with delicious scenarios requiring no more than simple household items and a little imagination, this guide to DIY S&M will explode the myth that adventurous sex requires a dungeonful of expensive custom-made paraphernalia.

JEAN SADDLER
THE FASCINATING TYRANT
$6.95/569-7
A reprint of a classic tale from the 1930s of erotic dictatorship. Jean Saddler's most famous novel, *The Fascinating Tyrant* is a riveting glimpse of sexual extravagance in which a young man discovers his penchant for flagellation and sadomasochism.

ROBERT SEWALL
THE DEVIL'S ADVOCATE
$6.95/553-0
Clara Reeves appeals to Conrad Garnett, a New York district attorney, for help in tracking down her missing sister, Rita. Clara soon finds herself being "persuaded" to accompany Conrad on his descent into a modern-day hell, where unspeakable pleasures await....

LUCY TAYLOR
UNNATURAL ACTS
$7.95/552-2
"A topnotch collection"   —*Science Fiction Chronicle*

Unnatural Acts plunges deep into the dark side of the psyche and brings to life a disturbing vision of erotic horror. Unrelenting angels and hungry gods play with souls and bodies in Taylor's murky cosmos: where heaven and hell are merely differences of perspective.

OLIVIA M. RAVENSWORTH
THE DESIRES OF REBECCA
$6.50/532-8
Rebecca follows her passions from the simple love of the girl next door to the lechery of London's most notorious brothel, hoping for the ultimate thrill. She casts her lot with a crew of sapphic buccaneers, each of whom is more than capable of matching Rebecca's lust.

THE MISTRESS OF
CASTLE ROHMENSTADT
$5.95/372-4
Lovely Katherine inherits a secluded European castle from a mysterious relative. Upon arrival she discovers, much to her delight, that the castle is a haven of sexual perversion. Before long, Katherine is truly Mistress of the house!

MASQUERADE BOOKS

GERALD GREY
LONDON GIRLS
$6.50/531-X

In 1875, Samuel Brown arrives in London, determined to take the glorious city by storm. Samuel quickly distinguishes himself as one of the city's most notorious rakehells. Young Mr. Brown knows well the many ways of making a lady weak at the knees—and uses them not only to his delight, but to his enormous profit!

ERICA BRONTE
LUST, INC.
$6.50/467-4

Explore the extremes of passion that lurk beneath even the most businesslike exteriors. Join in the sexy escapades of a group of professionals whose idea of office decorum is like nothing you've ever encountered!

ATAULLAH MARDAAN
KAMA HOURI/DEVA DASI
$7.95/512-3

"Mardaan excels in crowding her pages with the sights and smells of India, and her erotic descriptions are convincingly realistic."
—Michael Perkins,
The Secret Record: Modern Erotic Literature

Kama Houri details the life of a sheltered Western woman who finds herself living within the confines of a harem. *Deva Dasi* is a tale dedicated to the sacred women of India who devoted their lives to the fulfillment of the senses.

VISCOUNT LADYWOOD
GYNECOCRACY
$9.95/511-5

Julian is sent to a private school, and discovers that his program of study has been devised by stern Mademoiselle de Chambonnard. In no time, Julian is learning the many ways of pleasure and pain—under the firm hand of this beautifully demanding headmistress.

N. T. MORLEY
THE CONTRACT
$6.95/575-1

Meet Carlton and Sarah, two true connoisseurs of discipline. Sarah is experiencing some difficulty in training her current submissive. Carlton proposes an unusual wager: if Carlton is unsuccessful in bringing Tina to a full appreciation of Sarah's domination, Carlton himself will become Sarah's devoted slave....

THE LIMOUSINE
$6.95/555-7

Brenda was enthralled with her roommate Kristi's illicit sex life: a never ending parade of men who satisfied Kristi's desire to be dominated. Brenda decides to embark on a trip into submission, beginning in the long, white limousine where Kristi first met the Master.

THE CASTLE
$6.95/530-1

Tess Roberts is held captive by a crew of disciplinarians intent on making all her dreams come true—even those she'd never admitted to herself. While anyone can arrange for a stay at the Castle, Tess proves herself one of the most gifted applicants yet....

THE PARLOR
$6.50/496-8

The mysterious John and Sarah ask Kathryn to be their slave—an idea that turns her on so much that she can't refuse! Little by little, Kathryn not only learns to serve, but comes to know the inner secrets of her keepers.

J. A. GUERRA, ED.
COME QUICKLY:
For Couples on the Go
$6.50/461-5

The increasing pace of daily life is no reason to forgo a little carnal pleasure whenever the mood strikes. Here are over sixty of the hottest fantasies around—all designed especially for modern couples on a hectic schedule.

VANESSA DURIÈS
THE TIES THAT BIND
$6.50/510-7

This true story will keep you gasping with its vivid depictions of sensual abandon. At the hand of Masters Georges, Patrick, Pierre and others, this submissive seductress experiences pleasures she never knew existed.... One of modern erotica's best-selling accounts of real-life dominance and submission.

M. S. VALENTINE
THE GOVERNESS
$6.95/562-X

Lovely Miss Hunnicut eagerly embarks upon a career as a governess, hoping to escape the memories of her broken engagement. Little does she know that Crawleigh Manor is far from the upstanding household it appears. Mr. Crawleigh, in particular, devotes himself to Miss Hunnicut's thorough defiling.

BUY ANY 4 BOOKS & CHOOSE 1 ADDITIONAL BOOK, OF EQUAL OR LESSER VALUE, AS YOUR FREE GIFT

MASQUERADE BOOKS

ELYSIAN DAYS AND NIGHTS
$6.95/536-0
From around the world, neglected young wives arrive at the Elysium Spa intent on receiving a little heavy-duty pampering. Luckily for them, the spa's proprietor is a true devotee of the female form—and has dedicated himself to the pure pleasure of every woman who steps foot across their threshold....

THE CAPTIVITY OF CELIA
$6.50/453-4
Celia's lover, Colin, is considered the prime suspect in a murder, forcing him to seek refuge with his cousin, Sir Jason Hardwicke. In exchange for Colin's safety, Jason demands Celia's unquestioning submission....

AMANDA WARE
BINDING CONTRACT
$6.50/491-7
Louise was responsible for bringing many clients into Claremont's salon—so he was more than willing to have her miss a little work in order to pleasure one of his most important customers. But Eleanor Cavendish had her mind set on something more rigorous than a simple wash and set—dooming Louise to a life of sexual slavery! Soon, Louise is a slave to not only Eleanor, but her own rampant desire.

BOUND TO THE PAST
$6.50/452-6
Doing research in an old Tudor mansion, Anne finds herself aroused by James, a descendant of the property's owners. Together they uncover the perverse desires of the mansion's long-dead master—desires that bind Anne inexorably to the past—not to mention the bedpost!

SACHI MIZUNO
SHINJUKU NIGHTS
$6.50/493-3
A tour through the lives and libidos of the seductive East. Using Tokyo's infamous red light district as his backdrop, Sachi Mizuno weaves an intricate web of sensual desire, wherein many characters are ensnared and enraptured by the demands of their carnal natures.

PASSION IN TOKYO
$6.50/454-2
Tokyo—one of Asia's most historic and seductive cities. Come behind the closed doors of its citizens, and witness the many pleasures that await. Lusty men and women from every stratum of society free themselves of all inhibitions in this delirious tour through the libidinous East.

MARTINE GLOWINSKI
POINT OF VIEW
$6.50/433-X
The story of one woman's extraordinary erotic awakening. With the assistance of her new, unexpectedly kinky lover, she discovers and explores her virtual exhibitionist tendencies—until there is virtually nothing she won't do before the horny audiences her man arranges. Soon she is infamous for her unabashed sexual performances!

RICHARD McGOWAN
A HARLOT OF VENUS
$6.50/425-9
A highly fanciful, epic tale of lust on Mars! Cavortia—the most famous and sought-after courtesan in the cosmopolitan city of Venus—finds love and much more during her adventures with some cosmic characters. A sexy, sci-fi fairytale.

M. ORLANDO
THE SLEEPING PALACE
$6.95/582-4
Another thrilling volume of erotic reveries from the author of *The Architecture of Desire*. *Maison Bizarre* is the scene of unspeakable erotic cruelty; the *Lust Akademie* holds captive only the most luscious students of the sensual arts; *Baden-Eros* is the luxurious retreat of one's nastiest dreams.

CHET ROTHWELL
KISS ME, KATHERINE
$5.95/410-0
Beautiful Katherine can hardly believe her luck. Not only is she married to the charming Nelson, she's free to live out all her erotic fantasies with other men. Katherine's desires are more than any one man can handle—and plenty of men wait to fulfill her extraordinary needs!

MARCO VASSI
THE STONED APOCALYPSE
$5.95/401-1/Mass market
"Marco Vassi is our champion sexual energist."   —VLS

During his lifetime, Marco Vassi's reputation as a champion of sexual experimentation was worldwide. Funded by his groundbreaking erotic writing, *The Stoned Apocalypse* is Vassi's autobiography; chronicling a cross-country trip on America's erotic byways, it offers a rare an stimulating glimpse of a generation's sexual imagination.

MASQUERADE BOOKS

THE SALINE SOLUTION
$6.95/568-9/Mass market
"I've always read Marco's work with interest and I have the highest opinion not only of his talent but his intellectual boldness."
—Norman Mailer

During the Sexual Revolution, Vassi established himself as an explorer of an uncharted sexual landscape. Through this story of one couple's brief affair and the events that lead them to desperately reassess their lives, Vassi examines the dangers of intimacy in an age of extraordinary freedom.

ROBIN WILDE
TABITHA'S TEASE
$6.95/597-2
When poor Robin arrives at The Valentine Academy, he finds himself subject to the torturous teasing of Tabitha—the Academy's most notoriously domineering co-ed. But Tabitha is pledge-mistress of a secret sorority dedicated to enslaving young men. Robin finds himself the and wildly excited captive of Tabitha & Company's weird desires!

TABITHA'S TICKLE
$6.50/468-2
Once again, men fall under the spell of scrumptious co-eds and find themselves enslaved to demands and desires they never dreamed existed. Think it's a man's world? Guess again. With Tabitha around, no man gets what he wants until she's completely satisfied....

ERICA BRONTE
PIRATE'S SLAVE
$5.95/376-7
Lovely young Erica is stranded in a country where lust knows no bounds. Desperate to escape, she finds herself trading her firm, luscious body to any and all men willing and able to help her. Her adventure has its ups and downs, ins and outs—all to the pleasure of the increasingly lusty Erica!

CHARLES G. WOOD
HELLFIRE
$5.95/358-9
A vicious murderer is running amok in New York's sexual underground—and Nick O'Shay, a virile detective with the NYPD, plunges deep into the case. He soon becomes embroiled in the Big Apples notorious nightworld of dungeons and sex clubs, hunting a madman seeking to purge America with fire and blood sacrifices.

CHARISSE VAN DER LYN
SEX ON THE NET
$5.95/399-6
Electrifying erotica from one of the Internet's hottest authors. Encounters of all kinds—straight, lesbian, dominant/submissive and all sorts of extreme passions—are explored in thrilling detail.

STANLEY CARTEN
NAUGHTY MESSAGE
$5.95/333-3
Wesley Arthur discovers a lascivious message on his answering machine. Aroused beyond his wildest dreams by the acts described, he becomes obsessed with tracking down the woman behind the seductive voice. His search takes him through strip clubs, sex parlors and no-tell motels—before finally leading him to his randy reward....

AKBAR DEL PIOMBO
THE FETISH CROWD
$6.95/556-5
An infamous trilogy presented in one special volume guaranteed to appeal to the modern sophisticate. Separately, *Paula the Piquôse*, the infamous *Duke Cosimo*, and *The Double-Bellied Companion* are rightly considered masterpieces.

A CRUMBLING FAÇADE
$4.95/3043-1
The return of that incorrigible rogue, Henry Pike, who continues his pursuit of sex, fair or otherwise, in the homes of the most debauched aristocrats. Ultimately, every woman succumbs to Pike's charms—and submits to his whims!

CAROLE REMY
FANTASY IMPROMPTU
$6.50/513-1
Kidnapped to a remote island retreat, Chantal finds herself catering to every sexual whim of the mysterious Bran. Bran is determined to bring Chantal to a full embracing of her sensual nature, even while revealing himself to be something far more than human....

BEAUTY OF THE BEAST
$5.95/332-5
A shocking tell-all, written from the point-of-view of a prize-winning reporter. All the licentious secrets of an uninhibited life are revealed.

BUY ANY 4 BOOKS & CHOOSE 1 ADDITIONAL BOOK, OF EQUAL OR LESSER VALUE, AS YOUR FREE GIFT

MASQUERADE BOOKS

ANONYMOUS
DANIELLE: DIARY OF A SLAVE GIRL
$6.95/591-3
At the age of 19, Danielle Appleton vanishes. The frantic efforts of her family notwithstanding, she is never seen by them again. After her disappearance, Danielle finds herself doomed to a life of sexual slavery, obliged to become the ultimate instrument of pleasure to the man—or men—who own her and dictate her every move and desire.

SUBURBAN SOULS
$9.95/563-8/Trade paperback
One of American erotica's first classics. Focusing on the May–December sexual relationship of nubile Lillian and the more experienced Jack, all three volumes of *Suburban Souls* now appear in one special edition—guaranteed to enrapture modern readers with its lurid detail.

ROMANCE OF LUST
$9.95/604-9
"Truly remarkable...all the pleasure of fine historical fiction combined with the most intimate descriptions of explicit love-making."
—*The Times*

One of the most famous erotic novels of the century! First issued between 1873 and 1876, this titillating collaborative work of sexual awakening in Victorian England was repeatedly been banned for its "immorality"—and much sought after for its vivid portrayals of sodomy, sexual initiation, and flagellation. The novel that inspired Steven Marcus to coin the term "pornotopic," *Romance of Lust* not only offers the reader a linguistic tour de force, but also delivers a long look at the many possibilities of heterosexual love.

THE MISFORTUNES OF COLETTE
$7.95/564-6
The tale of one woman's erotic suffering at the hands of the sadistic man and woman who take her in hand. Beautiful Colette is the victim of an obscene plot guaranteed to keep her in erotic servitude—first to her punishing guardian, then to the man who takes her as his wife. Passed from one lustful tormentor to another, Colette wonders whether she is destined to find her greatest pleasures in punishment!

LOVE'S ILLUSION
$6.95/549-2
Elizabeth Renard yearned for the body of rich and successful Dan Harrington. Then she discovered Harrington's secret weakness: a need to be humiliated and punished. She makes him her slave, and together they commence a thrilling journey into depravity that leaves nothing to the imagination!

NADIA
$5.95/267-1
Follow the delicious but neglected Nadia as she works to wring every drop of pleasure out of life—despite an unhappy marriage. With the help of some very eager men, Nadia soon experiences the erotic pleaures she had always dreamed of.... A classic title providing a peek into the secret sexual lives of another time and place.

TITIAN BERESFORD
CHIDEWELL HOUSE AND OTHER STORIES
$6.95/554-9
What keeps Cecil a virtual, if willing, prisoner of Chidewell House? One man has been sent to investigate the sexy situation—and reports back with tales of such depravity that no expense is spared in attempting Cecil's rescue. But what man would possibly desire release from the breathtakingly beautiful and corrupt Elizabeth?

CINDERELLA
$6.50/500-X
Beresford triumphs again with this intoxicating tale, filled with castle dungeons and tightly corseted ladies-in-waiting, naughty viscounts and impossibly cruel masturbatrixes—nearly every conceivable method of erotic torture is explored and described in lush, vivid detail.

JUDITH BOSTON
$6.50/525-5
A bestselling chronicle of female domination. Edward would have been lucky to get the stodgy companion he thought his parents had hired for him. But an exquisite woman arrives at his door, and Edward finds—to his increasing delight—that his lewd behavior never goes unpunished by the unflinchingly severe Judith Boston.

THE WICKED HAND
$5.95/343-0
With an Introduction by *Leg Show*'s Dian Hanson.
A collection of fanciful fetishistic tales featuring the absolute subjugation of men by lovely, domineering women.

NINA FOXTON
$5.95/443-7
An erotic classic! An aristocrat finds herself bored by the run-of-the-mill amusements deemed appropriate for "ladies of good breeding." Instead of taking tea with proper gentlemen, naughty Nina "milks" them of their most private essences. No man ever says "No" to Nina!

MASQUERADE BOOKS

TINY ALICE
THE GEEK
$5.95/341-4
The Geek is told from the point of view of, well, a chicken who reports on the various perversities he witnesses as part of a traveling carnival. When a gang of renegade lesbians kidnaps Chicken and his geek, all hell breaks loose. A strange but highly arousing tale, filled with outrageous erotic oddities, that finally returns to print after years of infamy.

LYN DAVENPORT
THE GUARDIAN II
$6.50/505-0
The tale of submissive Felicia Brookes continues. No sooner has Felicia come to love Rodney than she discovers that she has been sold—and must now accustom herself to the guardianship of the debauched Duke of Smithton. Surely Rodney will rescue her from the domination of this depraved stranger. Won't he?

GWYNETH JAMES
DREAM CRUISE
$4.95/3045-8
Angelia has it all—exciting career and breathtaking beauty. But she longs to kick up her high heels and have some fun, so she takes an island vacation and vows to leave her inhibitions behind. From the moment her plane takes off, she finds herself in one steamy encounter after another—and wishes her horny holiday would never end!

LIZBETH DUSSEAU
MEMBER OF THE CLUB
$6.95/608-1
A restless woman yearns to realize her most secret, licentious desires. There is a club that exists for the fulfillment of such fantasies—a club devoted to the pleasures of the flesh, and the gratification of every hunger. When its members call she is compelled to answer—and serve each in an endless quest for satisfaction.... The ultimate sex club.

SPANISH HOLIDAY
$4.95/185-3
Lauren didn't mean to fall in love with the enigmatic Sam, but a once-in-a-lifetime European vacation gives her all the evidence she needs that this hot, insatiable man might be the one for her....Soon, both lovers are eagerly exploring the furthest reaches of their desires.

ANTHONY BOBARZYNSKI
STASI SLUT
$4.95/3050-4
Adina lives in East Germany, where she can only dream about the sexual freedoms of the West. But then she meets a group of ruthless and corrupt STASI agents. They use her body for their own gratification, while she opts to use her sensual talents in a bid for total freedom!

JOCELYN JOYCE
PRIVATE LIVES
$4.95/309-0
The dirty habits of the illustrious make for a sizzling tale of French erotic life. A widow has a craving for a young busboy; he's sleeping with a rich businessman's wife; her husband is minding his sex business elsewhere!

SABINE
$4.95/3046-6
There is no one who can refuse her once she casts her spell; no lover can do anything less than give up his whole life for her. Great men and empires fall at her feet; but she is haughty, distracted, impervious. It is the eve of WW II, and Sabine must find a new lover equal to her talents and her tastes.

THE JAZZ AGE
$4.95/48-3
An attorney becomes suspicious of his mistress while his wife has an interlude with a lesbian lover. A romp of erotic realism from the heyday of the flapper and the speakeasy—when rules existed to be broken!

SARA H. FRENCH
MASTER OF TIMBERLAND
$6.95/595-6
A tale of sexual slavery at the ultimate paradise resort—where sizzling submissives serve their masters without question. One of our bestselling titles, this trek to Timberland has ignited passions the world over—and stands poised to become one of modern erotica's legendary tales.

MARY LOVE
ANGELA
$6.95/545-X
Angela's game is "look but don't touch," and she drives everyone mad with desire, dancing for their pleasure but never allowing a single caress. Soon her sensual spell is cast, and she's the only one who can break it!

BUY ANY 4 BOOKS & CHOOSE 1 ADDITIONAL BOOK, OF EQUAL OR LESSER VALUE, AS YOUR FREE GIFT

MASQUERADE BOOKS

MASTERING MARY SUE
$5.95/351-1
Mary Sue is a rich nymphomaniac whose husband is determined to declare her mentally incompetent and gain control of her fortune. He brings her to a castle where, to Mary Sue's delight, she is unleashed for a veritable sex-fest!

AMARANTHA KNIGHT
The Darker Passions: CARMILLA
$6.95/578-6
Captivated by the portrait of a beautiful woman, a young man finds himself becoming obsessed with her remarkable story. Little by little, he uncovers the many blasphemies and debaucheries with which the beauteous Laura filled her hours—even as an otherworldly presence began feasting upon her....

The Darker Passions:
THE PICTURE OF DORIAN GRAY
$6.50/342-2
One woman finds her most secret desires laid bare by a portrait far more revealing than she could have imagined. Soon she benefits from a skillful masquerade, indulging her previously hidden and unusual whims.

THE DARKER PASSIONS READER
$6.50/432-1
Here are the most eerily erotic passages from the acclaimed sexual reworkings of *Dracula*, *Frankenstein*, *Dr. Jekyll & Mr. Hyde* and *The Fall of the House of Usher*.

The Darker Passions:
DR. JEKYLL AND MR. HYDE
$4.95/227-2
It is a story of incredible transformations. Explore the steamy possibilities of a tale where no one is quite who they seem. Victorian bedrooms explode with hidden demons!

The Darker Passions: DRACULA
$5.95/326-0
"Well-written and imaginative...taking us through the sexual and sadistic scenes with details that keep us reading.... A classic in itself has been added to the shelves." —*Divinity*

The infamous erotic revisioning of Bram Stoker's classic.

THE PAUL LITTLE LIBRARY
TEARS OF THE INQUISITION
$6.95/612-X
Paul Little delivers a staggering account of pleasure. "There was a tickling inside her as her nervous system reminded her she was ready for sex. But before her was...the Inquisitor!" Titillating accusations ring through the chambers of the Inquisitor as men and women confess their every desire....

CHINESE JUSTICE
$6.95/596-4
The notorious Paul Little indulges his penchant for discipline in these wild tales. *Chinese Justice* is already a classic—the story of the excruciating pleasures and delicious punishments inflicted on foreigners under the tyrannical leaders of the Boxer Rebellion.

FIT FOR A KING/BEGINNER'S LUST
$8.95/571-9/Trade paperback
Two complete novels from this master of modern lust. Voluptuous and exquisite, she is a woman *Fit for a King*—but could she withstand the fantastic force of his carnality? *Beginner's Lust* pays off handsomely for a novice in the many ways of sensuality.

SENTENCED TO SERVITUDE
$8.95/565-4/Trade paperback
A haughty young aristocrat learns what becomes of excessive pride when she is abducted and forced to submit to ordeals of sensual torment. Trained to accept her submissive state, the icy young woman soon melts under the heat of her owners....

ROOMMATE'S SECRET
$8.95/557-3/Trade paperback
A woman is forced to make ends meet by the most ancient of methods. From the misery of early impoverishment to the delight of ill-gotten gains, Elda learns to rely on her considerable sensual talents.

TUTORED IN LUST
$6.95/547-6
This tale of the initiation and instruction of a carnal college co-ed and her fellow students unlocks the sex secrets of the classroom.

LOVE SLAVE/
PECULIAR PASSIONS OF MEG
$8.95/529-8/Trade paperback
What does it take to acquire a willing *Love Slave* of one's own? What are the appetites that lurk within *Meg*? The notoriously depraved Paul Little spares no lascivious detail in these two relentless tales!

CELESTE
$6.95/544-1
It's definitely all in the family for this female duo of sexual dynamics. While traveling through Europe, these two try everything and everyone on their horny holiday.

ALL THE WAY
$6.95/509-3
Two hot Little tales in one big volume! *Going All the Way* features an unhappy man who tries to purge himself of the memory of his lover with a series of quirky and uninhibited vixens. *Pushover* tells the story of a serial spanker and his celebrated exploits.

MASQUERADE BOOKS

THE END OF INNOCENCE
$6.95/546-8
The early days of Women's Emancipation are the setting for this story of very independent ladies. These women were willing to go to any lengths to fight for their sexual freedom, and willing to endure any punishment in their desire for total liberation.

THE BEST OF PAUL LITTLE
$6.50/469-0
Known for his fantastic portrayals of punishment and pleasure, Little never fails to push readers over the edge of sensual excitement. His best scenes are here collected for the enjoyment of all erotic connoisseurs.

CAPTIVE MAIDENS
$5.95/440-2
Three young women find themselves powerless against the debauched landowners of 1824 England. They are banished to a sex colony, where they are subjected to unspeakable perversions.

THE PRISONER
$5.95/330-9
Judge Black has built a secret room below a penitentiary, where he sentences his female prisoners to hours of exhibition and torment while his friends watch. Judge Black's brand of rough justice keeps his captives on the brink of utter pleasure!

TEARS OF THE INQUISITION
$4.95/146-2
A staggering account of pleasure and punishment, set during a viciously immoral age. "There was a tickling inside her as her nervous system reminded her she was ready for sex. But before her was...the Inquisitor!"

DOUBLE NOVEL
$6.95/86-6
The Metamorphosis of Lisette Joyaux tells the story of a young woman initiated into an incredible world world of lesbian lusts. *The Story of Monique* reveals the twisted sexual rituals that beckon the ripe and willing Monique.

SLAVE ISLAND
$5.95/441-0
A leisure cruise is waylaid by Lord Henry Philbrock, a sadistic genius. The ship's passengers are kidnapped and spirited to his island prison, where the women are trained to accommodate the most bizarre sexual cravings of the rich and perverted. A perennially bestselling title.

ALIZARIN LAKE

CLARA
$6.95/548-4
The mysterious death of a beautiful woman leads her old boyfriend on a harrowing journey of discovery. His search uncovers an unimaginably sensuous woman embarked on a quest for deeper and more unusual sensations, each more shocking than the one before!

SEX ON DOCTOR'S ORDERS
$5.95/402-X
A tale of true devotion to mankind! Naughty Beth, a nubile young nurse, uses her considerable skills to further medical science by offering insatiable assistance in the gathering of important specimens. Soon she's involved everyone in her horny work—and no one leaves without surrendering exactly what Beth wants!

THE EROTIC ADVENTURES OF HARRY TEMPLE
$4.95/127-6
Harry Temple's memoirs chronicle his incredibly amorous adventures—from his initiation at the hands of insatiable sirens, through his stay at a house of hot repute, to his encounters with a chastity-belted nympho, and much more! A modern classic!

LUSCIDIA WALLACE

THE ICE MAIDEN
$6.95/613-8
Edward Canton has everything he wants in life, with one exception: Rebecca Esterbrook. He kidnaps her and whisks her away to his remote island compound, where she learns to shed her inhibitions with both men and women. Fully aroused for the first time in her life, she becomes a slave to his—and her—desires!

JOHN NORMAN

CAPTIVE OF GOR
$6.95/581-6
On Earth, Elinor Brinton was accustomed to having it all—wealth, beauty, and a host of men wrapped around her little finger. But Elinor's spoiled existence is a thing of the past. She is now a pleasure slave of Gor—a world whose society insists on her subservience to any man who calls her his own. And despite her headstrong past, Elinor finds herself succumbing—with pleasure—to her powerful Master....

BUY ANY 4 BOOKS & CHOOSE 1 ADDITIONAL BOOK, OF EQUAL OR LESSER VALUE, AS YOUR FREE GIFT

MASQUERADE BOOKS

TARNSMAN OF GOR
$6.95/486-0
This controversial series returns! Tarl Cabot is transported to Gor. He must quickly accustom himself to the ways of this world, including the caste system which exalts some as Priest-Kings or Warriors, and debases others as slaves. The beginning of the epic which made Norman a household name among fans of both sci-fi and dominance/submission.

OUTLAW OF GOR
$6.95/487-9
Tarl Cabot returns to Gor. Upon arriving, he discovers that his name, his city and the names of those he loves have become unspeakable. Once a respected Tarnsman, Cabot has become an outlaw, and must discover his new purpose on this strange planet, where even simple answers have their price....

PRIEST-KINGS OF GOR
$6.95/488-7
Tarl Cabot searches for his lovely wife Talena. Does she live, or was she destroyed by the all-powerful Priest-Kings? Cabot is determined to find out—though no one who has approached the mountain stronghold of the Priest-Kings has ever returned alive....

NOMADS OF GOR
$6.95/527-1
Cabot finds his way across Gor, pledged to serve the Priest-Kings. Unfortunately for Cabot, his mission leads him to the savage Wagon People—nomads who may very well kill before surrendering any secrets....

ASSASSIN OF GOR
$6.95/538-7
The chronicles of Counter-Earth continue with this examination of Gorean society. Here is the caste system of Gor: from the Assassin Kuurus, on a mission of vengeance, to Pleasure Slaves, trained in the ways of personal ecstasy.

RAIDERS OF GOR
$6.95/558-1
Tarl Cabot descends into the depths of Port Kar—the most degenerate port city of the Counter-Earth. There Cabot learns the ways of Kar, whose residents are renowned for the grip in which they hold their voluptuous slaves....

SYDNEY ST. JAMES
RIVE GAUCHE
$5.95/317-1
The Latin Quarter, Paris, circa 1920. Expatriate bohemians couple wildly—before eventually abandoning their ambitions amidst the temptations waiting to be indulged in every bedroom.

DON WINSLOW
THE BEST OF DON WINSLOW
$6.95/607-3
Internationally best-selling fetish author Don Winslow personally selected his hottest passages for this special collection. Sizzling excerpts from *Claire's Girls, Gloria's Indiscretion, Katerina in Charge, The Insatiable Mistress of Rosedale, Secrets of Cheatem Manor,* and *The Many Pleasures of Ironwood* are artfully woven together to make this an extraordinary overview of Winslow's greatest hits.

SLAVE GIRLS OF ROME
$6.95/577-8
Never were women so relentlessly used as were ancient Rome's voluptuous slaves! With no choice but to serve their lustful masters, these captive beauties learn to perform their duties with the passion of Venus herself.

THE FALL OF THE ICE QUEEN
$6.50/520-4
Rahn the Conqueror chose a true beauty as his Consort. But the regal disregard with which she treated Rahn was not to be endured. It was decided that she would submit to his will—and as so many had learned, Rahn's depraved expectations have made his court infamous.

PRIVATE PLEASURES
$6.50/504-2
Frantic voyeurs and licentious exhibitionists are here displayed in all their wanton glory—laid bare by the perverse and probing eye of Don Winslow.

THE INSATIABLE MISTRESS OF ROSEDALE
$6.50/494-1
Edward and Lady Penelope reside in Rosedale manor. While Edward is a connoisseur of sexual perversion, it is Lady Penelope whose mastery of complete sensual pleasure makes their home infamous. Indulging one another's bizarre whims is a way of life for this wicked couple....

SECRETS OF CHEATEM MANOR
$6.50/434-8
Edward returns to oversee his late father's estate, only to find it being run by the majestic Lady Amanda—assisted by her two beautiful daughters, Catherine and Prudence. What the randy young man soon comes to realize is the love of discipline that all three beauties share.

KATERINA IN CHARGE
$5.95/409-7
When invited to a country retreat by a mysterious couple, two randy young ladies can hardly resist! Soon after they arrive, the imperious Katerina makes her desires known—and demands that they be fulfilled...

MASQUERADE BOOKS

THE MANY PLEASURES OF IRONWOOD
$5.95/310-4
Seven lovely young women are employed by The Ironwood Sportsmen's Club, where their natural talents in the sensual arts are put to creative use. Winslow explores the ins and outs of this small and exclusive club—where members live out each of their fantasies with one (or all!) of these seven carefully selected sexual playthings.

CLAIRE'S GIRLS
$5.95/442-9
You knew when she walked by that she was something special. She was one of Claire's girls, a woman carefully dressed and groomed to fill a role, to capture a look, to fit an image crafted by the sophisticated proprietress of an exclusive escort agency. High-class whores blow the roof off!

MARCUS VAN HELLER
KIDNAP
$4.95/90-4
P.I. Harding is called in to investigate a kidnapping case involving the rich and powerful. Along the way he has the pleasure of "interrogating" an exotic dancer and a beautiful English reporter, as he finds himself enmeshed in the sleazy international underworld.

ALEXANDER TROCCHI
YOUNG ADAM
$4.95/63-7
A classic of intrigue and perversion. Two British barge operators discover a girl drowned in the river Clyde. Her lover, a plumber, is arrested for her murder. But he is innocent. Joe, the barge assistant, knows that. As the plumber is tried and sentenced to hang, this knowledge lends poignancy to Joe's romances with the women along the river whom he will love then... well, read on.

N. WHALLEN
THE EDUCATION OF SITA MANSOOR
$6.95/567-0
On the eve of her wedding, Sita Mansoor is left without a bridegroom. Sita travels to America, where she hopes to become educated in the ways of a permissive society. She could never have imagined the wide variety of tutors—both male and female—who would be waiting to take on so beautiful a pupil. The ultimate in Sex Ed!

TAU'TEVU
$6.50/426-7
Statuesque and beautiful Vivian learns to subject herself to the hand of a domineering man. He systematically helps her prove her own strength, and brings to life in her an unimagined sensual fire.

ISADORA ALMAN
ASK ISADORA
$4.95/61-0
Six years' worth of Isadora's syndicated columns on sex and relationships. Alman's been called a "hip Dr. Ruth," and a "sexy Dear Abby," based upon the wit of her advice. Today's world is more perplexing than ever—and Alman is just the expert to help untangle the most personal of knots.

THE CLASSIC COLLECTION
THE ENGLISH GOVERNESS
$5.95/373-2
When Lord Lovell's son was expelled from his prep school for masturbation, his father hired a very proper governess to tutor the boy—giving her strict instructions not to spare the rod to break him of his bad habits. Luckily, Harriet Marwood was addicted to domination.

PROTESTS, PLEASURES, RAPTURES
$5.95/400-3
Invited for an allegedly quiet weekend at a country vicarage, a young woman is stunned to find herself surrounded by shocking acts of sexual sadism. Soon she begins to explore her own capacities for delicious sexual cruelty.

THE YELLOW ROOM
$5.95/378-3
The "yellow room" holds the secrets of lust, lechery, and the lash. There, bare-bottomed, spread-eagled, and open to the world, demure Alice Darvell soon learns to love her lickings.

SCHOOL DAYS IN PARIS
$5.95/325-2
Few Universities provide the profound and pleasurable lessons one learns in after-hours study— particularly if one is young and available, and lucky enough to have Paris as a playground. Here are all the randy pursuits of young adulthood.

MAN WITH A MAID
$4.95/307-4
The adventures of Jack and Alice have delighted readers for eight decades! A classic of its genre, *Man with a Maid* tells a tale of desire, revenge, and submission.

BUY ANY 4 BOOKS & CHOOSE 1 ADDITIONAL BOOK, OF EQUAL OR LESSER VALUE, AS YOUR FREE GIFT

MASQUERADE BOOKS

MASQUERADE READERS
INTIMATE PLEASURES
$4.95/38-6
Indulge your most private penchants with this specially chosen selection of Masquerade's hottest moments. Try a tempting morsel of *The Prodigal Virgin* and *Eveline*, the bizarre public displays of carnality in *The Gilded Lily* or the relentless and shocking carnality of *The Story of Monique*.

CLASSIC EROTIC BIOGRAPHIES
JENNIFER AGAIN
$4.95/220-5
The uncensored life of one of modern erotica's most popular heroines. Once again, the insatiable Jennifer seizes the day and extracts every last drop of sensual pleasure! A thrilling peak at the mores of the uninhibited 1970s.

JENNIFER #3
$5.95/292-2
The adventures of erotica's most daring heroine. Jennifer has a photographer's eye for details—particularly of the male variety! One by one, her subjects submit to her demands for pleasure.

PAULINE
$4.95/129-2
From rural America to the royal court of Austria, Pauline follows her ever-growing sexual desires: "I would never see them again. Why shouldn't I give myself to them that they might become more and more inspired to deeds of greater lust!"

RHINOCEROS

M. CHRISTIAN, ED.
EROS EX MACHINA
$7.95/593-X
As the millennium approaches, technology is not only an inevitable, but a deeply desirable addition to daily life. *Eros Ex Machina: Eroticising the Mechanical* explores the thrill of machines—our literal and literary love of technology. Join over 25 of today's hottest writers as they explore erotic relationships with all kinds of gizmos, gadgets, and devices.

LEOPOLD VON SACHER-MASOCH
VENUS IN FURS
$7.95/589-1
The alliance of Severin and Wanda epitomizes Sacher-Masoch's obsession with a cruel goddess and the urges that drive the man held in her thrall. Exclusive to this edition are letters exchanged between Sacher-Masoch and Emilie Mataja—an aspiring writer he sought as the avatar of his desires.

JOHN NORMAN
IMAGINATIVE SEX
$7.95/561-1
The author of the Gor novels outlines his philosophy on relations between the sexes, and presents fifty-three scenarios designed to reintroduce fantasy to the bedroom.

KATHLEEN K.
SWEET TALKERS
$6.95/516-6
"If you enjoy eavesdropping on explicit conversations about sex... this book is for you." —*Spectator*

Kathleen K. ran a phone-sex company in the late 80s, and she opens up her diary for a peek at the life of a phone-sex operator. Transcripts of actual conversations are included.
Trade /$12.95/192-6

THOMAS S. ROCHE
DARK MATTER
$6.95/484-4
"*Dark Matter* is sure to please gender outlaws, bodymod junkies, goth vampires, boys who wish they were dykes, and anybody who's not to sure where the fine line should be drawn between pleasure and pain. It's a handful."—Pat Califia

"Here is the erotica of the cumming millennium.... You will be deliciously disturbed, but never disappointed."
—Poppy Z. Brite

NOIROTICA 2: PULP FRICTION
$7.95/584-0
Another volume of criminally seductive stories set in the murky terrain of the erotic and noir genres. Thomas Roche has gathered the darkest jewels from today's edgiest writers to create this provocative collection. A must for all fans of contemporary erotica.

NOIROTICA: An Anthology of Erotic Crime Stories (Ed.)
$6.95/390-2
A collection of darkly sexy tales, taking place at the crossroads of the crime and erotic genres. Here are some of today's finest writers, all of whom explore the arousing terrain where desire runs irrevocably afoul of the law.

DAVID MELTZER
UNDER
$6.95/290-6
The story of a 21st century sex professional living at the bottom of the social heap. After surgeries designed to increase his physical allure, corrupt government forces drive the cyber-gigolo underground, where even more bizarre cultures await....

MASQUERADE BOOKS

ORF
$6.95/110-1
Meltzer's celebrated exploration of Eros and modern mythology returns. Orf is the ultimate hero—the idol of thousands, the fevered dream of many more. Every last drop of feeling is squeezed from a modern-day troubadour and his lady love in this psychedelic bacchanal.

LAURA ANTONIOU, ED.
SOME WOMEN
$7.95/573-5
Introduction by Pat Califia
"Makes the reader think about the wide range of SM experiences, beyond the glamour of fiction and fantasy, or the clever-clever prose of the perverati." —SKIN TWO

Over forty essays written by women actively involved in consensual dominance and submission. Professional mistresses, lifestyle leatherdykes, whipmakers, titleholders—women from every conceivable walk of life lay bare their true feelings about issues as explosive as feminism, abuse, pleasure and public image. A bestselling title, Some Women is a valuable resource for anyone interested in sexuality.

NO OTHER TRIBUTE
$7.95/603-0
Tales of women kept in bondage to their lovers by their deepest passions. Love pushes these women beyond acceptable limits, rendering them helpless to deny anything to the men and women they adore. A volume certain to challenge political correctness as few have before.

BY HER SUBDUED
$6.95/281-7
These tales all involve women in control—of their lives and their lovers. So much in control that they can remorselessly break rules to become powerful goddesses of those who sacrifice all to worship at their feet.

AMELIA G, ED.
BACKSTAGE PASSES:
Rock n' Roll Erotica from the Pages of *Blue Blood* Magazine
$6.95/438-0
Amelia G, editor of the goth-sex journal *Blue Blood*, has brought together some of today's most irreverent writers, each of whom has outdone themselves with an edgy, antic tale of modern lust.

ROMY ROSEN
SPUNK
$6.95/492-5
Casey, a lovely model poised upon the verge of super-celebrity, falls for an insatiable young rock singer—not suspecting that his sexual appetite has led him to experiment with an dangerous new aphrodisiac. Soon, Casey becomes addicted to the drug, and her craving plunges her into a strange underworld, and into an alliance with a shadowy young man with secrets of his own....

MOLLY WEATHERFIELD
CARRIE'S STORY
$6.95/485-2
"I was stunned by how well it was written and how intensely foreign I found its sexual world.... And, since this is a world I don't frequent... I thoroughly enjoyed the National Geo tour."
—bOING bOING

"Hilarious and harrowing... just when you think things can't get any wilder, they do." —Black Sheets

Weatherfield's bestselling examination of dominance and submission. "I had been Jonathan's slave for about a year when he told me he wanted to sell me at an auction...." A rare piece of erotica, both thoughtful and hot!

CYBERSEX CONSORTIUM
CYBERSEX: The Perv's Guide to Finding Sex on the Internet
$6.95/471-2
You've heard the objections: cyberspace is soaked with sex, mired in immorality. Okay—so where is it!? Tracking down the good stuff—the real good stuff—can waste an awful lot of expensive time, and frequently leave you high and dry. The Cybersex Consortium presents an easy-to-use guide for those intrepid adults who know what they want.

LAURA ANTONIOU
("Sara Adamson")
"Ms. Adamson's friendly, conversational writing style perfectly couches what to some will be shocking material. Ms. Adamson creates a wonderfully diverse world of lesbian, gay, straight, bi and transgendered characters, all mixing delightfully in the melting pot of sadomasochism and planting the genre more firmly in the culture at large. I for one am cheering her on!"
—Kate Bornstein

BUY ANY 4 BOOKS & CHOOSE 1 ADDITIONAL BOOK, OF EQUAL OR LESSER VALUE, AS YOUR FREE GIFT

MASQUERADE BOOKS

THE MARKETPLACE
$7.95/602-2
The first title in Antoniou's thrilling Marketplace Trilogy, following the lives an lusts of those who have been deemed worthy to participate in the ultimate BDSM arena.

THE SLAVE
$7.95/601-4
The Slave covers the experience of one talented submissive who longs to join the ranks of those who have proven themselves worthy of entry into the Marketplace. But the price, while delicious, is staggeringly high....

THE TRAINER
$6.95/249-3
The Marketplace Trilogy concludes with the story of the trainers, and the desires and paths that led them to become the ultimate figures of authority.

GERI NETTICK WITH BETH ELLIOT

MIRRORS: Portrait of a Lesbian Transsexual
$6.95/435-6
Born a male, Geri Nettick knew something just didn't fit. Even after coming to terms with her own gender dysphoria she still fought to be accepted by the lesbian feminist community to which she felt she belonged. A true story.

TRISTAN TAORMINO & DAVID AARON CLARK, EDS.

RITUAL SEX
$6.95/391-0
The contributors to *Ritual Sex* know that body and soul share more common ground than society feels comfortable acknowledging. From memoirs of ecstatic revelation, to quests to reconcile sex and spirit, *Ritual Sex* provides an unprecedented look at private life.

TAMMY JO ECKHART

AMAZONS: Erotic Explorations of Ancient Myths
$7.95/534-4
The Amazon—the fierce woman warrior—appears in the traditions of many cultures, but never before has the erotic potential of this archetype been explored with such imagination. Powerful pleasures await anyone lucky enough to encounter Eckhart's spitfires.

PUNISHMENT FOR THE CRIME
$6.95/427-5
Stories that explore dominance and submission. From an encounter between two of society's most despised individuals, to the explorations of longtime friends, these tales take you where few others have ever dared....

AMARANTHA KNIGHT, ED.

SEDUCTIVE SPECTRES
$6.95/464-X
Tours through the erotic supernatural via the imaginations of today's best writers. Never have ghostly encounters been so alluring, thanks to otherworldly characters well-acquainted with the pleasures of the flesh.

SEX MACABRE
$6.95/392-9
Horror tales designed for dark and sexy nights—sure to make your skin crawl, and heart beat faster.

FLESH FANTASTIC
$6.95/352-X
Humans have long toyed with the idea of "playing God": creating life from nothingness, bringing life to the inanimate. Now Amarantha Knight collects stories exploring not only the act of Creation, but the lust that follows.

GARY BOWEN

DIARY OF A VAMPIRE
$6.95/331-7
"Gifted with a darkly sensual vision and a fresh voice, [Bowen] is a writer to watch out for."   —Cecilia Tan

Rafael, a red-blooded male with an insatiable hunger for the same, is the perfect antidote to the effete malcontents haunting bookstores today. The emergence of a bold and brilliant vision, rooted in past and present.

RENÉ MAIZEROY

FLESHLY ATTRACTIONS
$6.95/299-X
Lucien was the son of the wantonly beautiful actress, Marie-Rose Hardanges. When she decides to let a "friend" introduce her son to the pleasures of love, Marie-Rose could not have foretold the excesses that would lead to her own ruin and that of her cherished son.

GRANT ANTREWS

LEGACIES
$7.95/605-7
Kathi Lawton discovers that she has inherited the troubling secret of her late mother's scandalous sexuality. In an effort to understand what motivated her mother's desires, Kathi embarks on an exploration of SM that leads her into the arms of Horace Moore, a mysterious man who seems to see into her very soul. As she begins falling for her new master, Kathi finds herself wondering just how far she'll go to prove her love.... Another moving exploration from the author of *My Darling Dominatrix*.

MASQUERADE BOOKS

ROGUES GALLERY
$6.95/522-0
A stirring evocation of dominant/submissive love. Two doctors meet and slowly fall in love. Once Beth reveals her hidden desires to Jim, the two explore the forbidden acts that will come to define their distinctly exotic affair.

MY DARLING DOMINATRIX
$7.95/566-2
When a man and a woman fall in love, it's supposed to be simple, uncomplicated, easy—unless that woman happens to be a dominatrix. This highly praised and unpretentious love story captures the richness and depth of this very special kind of love without leering or smirking.

SUBMISSIONS
$6.95/207-8
Antrews portrays the very special elements of the dominant/submissive relationship with restraint—this time with the story of a lonely man, a winning lottery ticket, and a demanding dominatrix.

JEAN STINE
THRILL CITY
$6.95/411-9
Thrill City is the seat of the world's increasing depravity, and this classic novel transports you there with a vivid style you'd be hard pressed to ignore. No writer is better suited to describe the extremes of this modern Babylon.

SEASON OF THE WITCH
$6.95/268-X
"A future in which it is technically possible to transfer the total mind...of a rapist killer into the brain dead but physically living body of his female victim. Remarkable for intense psychological technique. There is eroticism but it is necessary to mark the differences between the sexes and the subtle altering of a man into a woman." —*The Science Fiction Critic*

Jean Stine's undisputed masterpiece, and one of the earliest science-fiction novels to explore the complexities and contradictions of gender.

JOHN WARREN
THE TORQUEMADA KILLER
$6.95/367-8
Detective Eva Hernandez gets her first "big case": a string of murders taking place within New York's SM community. Eva assembles the evidence, revealing a picture of a world misunderstood and under attack—and gradually comes to face her own hidden longings.

THE LOVING DOMINANT
$7.95/600-6
Everything you need to know about an infamous sexual variation, and an unspoken type of love. Warren guides readers through this rarely seen world, and offers clear-eyed advice guaranteed to enlighten the most jaded erotic explorers.

DAVID AARON CLARK
SISTER RADIANCE
$6.95/215-9
A meditation on love, sex, and death. The vicissitudes of lust and romance are examined against a backdrop of urban decay in this testament to the allure of the forbidden.

THE WET FOREVER
$6.95/117-1
The story of Janus and Madchen—a small-time hood and a beautiful sex worker on the run—examines themes of loyalty, sacrifice, redemption and obsession amidst Manhattan's sex parlors and underground S/M clubs.

MICHAEL PERKINS
EVIL COMPANIONS
$6.95/3067-9
Evil Companions has been hailed as "a frightening classic." A young couple explores the nether reaches of the erotic unconscious in a confrontation with the extremes of passion.

THE SECRET RECORD:
Modern Erotic Literature
$6.95/3039-3
Michael Perkins surveys the field with authority and unique insight. Updated and revised to include the latest trends, tastes, and developments in this misunderstood genre.

AN ANTHOLOGY OF CLASSIC ANONYMOUS EROTIC WRITING
$6.95/140-3
Michael Perkins has collected the best passages from the world's erotic writing. "Anonymous" is one of the most infamous bylines in publishing history—and these excerpts show why!

HELEN HENLEY
ENTER WITH TRUMPETS
$6.95/197-7
Helen Henley was told that women just don't write about sex. So Henley did it alone, flying in the face of "tradition" by writing this touching tale of arousal and devotion in one couple's kinky relationship.

BUY ANY 4 BOOKS & CHOOSE 1 ADDITIONAL BOOK, OF EQUAL OR LESSER VALUE, AS YOUR FREE GIFT

MASQUERADE BOOKS

ALICE JOANOU
CANNIBAL FLOWER
$4.95/72-6
"She is waiting in her darkened bedroom, as she has waited throughout history, to seduce the men who are foolish enough to be blinded by her irresistible charms.... She is the goddess of sexuality, and *Cannibal Flower* is her haunting siren song." —Michael Perkins

BLACK TONGUE
$6.95/258-2
"Joanou has created a series of sumptuous, brooding, dark visions of sexual obsession, and is undoubtedly a name to look out for in the future." —Redeemer

Exploring lust at its most florid and unsparing, *Black Tongue* is redolent of forbidden passions.

TOURNIQUET
$6.95/3060-1
A heady collection of stories and effusions. A riveting series of meditations on desire.

LIESEL KULIG
LOVE IN WARTIME
$6.95/3044-X
Madeleine knew that the handsome SS officer was dangerous, but she was just a cabaret singer in Nazi-occupied Paris, trying to survive in a perilous time. When Josef fell in love with her, he discovered that a beautiful woman can be as dangerous as any warrior.

SAMUEL R. DELANY
THE MAD MAN
$8.99/408-9/Mass market
"Delany develops an insightful dichotomy between [his protagonist]'s two worlds: the one of cerebral philosophy and dry academia, the other of heedless, 'impersonal' obsessive sexual extremism. When these worlds finally collide...the novel achieves a surprisingly satisfying resolution...." —Publishers Weekly

Graduate student John Marr researches the life of Timothy Hasler: a philosopher whose career was cut tragically short over a decade earlier. Marr begins to find himself increasingly drawn toward shocking sexual encounters with the homeless men, until it begins to seem that Hasler's death might hold some key to his own life as a gay man in the age of AIDS.

DANIEL VIAN
ILLUSIONS
$6.95/3074-1
Two tales of danger and desire in Berlin on the eve of WWII. From private homes to lurid cafés, passion is exposed in stark contrast to the brutal violence of the time, as desperate people explore their darkest sexual desires.

PERSUASIONS
$4.95/183-7
"The stockings are drawn tight by the suspender belt, tight enough to be stretched to the limit just above the middle part of her thighs, tight enough so that her calves glow through the sheer silk..." A double novel, including the classics *Adagio* and *Gabriela and the General*, this volume traces lust around the globe.

PHILIP JOSÉ FARMER
A FEAST UNKNOWN
$6.95/276-0
"Sprawling, brawling, shocking, suspenseful, hilarious..." —Theodore Sturgeon

Lord Grandrith—armed with the belief that he is the son of Jack the Ripper—tells the story of his remarkable life. His story progresses to encompass the furthest extremes of human behavior.

FLESH
$6.95/303-1
Stagg explored the galaxies for 800 years. Upon his return, the hero Stagg is made the centerpiece of an incredible public ritual—one that will take him to the heights of ecstasy, and drag him toward the depths of hell.

ANDREI CODRESCU
THE REPENTANCE OF LORRAINE
$6.95/329-5
"One of our most prodigiously talented and magical writers." —NYT Book Review

An aspiring writer, a professor's wife, a secretary, gold anklets, Maoists, Roman harlots—and more—swirl through this spicy tale of a harried quest for a mythic artifact. Written when the author was a young man.

TUPPY OWENS
SENSATIONS
$6.95/3081-4
Tuppy Owens takes a rare peek behind the scenes of *Sensations*—the first big-budget sex flick. Originally commissioned to appear in book form after the release of the film in 1975, *Sensations* is finally available.

SOPHIE GALLEYMORE BIRD
MANEATER
$6.95/103-9
Through a bizarre act of creation, a man attains the "perfect" lover—by all appearances a beautiful, sensuous woman, but in reality something far darker. Once brought to life she will accept no mate, seeking instead the prey that will sate her hunger.

MASQUERADE BOOKS

BADBOY

DAVID MAY
MADRUGADA
$6.95/574-3
Set in San Francisco's gay leather community, *Madrugada* follows the lives of a group of friends—and their many acquaintances—as they tangle with the thorny issues of love and lust. Uncompromising, mysterious, and arousing, David May weaves a complex web of relationships in this unique story cycle.

PETER HEISTER
ISLANDS OF DESIRE
$6.95/480-1
Red-blooded lust on the wine-dark seas of classical Greece. Anacraeon yearns to leave his small, isolated island and find adventure in one of the overseas kingdoms. Accompanied by some randy friends, Anacraeon makes his dream come true—and discovers pleasures he never dreamed of!

KITTY TSUI WRITING AS "ERIC NORTON"
SPARKS FLY
$6.95/551-4
The highest highs—and most wretched depths—of life as Eric Norton, a beautiful wanton living San Francisco's high life. *Sparks Fly* traces Norton's rise, fall, and resurrection, vividly marking the way with the personal affairs that give life meaning.

BARRY ALEXANDER
ALL THE RIGHT PLACES
$6.95/482-8
Stories filled with hot studs in lust and love. From modern masters and slaves to medieval royals and their subjects, Alexander explores the mating rituals men have engaged in for centuries—all in the name of desire...

MICHAEL FORD, ED.
BUTCHBOYS:
Stories For Men Who Need It Bad
$6.50/523-9
A big volume of tales dedicated to the rough-and-tumble type who can make a man weak at the knees. Some of today's best erotic writers explore the many possible variations on the age-old fantasy of the thoroughly dominating man.

WILLIAM J. MANN, ED.
GRAVE PASSIONS:
Gay Tales of the Supernatural
$6.50/405-4
A collection of the most chilling tales of passion currently being penned by today's most provocative gay writers. Unnatural transformations, otherworldly encounters, and deathless desires make for a collection sure to keep readers up late at night.

J. A. GUERRA, ED.
COME QUICKLY:
For Boys on the Go
$6.50/413-5
Here are over sixty of the hottest fantasies around—all designed to get you going in less time than it takes to dial 976. Julian Anthony Guerra, the editor behind the popular *Men at Work* and *Badboy Fantasies*, has put together this volume especially for you—a busy man on a modern schedule, who still appreciates a little old-fashioned action.

JOHN PRESTON
HUSTLING: A Gentleman's Guide to the Fine Art of Homosexual Prostitution
$6.50/517-4
"Fun and highly literary. What more could you expect form such an accomplished activist, author and editor?" —*Drummer*

John Preston solicited the advice and opinions of "working boys" from across the country in his effort to produce the ultimate guide to the hustler's world. *Hustling* covers every practical aspect of the business, from clientele and payment to "specialties," and drawbacks.
Trade $12.95/137-3
MR. BENSON
$4.95/3041-5
Jamie is an aimless young man lucky enough to encounter Mr. Benson. He is soon learns to accept this man as his master. Jamie's incredible adventures never fail to excite—especially when the going gets rough!
TALES FROM THE DARK LORD
$5.95/323-6
Twelve stunning works from the man *Lambda Book Report* called "the Dark Lord of gay erotica." The relentless ritual of lust and surrender is explored in all its manifestations in this heart-stopping triumph of authority and vision.

BUY ANY 4 BOOKS & CHOOSE 1 ADDITIONAL BOOK, OF EQUAL OR LESSER VALUE, AS YOUR FREE GIFT

MASQUERADE BOOKS

TALES FROM THE DARK LORD II
$4.95/176-4
THE ARENA
$4.95/3083-0
Preston's take on the ultimate sex club—where men go to abolish all personal limits. Only the author of *Mr. Benson* could have imagined so perfect an institution for the satisfaction of male desire.

THE HEIR•THE KING
$4.95/3048-2
The Heir, written in the lyric voice of the ancient myths, tells the story of a world where slaves and masters create a new sexual society. *The King* tells the story of a soldier who discovers his monarch's most secret desires.

THE MISSION OF ALEX KANE
SWEET DREAMS
$4.95/3062-8
It's the triumphant return of gay action hero Alex Kane! In *Sweet Dreams*, Alex travels to Boston where he takes on a street gang that stalks gay teenagers.

GOLDEN YEARS
$4.95/3069-5
When evil threatens the plans of a group of older gay men, Kane's got the muscle to take it head on. Along the way, he wins the support—and very specialized attentions—of a cowboy plucked right out of the Old West.

DEADLY LIES
$4.95/3076-8
Politics is a dirty business and the dirt becomes deadly when a smear campaign targets gay men. Who better to clean things up than Alex Kane!

STOLEN MOMENTS
$4.95/3098-9
Houston's evolving gay community is victimized by a malicious newspaper editor who is more than willing to boost circulation by printing homophobic slander. He never counted on Alex Kane, fearless defender of gay dreams and desires.

SECRET DANGER
$4.95/111-X
Alex Kane and the faithful Danny are called to a small European country, where a group of gay tourists is being held hostage by brutal terrorists.

LETHAL SILENCE
$4.95/125-X
Chicago becomes the scene of the rightwing's most noxious plan—facilitated by unholy political alliances. Alex and Danny head to the Windy City to battle the mercenaries who would squash gay men underfoot.

MATT TOWNSEND
SOLIDLY BUILT
$6.50/416-X
The tale of the relationship between Jeff, a young photographer, and Mark, the butch electrician hired to wire Jeff's new home. For Jeff, it's love at first sight; Mark, however, has more than a few hang-ups.

JAY SHAFFER
SHOOTERS
$5.95/284-1
No mere catalog of random acts, *Shooters* tells the stories of a variety of stunning men and the ways they connect in sexual and non-sexual ways. Shaffer always gets his man.

ANIMAL HANDLERS
$4.95/264-7
In Shaffer's world, every man finally succumbs to the animal urges deep inside. And if there's any creature that promises a wild time, it's a beast who's been caged for far too long.

FULL SERVICE
$4.95/150-0
No-nonsense guys bear down hard on each other as they work their way toward release in this finely detailed assortment of fantasies.

D. V. SADERO
IN THE ALLEY
$4.95/144-6
Hardworking men bring their special skills and impressive tools to the most satisfying job of all: capturing and breaking the male animal.

SCOTT O'HARA
DO-IT-YOURSELF PISTON POLISHING
$6.50/489-5
Longtime sex-pro Scott O'Hara draws upon his acute powers of seduction to lure you into a world of hard, horny men long overdue for a tune-up.

SUTTER POWELL
EXECUTIVE PRIVILEGES
$6.50/383-X
No matter how serious or sexy a predicament his characters find themselves in, Powell conveys the sheer exuberance of their encounters with a warm humor rarely seen in contemporary erotica.

GARY BOWEN
WESTERN TRAILS
$6.50/477-1
Some of gay literature's brightest stars tell the sexy truth about the many ways a rugged stud found to satisfy himself—and his buddy—in the Very Wild West.

MASQUERADE BOOKS

MAN HUNGRY
$5.95/374-0
A riveting collection of stories from one of gay erotica's new stars. Dipping into a variety of genres, Bowen crafts tales of lust unlike anything being published today.

KYLE STONE
THE HIDDEN SLAVE
$6.95/580-8
"This perceptive and finely-crafted work is a joy to discover. Kyle Stone's fiction belongs on the shelf of every serious fan of gay literature."
—Pat Califia

"Once again, Kyle Stone proves that imagination, ingenuity, and sheer intellectual bravado go a long way in making porn hot. This book turns us on and makes us think. Who could ask for anything more?"
—Michael Bronski

HOT BAUDS 2
$6.50/479-8
Stone conducted another heated search through the world's randiest gay bulletin boards, resulting in one of the most scalding follow-ups ever published.

HOT BAUDS
$5.95/285-X
Stone combed cyberspace for the hottest fantasies of the world's horniest hackers. Sexy, shameless, and eminently user-friendly.

FIRE & ICE
$5.95/297-3
A collection of stories from the author of the adventures of PB 500. Stone's characters always promise one thing: enough hot action to burn away your desire for anyone else....

FANTASY BOARD
$4.95/212-4
Explore the future—through the intertwined lives of a collection of randy computer hackers. On the Lambda Gate BBS, every horny male is in search of virtual satisfaction!

THE CITADEL
$4.95/198-5
The sequel to PB 500. Micah faces new challenges after entering the Citadel. Only his master knows what awaits....

THE INITIATION OF PB 500
$4.95/141-1
He is a stranger on their planet, unschooled in their language, and ignorant of their customs. But Micah will soon be trained in every detail of erotic service. When his training is complete, he must prove himself worthy of the master who has chosen him....

RITUALS
$4.95/168-3
Via a computer bulletin board, a young man finds himself drawn into sexual rites that transform him into the willing slave of a mysterious stranger. His former life is thrown off, and he learns to live for his Master's touch....

ROBERT BAHR
SEX SHOW
$4.95/225-6
Luscious dancing boys. Brazen, explicit acts. Take a seat, and get very comfortable, because the curtain's going up on a very special show no discriminating appetite can afford to miss.

JASON FURY
THE ROPE ABOVE, THE BED BELOW
$4.95/269-8
A vicious murderer is preying upon New York's go-go boys. In order to solve this mystery and save lives, each studly suspect must lay bare his soul—and more!

ERIC'S BODY
$4.95/151-9
Follow the irresistible Jason through sexual adventures unlike any you have ever read—touching on the raunchy, the romantic, and a number of highly sensitive areas in between....

1 900 745-HUNG

THE connection for hot handfuls of eager guys! No credit card needed—so call now for access to the hottest party line available. Spill it all to bad boys from across the country! (Must be over 18.) Pick one up now.... $3.98 per min.

LARS EIGHNER
WANK: THE TAPES
$6.95/588-3
Lars Eighner gets back to basics with this look at every guy's favorite pastime. Horny studs bare it all and work up a healthy sweat during these provocative discussions about masturbation.

WHISPERED IN THE DARK
$5.95/286-8
A volume demonstrating Eighner's unique combination of strengths: poetic descriptive power, an unfailing ear for dialogue, and a finely tuned feeling for the nuances of male passion. An extraordinary collection of this influential writer's work.

BUY ANY 4 BOOKS & CHOOSE 1 ADDITIONAL BOOK, OF EQUAL OR LESSER VALUE, AS YOUR FREE GIFT

MASQUERADE BOOKS

AMERICAN PRELUDE
$4.95/170-5
Eighner is one of gay erotica's true masters, producing wonderfully written tales of all-American lust, peopled with red-blooded, oversexed studs.

DAVID LAURENTS, ED.
SOUTHERN COMFORT
$6.50/466-6
Editor David Laurents now unleashes a collection of tales focusing on the American South—stories reflecting the many sexy contributions the region has made to the iconography of the American Male.

WANDERLUST:
Homoerotic Tales of Travel
$5.95/395-3
A volume dedicated to the special pleasures of faraway places—and the horny men who lie in wait for intrepid tourists. Celebrate the freedom of the open road, and the allure of men who stray from the beaten path....

THE BADBOY BOOK OF EROTIC POETRY
$5.95/382-1
Erotic poetry has long been the problem child of the literary world—highly creative and provocative, but somehow too frank to be "art." *The Badboy Book of Erotic Poetry* restores eros to its place of honor in gay writing.

AARON TRAVIS
BIG SHOTS
$5.95/448-8
Two fierce tales in one electrifying volume. In *Beirut*, Travis tells the story of ultimate military power and erotic subjugation; *Kip*, Travis' hypersexed and sinister take on *film noir*, appears in unexpurgated form for the first time.

EXPOSED
$4.95/126-8
A unique glimpse of the horny gay male in his natural environment! Cops, college jocks, ancient Romans—even Sherlock Holmes and his loyal Watson—cruise these pages, fresh from the pen of one of our hottest authors.

BEAST OF BURDEN
$4.95/105-5
Innocents surrender to the brutal sexual mastery of their superiors, as taboos are shattered and replaced with the unwritten rules of masculine conquest. Intense and extreme.

IN THE BLOOD
$5.95/283-3
Early tales from this master of the genre. Includes "In the Blood"—a heart-pounding descent into sexual vampirism.

THE FLESH FABLES
$4.95/243-4
One of Travis' best collections. Includes "Blue Light," as well as other masterpieces that established him as the erotic writer to watch.

BOB VICKERY
SKIN DEEP
$4.95/265-5
So many varied beauties no one will go away unsatisfied. No tantalizing morsel of manflesh is overlooked—or left unexplored!

JR
FRENCH QUARTER NIGHTS
$5.95/337-6
Sensual snapshots of the many places where men get down and dirty—from the steamy French Quarter to the steam room at the old Everard baths.

TOM BACCHUS
RAHM
$5.95/315-5
Tom Bacchus brings to life an extraordinary assortment of characters, from the Father of Us All to the cowpoke next door, the early gay literati to rude, queercore mosh rats.

BONE
$4.95/177-2
Queer musings from the pen of one of today's hottest young talents. Tom Bacchus maps out the tricking ground of a new generation.

KEY LINCOLN
SUBMISSION HOLDS
$4.95/266-3
From tough to tender, the men between these covers stop at nothing to get what they want. These sweat-soaked tales show just how bad boys can really get.

CALDWELL/EIGHNER
QSFX2
$5.95/278-7
Other-worldly yarns from two master storytellers—Clay Caldwell and Lars Eighner. Both eroticists take a trip to the furthest reaches of the sexual imagination, sending back ten scalding sci-fi stories of male desire.

CLAY CALDWELL
JOCK STUDS
$6.95/472-0
Scalding tales of pumped bodies and raging libidos. Swimmers, runners, football players—whatever your sport might be, there's a man here waiting to work up a little sweat, peel off his uniform, and claim his reward for a game well-played....

MASQUERADE BOOKS

ASK OL' BUDDY
$5.95/346-5
Set in the underground SM world—where men initiate one another into the secrets of the rawest sexual realm of all. And when each stud's initiation is complete, he takes part in the training of another hungry soul....

STUD SHORTS
$5.95/320-1
"If anything, Caldwell's charm is more powerful, his nostalgia more poignant, the horniness he captures more sweetly, achingly acute than ever." —Aaron Travis

A new collection of this legend's latest sex-fiction. Caldwell tells all about cops, cadets, truckers, farmboys (and many more) in these dirty jewels.

TAILPIPE TRUCKER
$5.95/296-5
Trucker porn! Caldwell tells the truth about Trag and Curly—two men hot for the feeling of sweaty manflesh. Together, they pick up—and turn out—a couple of thrill-seeking punks.

SERVICE, STUD
$5.95/336-5
Another look at the gay future. The setting is the Los Angeles of a distant future. Here the all-male populace is divided between the served and the servants—guaranteeing the erotic satisfaction of all involved.

QUEERS LIKE US
$4.95/262-0
For years the name Clay Caldwell has been synonymous with the hottest, most finely crafted gay tales available. Queers Like Us is one of his best: the story of a randy mailman's trek through a landscape of available studs.

ALL-STUD
$4.95/104-7
This classic, sex-soaked tale takes place under the watchful eye of Number Ten: an omniscient figure who has decreed unabashed promiscuity as the law of his all-male land.

CLAY CALDWELL & AARON TRAVIS
TAG TEAM STUDS
$6.50/465-8
Wrestling will never seem the same, once you've made your way through this assortment of sweaty studs. But you'd better be wary—should one catch you off guard, you just might spend the night pinned to the mat....

LARRY TOWNSEND
LEATHER AD: M
$5.95/380-5
John's curious about what goes on between the leatherclad men he's fantasized about. He takes out a personal ad, and starts a journey of discovery that will leave no part of his life unchanged.

LEATHER AD: S
$5.95/407-0
The tale continues—this time told from a Top's perspective. A simple ad generates many responses, and one man puts these studs through their paces....

1 800 906-HUNK
Hardcore phone action for real men. A scorching assembly of studs is waiting for your call—and eager to give you the headtrip of your life! Totally live, guaranteed one-on-one encounters. (Must be over 18.) No credit card needed. $3.98 per minute.

BEWARE THE GOD WHO SMILES
$5.95/321-X
Two lusty young Americans are transported to ancient Egypt—where they are embroiled in warfare and taken as slaves by barbarians. The two finally discover that the key to escape lies within their own rampant libidos.

2069 TRILOGY
(This one-volume collection only $6.95)244-2
The early science-fiction trilogy in one volume! Here is the tight plotting and shameless all-male sex action that established Townsend as one of erotica's masters.

MIND MASTER
$4.95/209-4
Who better to explore the territory of erotic dominance than an author who helped define the genre—and knows that ultimate mastery always transcends the physical.

THE LONG LEATHER CORD
$4.95/201-9
Chuck's stepfather never lacks money or male visitors with whom he enacts intense sexual rituals. As Chuck comes to terms with his own desires, he begins to unravel the mystery behind his stepfather's secret life.

THE SCORPIUS EQUATION
$4.95/119-5
The story of a man caught between the demands of two galactic empires. Our randy hero must match wits—and more—with the incredible forces that rule his world.

BUY ANY 4 BOOKS & CHOOSE 1 ADDITIONAL BOOK, OF EQUAL OR LESSER VALUE, AS YOUR FREE GIFT

MASQUERADE BOOKS

MAN SWORD
$4.95/188-8
The *trés gai* tale of France's King Henri III, who encounters enough sexual schemers and politicos to alter one's picture of history forever! Witness the unbridled licentiousness of one of Europe's most notorious courts.

THE FAUSTUS CONTRACT
$4.95/167-5
Two cocky young hustlers get more than they bargained for in this story of lust and its discontents.

CHAINS
$4.95/158-6
Picking up street punks has always been risky, but here it sets off a string of events that must be read to be believed. The legendary Townsend at his grittiest.

KISS OF LEATHER
$4.95/161-6
A look at the acts and attitudes of an earlier generation of gay leathermen. Sensual pain and pleasure mix in this classic tale.

RUN, LITTLE LEATHER BOY
$4.95/143-8
The famous tale of sexual awakening. A chronic underachiever, Wayne seems to be going nowhere fast. He finds himself drawn to the masculine intensity of a dark and mysterious sexual underground, where he soon finds many goals worth pursuing....

RUN NO MORE
$4.95/152-7
The sequel to *Run, Little Leather Boy*. This volume follows the further adventures of Townsend's leatherclad narrator as he travels every sexual byway available to the S/M male.

THE SEXUAL ADVENTURES OF SHERLOCK HOLMES
$4.95/3097-0
A scandalously sexy take on the notorious sleuth. Via the unexpurgated diary of Holmes' horny sidekick Watson, "A Study in Scarlet" is transformed to expose the Diogenes Club as an S/M arena, and clues only the redoubtable–and horny—Sherlock Holmes could piece together.

THE GAY ADVENTURES OF CAPTAIN GOOSE
$4.95/169-1
Jerome Gander is sentenced to serve aboard a ship manned by the most hardened, unrepentant criminals. In no time, Gander becomes one of the most notorious rakehells Merrie Olde England had ever seen. On land or sea, Gander hunts down the Empire's hottest studs.

DONALD VINING
CABIN FEVER AND OTHER STORIES
$5.95/338-4
"Demonstrates the wisdom experience combined with insight and optimism can create." —*Bay Area Reporter*

Eighteen blistering stories in celebration of the most intimate of male bonding, reaffirming both love and lust in modern gay life.

DEREK ADAMS
MILES DIAMOND AND THE CASE OF THE CRETAN APOLLO
$6.95/381-3
Hired by a wealthy man to track a cheating lover, Miles finds himself involved in ways he could never have imagined! When the jealous Callahan threatens not only Diamond but his innocent an studly assistant, Miles counters with a little undercover work—involving as many horny informants as he can get his hands on!

PRISONER OF DESIRE
$6.50/439-9
Red-blooded, sweat-soaked excursions through the modern gay libido.

THE MARK OF THE WOLF
$5.95/361-9
The past comes back to haunt one well-off stud, whose desires lead him into the arms of many men—and the midst of a mystery.

MY DOUBLE LIFE
$5.95/314-7
Every man leads a double life, dividing his hours between the mundanities of the day and the pursuits of the night. Derek Adams shines a little light on the wicked things men do when no one's looking.

HEAT WAVE
$4.95/159-4
Derek Adams sexy short stories are guaranteed to jump start any libido—and *Heatwave* contains his very best.

MILES DIAMOND AND THE DEMON OF DEATH
$4.95/251-5
Miles always find himself in the stickiest situations—with any stud he meets! This adventure promises another carnal carnival, as Diamond investigates a host of horny guys.

THE ADVENTURES OF MILES DIAMOND
$4.95/118-7
The debut of this popular gay gumshoe. To Diamond's delight, "The Case of the Missing Twin" is packed with randy studs. Miles sets about uncovering all as he tracks down the delectable Daniel Travis.

MASQUERADE BOOKS

KELVIN BELIELE
IF THE SHOE FITS
$4.95/223-X
An essential volume of tales exploring a world where randy boys can't help but do what comes naturally—as often as possible! Sweaty male bodies grapple in pleasure.

JAMES MEDLEY
THE REVOLUTIONARY & OTHER STORIES
$6.50/417-8
Billy, the son of the station chief of the American Embassy in Guatemala, is kidnapped and held for ransom. Frightened at first, Billy gradually develops an unimaginably close relationship with Juan, the revolutionary assigned to guard him.

HUCK AND BILLY
$4.95/245-0
Young lust knows no bounds—and is often the hottest of one's life! Huck and Billy explore the desires that course through their bodies, determined to plumb the depths of passion.

FLEDERMAUS
FLEDERFICTION: STORIES OF MEN AND TORTURE
$5.95/355-4
Fifteen blistering paeans to men and their suffering. Unafraid of exploring the furthest reaches of pain and pleasure, Fledermaus unleashes his most thrilling tales in this volume.

VICTOR TERRY
MASTERS
$6.50/418-6
Terry's butchest tales. A powerhouse volume of boot-wearing, whip-wielding, bone-crunching bruisers who've got what it takes to make a grown man grovel.

SM/SD
$6.50/406-2
Set around a South Dakota town called Prairie, these tales offer evidence that the real rough stuff can still be found where men take what they want despite all rules.

WHIPs
$4.95/254-X
Cruising for a hot man? You'd better be, because one way or another, these WHIPs—officers of the Wyoming Highway Patrol—are gonna pull you over for a little impromptu interrogation....

MAX EXANDER
DEEDS OF THE NIGHT: Tales of Eros and Passion
$5.95/348-1
MAXimum porn! Exander's a writer who's seen it all—and is more than happy to describe every glorious inch of it in pulsating detail. A whirlwind tour of the hypermasculine libido.

LEATHERSEX
$4.95/210-8
Hard-hitting tales from merciless Max. This time he focuses on the leather clad lust that draws together only the most willing and talented of tops and bottoms—for an all-out orgy of limitless surrender and control....

MANSEX
$4.95/160-8
"Mark was the classic leatherman: a huge, dark stud in chaps, with a big black moustache, hairy chest and enormous muscles. Exactly the kind of men Todd liked—strong, hunky, masculine, ready to take control...."

TOM CAFFREY
TALES FROM THE MEN'S ROOM
$5.95/364-3
Male lust at its most elemental and arousing. The Men's Room is less a place than a state of mind—one that every man finds himself in, day after day....

HITTING HOME
$4.95/222-1
Titillating and compelling, the stories in *Hitting Home* make a strong case for there being only one thing on a man's mind.

"BIG" BILL JACKSON
EIGHTH WONDER
$4.95/200-0
"Big" Bill Jackson's always the randiest guy in town—no matter what town he's in. From the bright lights and back rooms of New York to the open fields and sweaty bods of a small Southern town, "Big" Bill always manages to cause a scene!

TORSTEN BARRING
GUY TRAYNOR
$6.50/414-3
Some call Guy Traynor a theatrical genius; others say he was a madman. All anyone knows for certain is that his productions were the result of blood, sweat and outrageous erotic torture!

BUY ANY 4 BOOKS & CHOOSE 1 ADDITIONAL BOOK, OF EQUAL OR LESSER VALUE, AS YOUR FREE GIFT

MASQUERADE BOOKS

PRISONERS OF TORQUEMADA
$5.95/252-3
Another volume sure to push you over the edge. How cruel is the "therapy" practiced at Casa Torquemada? Rest assured that Barring is just the writer to evoke such steamy sexual malevolence.

SHADOWMAN
$4.95/178-0
From spoiled aristocrats to randy youths sowing wild oats at the local picture show, Barring's imagination works overtime in these steamy vignettes of homolust.

PETER THORNWELL
$4.95/149-7
Follow the exploits of Peter Thornwell and his outrageously horny cohorts as he goes from misspent youth to scandalous stardom, all thanks to an insatiable libido and love for the lash. The first of Torsten Barring's popular SM novels.

THE SWITCH
$4.95/3061-X
Sometimes a man needs a good whipping, and The Switch certainly makes a case! Packed with hot studs and unrelenting passions, these stories established Barring as a writer to be watched.

BERT McKENZIE
FRINGE BENEFITS
$5.95/354-6
From the pen of a widely published short story writer comes a volume of highly immodest tales. Not afraid of getting down and dirty, McKenzie produces some of today's most visceral sextales.

CHRISTOPHER MORGAN
STEAM GAUGE
$6.50/473-9
This volume abounds in manly men doing what they do best—to, with, or for any hot stud who crosses their paths.

THE SPORTSMEN
$5.95/385-6
A collection of super-hot stories dedicated to the all-American athlete. These writers know just the type of guys that make up every red-blooded male's starting line-up....

MUSCLE BOUND
$4.95/3028-8
In the NYC bodybuilding scene, Tommy joins forces with sexy Will Rodriguez in a battle of wits and biceps at the hottest gym in town, where the weak are bound and crushed by iron-pumping gods.

SONNY FORD
REUNION IN FLORENCE
$4.95/3070-9
Follow Adrian and Tristan an a sexual odyssey that takes in all ports known to ancient man. From lustful Turks to insatiable Mamluks, these two spread pleasure throughout the classical world!

ROGER HARMAN
FIRST PERSON
$4.95/179-9
Each story takes the form of a confessional—told by men who've got plenty to confess! From the "first time ever" to firsts of different kinds....

J. A. GUERRA, ED.
SLOW BURN
$4.95/3042-3
Torsos get lean and hard, pecs widen, and stomachs ripple in these sexy stories of the power and perils of physical perfection.

DAVE KINNICK
SORRY I ASKED
$4.95/3090-3
Unexpurgated interviews with gay porn's rank and file. Get personal with the men behind (and under) the "stars," and discover the hot truth about the porn business.

SEAN MARTIN
SCRAPBOOK
$4.95/224-8
From the creator of Doc and Raider comes this hot collection of life's horniest moments—all involving studs sure to set your pulse racing!

CARO SOLES & STAN TAL, EDS.
BIZARRE DREAMS
$4.95/187-X
An anthology of voices dedicated to exploring the dark side of human fantasy. Here are the most talented practitioners of "dark fantasy," the most forbidden sexual realm of all.

MICHAEL LOWENTHAL, ED.
THE BADBOY EROTIC LIBRARY Volume 1
$4.95/190-X
Excerpts from A Secret Life, Imre, Sins of the Cities of the Plain, Teleny and others.

THE BADBOY EROTIC LIBRARY Volume 2
$4.95/211-6
This time, selections are taken from Mike and Me, Muscle Bound, Men at Work, Badboy Fantasies, and Slowburn.

MASQUERADE BOOKS

ERIC BOYD
MIKE AND ME
$5.95/419-4
Mike joined the gym squad to bulk up on muscle. Little did he know he'd be turning on every sexy muscle jock in Minnesota! Hard bodies collide in a series of horny workouts.

MIKE AND THE MARINES
$6.50/497-6
Mike takes on America's most elite corps of studs! Join in on the never-ending sexual escapades of this singularly lustful platoon!

ANONYMOUS
A SECRET LIFE
$4.95/3017-2
Meet Master Charles: eighteen and quite innocent, until his arrival at the Sir Percival's Academy, where the lessons are supplemented with a crash course in pure sexual heat!

SINS OF THE CITIES OF THE PLAIN
$5.95/322-8
indulge yourself in the scorching memoirs of young man-about-town Jack Saul. Jack's sinful escapades grow wilder with every chapter!

IMRE
$4.95/3019-9
An extraordinary lost classic of obsession, gay erotic desire, and romance in a small European town on the eve of WWI.

TELENY
$4.95/3020-2
Often attributed to Oscar Wilde. A young man dedicates himself to a succession of forbidden pleasures.

THE SCARLET PANSY
$4.95/189-6
Randall Etrange travels the world in search of true love. Along the way, his journey becomes a sexual odyssey of truly epic proportions.

PAT CALIFIA, ED.
THE SEXPERT
$4.95/3034-2
From penis size to toy care, bar behavior to AIDS awareness, The Sexpert responds to real concerns with uncanny wisdom and a razor wit.

HARD CANDY

ELISE D'HAENE
LICKING OUR WOUNDS
$7.95/605-7
"A fresh, engagingly sarcastic and determinedly bawdy voice. D'Haene is blessed with a savvy, iconoclastic view of the world that is mordant but never mean." —*Publisher's Weekly*

Licking Our Wounds, Elise D'Haene's acclaimed debut novel, is the story of Maria, a young woman coming to terms with the complexities of life in the age of AIDS. Abandoned by her lover and faced with the deaths of her friends, Maria struggles along with the help of Peter, HIV-positive and deeply conflicted about the changes in his own life, and Christie, a lover who is full of her own ideas about truth and the meaning of life.

CHEA VILLANUEVA
BULLETPROOF BUTCHES
$7.95/560-3
"...Gutsy, hungry, and outrageous, but with a tender core... Villanueva is a writer to watch out for: she will teach us something." —Joan Nestle

One of lesbian literature's most uncompromising voices. Never afraid to address the harsh realities of working-class lesbian life, Chea Villanueva charts territory frequently overlooked in the age of "lesbian chic."

KEVIN KILLIAN
ARCTIC SUMMER
$6.95/514-X
An examination of the emptiness lying beneath the rich exterior of America in the 50s. With the story of Liam Reilly—a young gay man of considerable means and numerous secrets—Killian exposes the contradictions of the American Dream.

MICHAEL ROWE
WRITING BELOW THE BELT:
Conversations with Erotic Authors
$7.95/540-9
"An in-depth and enlightening tour of society's love/hate relationship with sex, morality, and censorship."
—*James White Review*

Michael Rowe interviewed the best and brightest erotic writers and presents the collected wisdom in *Writing Below the Belt*. Includes interviews with such cult sensations as John Preston, Larry Townsend, Pat Califia, and others.

BUY ANY 4 BOOKS & CHOOSE 1 ADDITIONAL BOOK, OF EQUAL OR LESSER VALUE, AS YOUR FREE GIFT

MASQUERADE BOOKS

PAUL T. ROGERS
SAUL'S BOOK
$7.95/462-3
Winner of the Editors' Book Award

"A first novel of considerable power... Speaks to us all."
—*New York Times Book Review*

The story of a Times Square hustler, Sinbad the Sailor, and Saul, a brilliant, self-destructive, alcoholic, dominating character who may be the only love Sinbad will ever know. A classic tale of desire, obsession and the terrible wages of love.

STAN LEVENTHAL
BARBIE IN BONDAGE
$6.95/415-1
Widely regarded as one of the most clear-eyed interpreters of big city gay male life, Leventhal here provides a series of explorations of love and desire between men.

SKYDIVING ON CHRISTOPHER STREET
$6.95/287-6
"Positively addictive." —Dennis Cooper

Aside from a hateful job, a hateful apartment, a hateful world and an increasingly hateful lover, life seems, well, all right for the protagonist of Stan Leventhal's latest novel. An insightful tale of contemporary urban gay life.

BRAD GOOCH
THE GOLDEN AGE OF PROMISCUITY
$7.95/550-6
"The next best thing to taking a time-machine trip to grovel in the glorious '70s gutter." —*San Francisco Chronicle*

"A solid, unblinking, unsentimental look at a vanished era. Gooch tells us everything we ever wanted to know about the dark and decadent gay subculture in Manhattan before AIDS altered the landscape." —*Kirkus Reviews*

RED JORDAN AROBATEAU
DIRTY PICTURES
$5.95/345-7
Dirty Pictures is the story of a lonely butch tending bar—and the femme she finally calls her own.

LUCY AND MICKEY
$6.95/311-2
"A necessary reminder to all who blissfully—some may say ignorantly—ride the wave of lesbian chic into the mainstream." —Heather Findlay

The story of Mickey—an uncompromising butch—and her long affair with Lucy, the femme she loves.

PATRICK MOORE
IOWA
$6.95/423-2
"Full of terrific characters etched in acid-sharp prose, soaked through with just enough ambivalence to make it thoroughly romantic." —Felice Picano

The raw tale of one gay man's journey into adulthood, and the roads that bring him home again.

WALTER R. HOLLAND
THE MARCH
$6.95/429-1
Beginning on a hot summer night in 1980, *The March* revolves around a circle of young gay men, and the many others their lives touch. Over time, each character changes in unexpected ways; lives and loves come together and fall apart, as society itself is horribly altered by the onslaught of AIDS.

DONALD VINING
A GAY DIARY
$8.95/451-8
"*A Gay Diary* is, unquestionably, the richest historical document of gay male life in the United States that I have ever encountered...." —*Body Politic*

Vining's *Diary* portrays a vanished age and the lifestyle of a generation frequently forgotten.

LARS EIGHNER
GAY COSMOS
$6.95/236-1
An analysis of gay culture. Praised by the press, *Gay Cosmos* is an important contribution to the area of Gay and Lesbian Studies.

FELICE PICANO
AMBIDEXTROUS
$6.95/275-2
"Makes us remember what it feels like to be a child..." —*The Advocate*

Picano tells all about his formative years: home life, school face-offs, the ingenuous sophistications of his first sexual steps.

MEN WHO LOVED ME
$6.95/274-4
"Zesty...spiked with adventure and romance...a distinguished and humorous portrait of a vanished age." —*Publishers Weekly*

In 1966, Picano abandoned New York, determined to find true love in Europe. He becomes embroiled in a romance with Djanko, and lives *la dolce vita* to the fullest. Upon returning to the US, he plunges into the city's thriving gay community of the 1970s.

MASQUERADE BOOKS

THE LURE
$6.95/398-8
A Book-of-the-Month-Club Selection
After witnessing a brutal murder, Noel is recruited by the police, to assist as a lure for the killer. Undercover, he moves deep into the freneticism of gay highlife in 1970s Manhattan—where he discovers his own hidden desires.

WILLIAM TALSMAN
THE GAUDY IMAGE
$6.95/263-9
"To read *The Gaudy Image* now...it is to see first-hand the very issues of identity and positionality with which gay men were struggling in the decades before Stonewall. For. what Talsman is dealing with...is the very question of how we conceive ourselves gay." —from the introduction by Michael Bronski

ROSEBUD

THE ROSEBUD READER
$5.95/319-8
Rosebud has contributed greatly to the burgeoning genre of lesbian erotica, introducing new writers and adding contemporary classics to the shelves. Here are the finest moments from Rosebud's runaway successes.

DANIELLE ENGLE
UNCENSORED FANTASIES
$6.95/572-7
In a world where so many stifle their emotions, who doesn't find themselves yearning for a little old-fashioned honesty—even if it means bearing one's own secret desires? Danielle Engle's heroines do just that—and a great deal more—in their quest for total sexual pleasure.

LESLIE CAMERON
WHISPER OF FANS
$6.50/542-5
A thrilling chronicle of love between women, written with a sure eye for sensual detail. One woman discovers herself through the sensual devotion of another.

RACHEL PEREZ
ODD WOMEN
$6.50/526-3
These women are sexy, smart, tough— some say odd. But who cares! An assortment of Sapphic sirens proves once and for all that comely ladies come best in pairs.

RED JORDAN AROBATEAU
STREET FIGHTER
$6.95/583-2
Another blast of truth from one of today's most notorious plain-speakers. An unsentimental look at the life of a street butch— Woody, the consummate outsider, living on the fringes of San Francisco.

SATAN'S BEST
$6.95/539-5
An epic tale of life with the Outlaws—the ultimate lesbian biker gang. Angel, a lonely butch, joins the Outlaws, and finds herself loving a new breed of woman and facing a new brand of danger on the open road....

ROUGH TRADE
$6.50/470-4
Famous for her unflinching portrayal of lower-class dyke life and love, Arobateau outdoes herself with these tales of butch/femme affairs and unrelenting passions.

BOYS NIGHT OUT
$6.50/463-1
Incendiary short fiction from this lesbian literary sensation. As always, Arobateau takes a good hard look at the lives of everyday women, noting well the struggles and triumphs each experiences.

RANDY TUROFF
LUST NEVER SLEEPS
$6.50/475-5
Highly erotic, powerfully real fiction. Turoff depicts a circle of modern women connected through the bonds of love, friendship, ambition, and lust with accuracy and compassion.

ALISON TYLER
THE SILVER KEY:
MADAME VICTORIA'S FINISHING SCHOOL
$6.95/614-6
In the rarefied atmosphere of a Victorian finishing school, a circle of randy young ladies share a diary. Molly records an explicit description of her initiation into the ways of physical love; Colette reports on a ghostly encounter. Eden tells of how it feels to wield a switch; and Katherine transcribes the journey of her love affair with the wickedly wanton Eden. Each of these thrilling tales is recounted in loving detail, making *The Silver Key* a treasure trove of scalding prose....

BUY ANY 4 BOOKS & CHOOSE 1 ADDITIONAL BOOK, OF EQUAL OR LESSER VALUE, AS YOUR FREE GIFT

MASQUERADE BOOKS

COME QUICKLY:
For Girls on the Go
$6.95/428-3
Here are over sixty of the hottest fantasies around. A volume designed a modern girl on a modern schedule, who still appreciates a little old-fashioned action.

VENUS ONLINE
$6.50/521-2
Lovely Alexa spends her days in a boring bank job, saving her energies for the night. That's when she goes online... Soon Alexa—aka Venus—finds her real and online lives colliding deliciously.

DARK ROOM:
An Online Adventure
$6.50/455-0
Dani, a successful photographer, can't bring herself to face the death of her lover, Kate. Determined to keep the memory of her lover alive, Dani goes online under Kate's screen alias—and begins to uncover the truth behind Kate's shocking death....

BLUE SKY SIDEWAYS
& OTHER STORIES
$6.50/394-5
A variety of women, and their many breathtaking experiences with lovers, friends—and even the occasional sexy stranger.

DIAL "L" FOR LOVELESS
$5.95/386-4
Katrina Loveless—a sexy private eye talented enough to give Sam Spade a run for his money. In her first case, Katrina investigates a murder implicating a host of lovely, lusty ladies.

THE VIRGIN
$5.95/379-1
Seeking the fulfillment of her deepest sexual desires, Veronica answers a personal ad in the "Women Seeking Women" category—and discovers a whole sensual world she had only dreamed existed!

K. T. BUTLER
TOOLS OF THE TRADE
$5.95/420-8
A sparkling mix of lesbian erotica and humor. An encounter with ice cream, cappuccino and chocolate cake; an affair with a complete stranger; a pair of faulty handcuffs; and more.

LOVECHILD
GAG
$5.95/369-4
One of the bravest young writers you'll ever encounter. These poems take on hypocrisy with uncommon energy, and announce Lovechild as a writer of unforgettable rage.

ELIZABETH OLIVER
THE SM MURDER:
Murder at Roman Hill
$5.95/353-8
Intrepid lesbian P.I.s Leslie Patrick and Robin Penny take on a really hot case: the murder of the notorious Felicia Roman. The circumstances of the crime lead them through the leatherdyke underground, where motives—and desires—run deep.

SUSAN ANDERS
CITY OF WOMEN
$5.95/375-9
Stories dedicated to women and the passions that draw them together. Designed strictly for the sensual pleasure of women, these tales are set to ignite flames of passion in any reader.

PINK CHAMPAGNE
$5.95/282-5
Tasty, torrid tales of butch/femme couplings. Tough as nails or soft as silk, these women seek out their antitheses, intent on working out the details of their own personal theory of difference.

LAURA ANTONIOU, ED.
LEATHERWOMEN
$6.95/598-0
"...a great new collection of fiction by and about SM dykes."
—SKIN TWO

A groundbreaking anthology. These fantasies, from the pens of new or emerging authors, break every rule imposed on women's fantasies. The hottest stories from some of today's newest writers make this an unforgettable exploration of the female libido. A bestselling title.

LEATHERWOMEN II
$4.95/229-9
Another groundbreaking volume of writing from women on the edge, sure to ignite libidinal flames in any reader. Leave taboos behind, because these Leatherwomen know no limits....

AARONA GRIFFIN
LEDA AND THE HOUSE OF SPIRITS
$6.95/585-9
Two steamy novellas in one volume. Ten years into her relationship with Chrys, *Leda* decides to take a one-night vacation—at a local lesbian sex club. She soon finds herself reveling in sensual abandon. In the second story, lovely Lydia thinks she has her grand new home all to herself—until strange dreams begin to suggest that this *House of Spirits* harbors other souls, determined to do some serious partying.

MASQUERADE BOOKS

PASSAGE & OTHER STORIES
$6.95/599-9
"A tale of a woman who is brave enough to follow her desire, even if it leads her into the arms of dangerous women."
—Pat Califia

An SM romance. Lovely Nina leads a "safe" life—until she finds herself infatuated with a woman she spots at a local café. One night, Nina follows her, only to find herself enmeshed in an endless maze leading to a mysterious world of pain and pleasure where women test the edges of sexuality and power.

VALENTINA CILESCU

MY LADY'S PLEASURE:
Mistress with a Maid, Volume 1
$5.95/412-7
Claudia Dungarrow, a lovely, powerful professor, attempts to seduce Elizabeth Stanbridge, setting off a chain of events that eventually ruins her career. Claudia vows revenge—and makes her foes pay deliciously....

DARK VENUS:
Mistress with a Maid, Volume 2
$6.50/481-X
Claudia Dungarrow's quest for ultimate erotic dominance continues in this scalding second volume! How many maidens will fall prey to her insatiable appetite?

BODY AND SOUL:
Mistress with a Maid, Volume 3
$6.50/515-8
Dr. Claudia Dungarrow returns for yet another tour of depravity, subjugating every maiden in sight to her sexual whims. But she has yet to hold Elizabeth in submission. Will she ever?

THE ROSEBUD SUTRA
$4.95/242-6
A look at the ultimate guide to lesbian love. The Rosebud Sutra explores the secrets women keep from everyone—everyone but one another, that is...

MISTRESS MINE
$6.50/502-6
Sophia Cranleigh sits in prison, accused of authoring the "obscene" *Mistress Mine*. What she has done, however, is merely chronicle the events of her life under the hand of Mistress Malin.

THE HAVEN
$4.95/165-9
J craves domination, and her perverse appetites lead her to the Haven: the isolated sanctuary Ros and Annie call home. Soon J forces her way into their world, bringing unspeakable lust into their staid lives.

LINDSAY WELSH

SEXUAL FANTASIES
$6.95/586-7
A volume of today's hottest lesbian erotica, selected by no less an authority than Lindsay Welsh, bestselling author of *Bad Habits* and *A Circle of Friends*. A dozen sexy stories, ranging from sweet to spicy, *Sexual Fantasies* offers a look at the many desires and depravities indulged in by modern women.

SECOND SIGHT
$6.50/507-7
The debut of lesbian superhero Dana Steel! During an attack by a gang of homophobic youths, Dana is thrown onto subway tracks. Miraculously, she survives, and finds herself the world's first lesbian superhero.

NASTY PERSUASIONS
$6.50/436-4
A hot peek into the behind-the-scenes operations of Rough Trade—one of the world's most famous lesbian clubs. Join Slash, Ramone, Cherry and many others as they bring one another to the height of ecstasy.

MILITARY SECRETS
$5.95/397-X
Colonel Candice Sproule heads a specialized boot camp. Assisted by three dominatrix sergeants, Colonel Sproule takes on the submissives sent to her by secret military contacts. Then along comes Jesse—whose pleasure in being served matches the Colonel's own.

ROMANTIC ENCOUNTERS
$5.95/359-7
Julie, the most powerful editor of romance novels in the industry, spends her days igniting women's passions through books—and her nights fulfilling those needs with a variety of lovers.

THE BEST OF LINDSAY WELSH
$5.95/368-6
Lindsay Welsh was one of Rosebud's early bestsellers, and remains one of our most popular writers. This sampler is set to introduce some of the hottest lesbian erotica to a wider audience.

NECESSARY EVIL
$5.95/277-9
When her Mistress proves too by-the-book, one lovely submissive takes the ultimate chance—creating a Mistress who'll fulfill her heart's desire. Little did she know how difficult it would be—and, in the end, rewarding....

BUY ANY 4 BOOKS & CHOOSE 1 ADDITIONAL BOOK, OF EQUAL OR LESSER VALUE, AS YOUR FREE GIFT

MASQUERADE BOOKS

A VICTORIAN ROMANCE
$5.95/365-1
A young woman realizes her dream—a trip abroad! Soon, Elaine comes to discover her own sexual talents, as a Parisian named Madelaine takes her Sapphic education in hand.

A CIRCLE OF FRIENDS
$6.50/524-7
A group of women pair off to explore all the possibilities of lesbian passion, until finally it seems that there is nothing—and no one—they have not dabbled in.

ANNABELLE BARKER
MOROCCO
$6.50/541-7
A young woman stands to inherit a fortune—if she can only withstand the ministrations of her guardian until her twentieth birthday. Lila makes a bid for freedom, only to find that liberty has its own delicious price....

A.L. REINE
DISTANT LOVE & OTHER STORIES
$4.95/3056-3
In the title story, Leah Michaels and her lover, Ranelle, have had four years of blissful, smoldering passion together. When Ranelle is out of town, Leah records an audio "Valentine:" a cassette filled with erotic reminiscences....

A RICHARD KASAK BOOK

LARRY TOWNSEND
THE LEATHERMAN'S HANDBOOK
$12.95/559-X
With introductions by John Preston, Jack Fritscher and Victor Terry

"The real thing, the book that started thousands of bikes roaring to the leather bars..." —John Preston

A special twenty-fifth anniversary edition of this guide to the gay leather underground, with additional material addressing the realities of sex in the 90s. A volume of historical value, the *Handbook* remains relevant to today's reader.

ASK LARRY
$12.95/289-2
For many years, Townsend wrote the "Leather Notebook" column for *Drummer* magazine. Now read Townsend's collected wisdom, as well as the author's contemporary commentary—a careful consideration of the way life has changed in the AIDS era.

PAT CALIFIA
DIESEL FUEL: Passionate Poetry
$12.95/535-2
"Dead-on direct, these poems burn, pierce, penetrate, soak, and sting.... Califia leaves no sexual stone unturned, clearing new ground for us all." —Gerry Gomez Pearlberg

Pat Califia reveals herself to be a poet of power and frankness, in this first collection of verse. A volume of extraordinary scope, and one of this year's must-read explorations of underground culture.

SENSUOUS MAGIC
$12.95/610-X
"*Sensuous Magic* is clear, succinct and engaging even for the reader for whom S/M isn't the sexual behavior of choice.... When she is writing about the dynamics of sex and the technical aspects of it, Califia is the Dr. Ruth of the alternative sexuality set...." —*Lambda Book Report*

"Captures the power of what it means to enter forbidden terrain, and to do so safely with someone else, and to explore the healing potential, spiritual aspects and the depth of S/M." —*Bay Area Reporter*

"Don't take a dangerous trip into the unknown—buy this book and know where you're going!" —*SKIN TWO*

SIMON LEVAY
ALBRICK'S GOLD
$20.95/518-2/Hardcover
"Well-plotted and imaginative... [Levay's] premise and execution are original and engaging." —*Publishers Weekly*

From the man behind the controversial "gay brain" studies comes a tale of medical experimentation run amok. Is Dr. Guy Albrick performing unethical experiments in an attempt at "correcting" homosexuality? Doctor Roger Cavendish is determined to find out, before Albrick's guinea pigs are let loose among an unsuspecting gay community... An edge-of-the-seat thriller based on today's cutting-edge science.

SHAR REDNOUR, ED.
VIRGIN TERRITORY 2
$12.95/506-9
Focusing on the many "firsts" of a woman's erotic life, *VT2* provides one of the sole outlets for serious discussion of the myriad possibilities available to and chosen by many lesbians.

VIRGIN TERRITORY
$12.95/457-7
An anthology of writing by women about their first-time erotic experiences with other women. A groundbreaking examination of contemporary lesbian desire.

MASQUERADE BOOKS

MICHAEL BRONSKI, ED.
TAKING LIBERTIES: Gay Men's Essays on Politics, Culture and Sex
$12.95/456-9
Lambda Literary Award Winner
"Offers undeniable proof of a heady, sophisticated, diverse new culture of gay intellectual debate. I cannot recommend it too highly." —Christopher Bram

An essential look at the state of the gay male community. Some of the gay community's foremost essayists—from radical left to neo-conservative— weigh in on such slippery topics as outing, identity, pornography, pedophilia, and much more.

FLASHPOINT:
Gay Male Sexual Writing
$12.95/424-0
Over twenty of the genre's best writers are included in this thrilling and enlightening look at contemporary gay porn. Accompanied by Bronski's insightful analysis, each story illustrates the many approaches to sexuality used by today's gay writers.

HEATHER FINDLAY, ED.
A MOVEMENT OF EROS:
25 Years of Lesbian Erotica
$12.95/421-6
A roster of stellar talents, each represented by their best work. Tracing the course of the genre from its pre-Stonewall roots to its current renaissance, Findlay examines each piece, placing it within the context of lesbian community and politics.

MICHAEL FORD, ED.
ONCE UPON A TIME:
Erotic Fairy Tales for Women
$12.95/449-6
How relevant to contemporary lesbians are traditional fairy tales? Some of the biggest names in lesbian literature retell their favorites, adding their own sexy—and surprising—twists.

HAPPILY EVER AFTER:
Erotic Fairy Tales for Men
$12.95/450-X
An eye-opening appreciation of these age-ol tales. Adapting some of childhood's beloved stories for the adult gay reader, the contributors to *Happily Ever After* dig up the erotic subtext of these hitherto "innocent" diversions.

CHARLES HENRI FORD & PARKER TYLER
THE YOUNG AND EVIL
$12.95/431-3
"*The Young and Evil* creates [its] generation as *This Side of Paradise* by Fitzgerald created his generation."—Gertrude Stein

Originally published in 1933, *The Young and Evil* was a sensation due to its portrayal of young gay artists living in Greenwich Village. From drag balls to bohemian flats, these characters followed love wherever it led them.

BARRY HOFFMAN, ED.
THE BEST OF GAUNTLET
$12.95/202-7
Gauntlet has always published the widest possible range of opinions. The most provocative articles have been gathered by editor-in-chief Barry Hoffman, to make *The Best of Gauntlet* a riveting exploration of American society's limits.

AMARANTHA KNIGHT, ED.
LOVE BITES
$12.95/234-5
A volume of tales dedicated to legend's sexiest demon—the Vampire. Not only the finest collection of erotic horror available—but a virtual who's who of promising new talent.

MICHAEL ROWE
WRITING BELOW THE BELT:
Conversations with Erotic Authors
$19.95/363-5
"An in-depth and enlightening tour of society's love/hate relationship with sex, morality, and censorship."
—James White Review

Rowe speaks frankly with cult favorites such as Pat Califia, crossover success stories like John Preston, and up-and-comers Michael Lowenthal and Will Leber.

MICHAEL LASSELL
THE HARD WAY
$12.95/231-0
"Lassell is a master of the necessary word. In an age of tepid and whining verse, his bawdy and bittersweet songs are like a plunge in cold champagne." —Paul Monette

The first collection of renowned gay writer Michael Lassell's poetry, fiction and essays. As much a chronicle of post-Stonewall gay life as a compendium of a remarkable writer's work.

BUY ANY 4 BOOKS & CHOOSE 1 ADDITIONAL BOOK, OF EQUAL OR LESSER VALUE, AS YOUR FREE GIFT

MASQUERADE BOOKS

WILLIAM CARNEY
THE REAL THING
$10.95/280-9

"Carney gives us a good look at the mores and lifestyle of the first generation of gay leathermen. —Pat Califia

With a new introduction by Michael Bronski. *The Real Thing* returns from exile more than twenty-five years after its initial release, detailing the attitudes and practices of an earlier generation of leathermen. An important piece of gay publishing history.

RANDY TUROFF, ED.
LESBIAN WORDS: State of the Art
$10.95/340-6

"This is a terrific book that should be on every thinking lesbian's bookshelf." —Nisa Donnelly

The best of lesbian nonfiction looking at not only the current fashionability the media has brought to the lesbian "image," but considerations of the lesbian past via historical inquiry and personal recollections.

ASSOTTO SAINT
SPELLS OF A VOODOO DOLL
$12.95/393-7
Lambda Literary Award Nominee.
"Angelic and brazen." —Jewelle Gomez

A spellbinding collection of the poetry, lyrics, essays and performance texts by one of the most important voices in the renaissance of black gay writing.

EURYDICE
F/32
$10.95/350-3
"It's wonderful to see a woman...celebrating her body and her sexuality by creating a fabulous and funny tale." —Kathy Acker

A funny, disturbing quest for unity, *f/32* tells the story of Ela and her vagina—the latter of whom embarks on one of the most hilarious road trips in recent fiction. An award-winning novel.

ROBERT PATRICK
TEMPLE SLAVE
$12.95/191-8
"One of the best ways to learn what it was like to be fabulous, gay, theatrical and loved in a time at once more and less dangerous to gay life than our own." —Genre

The story of Greenwich Village and the beginnings of gay theater, fictionalized by this world-famous playwright.

FELICE PICANO
DRYLAND'S END
$12.95/279-5

Dryland's End takes place in a fabulous techno-empire ruled by intelligent, powerful women. While the Matriarchy has ruled for over two thousand years and altered human society, it is now unraveling. Military rivalries, religious fanaticism and economic competition threaten to destroy the mighty empire.

SAMUEL R. DELANY
THE MOTION OF LIGHT IN WATER
$12.95/133-0
"A very moving, intensely fascinating literary biography from an extraordinary writer...The artist as a young man and a memorable picture of an age." —William Gibson

Samuel R. Delany's autobiography covers the early years of one of science fiction's most important voices. A self-portrait of one of today's most challenging writers.

THE MAD MAN
$23.95/193-4/Hardcover
"What Delany has done here is take the ideas of the Marquis de Sade one step further, by filtering extreme and obsessive sexual behavior through the sieve of post-modern experience...." —Lambda Book Report

"Delany develops an insightful dichotomy between [his protagonist]'s two worlds: the one of cerebral philosophy and dry academia, the other of heedless, 'impersonal' obsessive sexual extremism. When these worlds finally collide ... the novel achieves a surprisingly satisfying resolution...." —Publishers Weekly

For his thesis, graduate student John Marr researches the life and work of the brilliant Timothy Hasler: a philosopher whose career was cut tragically short over a decade earlier. Marr notices parallels between his life and that of his subject—and begins to believe that Hasler's death might hold some key to his own life as a gay man in the age of AIDS.

LUCY TAYLOR
UNNATURAL ACTS
$12.95/181-0
"A topnotch collection..." —Science Fiction Chronicle

A disturbing vision of erotic horror. Unrelenting angels and hungry gods play with souls and bodies in Taylor's murky cosmos: where heaven and hell are merely differences of perspective; where redemption and damnation lie behind the same shocking acts.

MASQUERADE BOOKS

TIM WOODWARD, ED.
THE BEST OF SKIN TWO
$12.95/130-6
Provocative essays by the finest writers working in the "radical sex" scene. Including interviews with cult figures Tim Burton, Clive Barker and Jean Paul Gaultier.

LAURA ANTONIOU, ED.
LOOKING FOR MR. PRESTON
$23.95/288-4/Hardcover
Interviews, essays and personal reminiscences of John Preston—a man whose career spanned the gay publishing industry. Ten percent of the proceeds from this book will go to the AIDS Project of Southern Maine, for which Preston served as President of the Board.

CARO SOLES, ED.
MELTDOWN!
An Anthology of Erotic Science Fiction and Dark Fantasy for Gay Men
$12.95/203-5
Meltdown! contains the very best examples of the increasingly popular sub-genre of erotic sci-fi/dark fantasy: stories meant to send a shiver down the spine and start a fire down below.

GUILLERMO BOSCH
RAIN
$12.95/232-9
In a quest to sate his hunger for some knowledge of the world, one man is taken through a series of extraordinary encounters that change the course of civilization around him.

RUSS KICK
OUTPOSTS:
A Catalog of Rare and Disturbing Alternative Information
$18.95/0202-8
A tour through the work of political extremists, conspiracy theorists, sexual explorers, and others whose work has been deemed "too far out" for consideration by the mainstream.

CECILIA TAN, ED.
SM VISIONS:
The Best of Circlet Press
$10.95/339-2
Circlet Press, publisher of erotic science fiction and fantasy genre, is now represented by the best of its very best—a most thrilling and eye-opening rides through the erotic imagination.

DAVID MELTZER
THE AGENCY TRILOGY
$12.95/216-7
"...'The Agency' is clearly Meltzer's paradigm of society; a mindless machine of which we are all 'agents,' including those whom the machine supposedly serves...." —Norman Spinrad

A vision of an America consumed and dehumanized by a lust for power.

MICHAEL PERKINS
THE GOOD PARTS: An Uncensored Guide to Literary Sexuality
$12.95/186-1
A survey of sex as seen/written about in the pages of over 100 major fiction and nonfiction volumes from the past twenty years.
COMING UP: The World's Best Erotic Writing
$12.95/370-8
Michael Perkins has scoured the field of erotic writing to produce an anthology sure to challenge the limits of the most seasoned reader.

MICHAEL LOWENTHAL, ED.
THE BEST OF THE BADBOYS
$12.95/233-7
The best Badboy writers are collected here, in this testament to the artistry that has catapulted them to bestselling status.

LARS EIGHNER
ELEMENTS OF AROUSAL
$12.95/230-2
A guideline for success with one of publishing's best kept secrets: the novice-friendly field of gay erotic writing. Eighner details his craft, providing the reader with sure advice.

JOHN PRESTON
MY LIFE AS A PORNOGRAPHER AND OTHER INDECENT ACTS
$12.95/135-7
"...essential and enlightening... *My Life as a Pornographer*] is a bridge from the sexually liberated 1970s to the more cautious 1990s, and Preston has walked much of that way as a standard-bearer to the cause for equal rights...." —*Library Journal*

A collection of author and social critic John Preston's essays, focusing on his work as an erotic writer, and proponent of gay rights.

BUY ANY 4 BOOKS & CHOOSE 1 ADDITIONAL BOOK, OF EQUAL OR LESSER VALUE, AS YOUR FREE GIFT

MASQUERADE BOOKS

MARCO VASSI
THE EROTIC COMEDIES
$12.95/136-5

"The comparison to [Henry] Miller is high praise indeed.... But reading Vassi's work, the analogy holds—for he shares with Miller an unabashed joy in sensuality, and a questing after experience that is the root of all great literature, erotic or otherwise...." —David L. Ulin, *The Los Angeles Reader*

Scathing and humorous, these stories reflect Vassi's belief in the power and primacy of Eros in American life.

THE STONED APOCALYPSE
$12.95/132-2
Vassi's autobiography, financed by the other erotic writing that made him a cult sensation.

A DRIVING PASSION
$12.95/134-9
Famous for the lectures he gave regarding sexuality, *A Driving Passion* collects these lectures, and distills the philosophy that made him a sensation.

THE SALINE SOLUTION
$12.95/180-2
The story of one couple's affair and the events that lead them to reassess their lives.

CHEA VILLANUEVA
JESSIE'S SONG
$9.95/235-3

"It conjures up the strobe-light confusion and excitement of urban dyke life.... Read about these dykes and you'll love them." —Rebecca Ripley

Touching, arousing portraits of working class butch/femme relations. An underground hit.

STAN TAL, ED.
BIZARRE SEX AND OTHER CRIMES OF PASSION
$12.95/213-2
Over twenty stories of erotic shock, guaranteed to titillate and terrify. This incredible volume includes such masters of erotic horror as Lucy Taylor and Nancy Kilpatrick.

ORDERING IS EASY

MC/VISA orders can be placed by calling our toll-free number
PHONE 800-375-2356/FAX 212-986-7355
HOURS M-F 9am—12am EDT Sat & Sun 12pm—8pm EDT
E-MAIL masqbks@aol.com
or mail this coupon to:
MASQUERADE DIRECT
DEPT. BMMQ98 801 2ND AVE., NY, NY 10017

BUY ANY FOUR BOOKS AND CHOOSE ONE ADDITIONAL BOOK, OF EQUAL OR LESSER VALUE, AS YOUR FREE GIFT

QTY.	TITLE	NO.	PRICE
			FREE

DEPT. BMMQ98 (please have this code available when placing your order)

We never sell, give or trade any customer's name.

SUBTOTAL
POSTAGE AND HANDLING
TOTAL

In the U.S., please add $1.50 for the first book and 75¢ for each additional book; in Canada, add $2.00 for the first book and $1.25 for each additional book. Foreign countries: add $4.00 for the first book and $2.00 for each additional book. No C.O.D. orders. Please make all checks payable to Masquerade/Direct. Payable in U.S. currency only. NY state residents add 8.25% sales tax. Please allow 4–6 weeks for delivery. Payable in U.S. currency only.

NAME _____
ADDRESS _____
CITY _____ STATE _____ ZIP _____
TEL( ) _____
E-MAIL _____
PAYMENT: ☐ CHECK ☐ MONEY ORDER ☐ VISA ☐ MC
CARD NO. _____ EXP. DATE _____